Of Dark and Bright

Kate Sherwood

This book is a work of fiction. Names, characters, places, and incidents either are products of the author's imagination or are used fictitiously. Any resemblance to actual events or locales or persons, living or dead, is entirely coincidental.

Published by Kate Sherwood

Cover Art by Justin James/Mara McKennen

Print ISBN #978-1-988752-35-8

Second Edition Issued 2019

Chapter One

Dan was having trouble concentrating on his work. It was fair, in a way, because right then his work was a three-year-old filly, and she seemed to be having trouble concentrating on *him* too. But he was the human. He was in charge.

Damn it. He shouldn't have thought about being in charge. He eased the filly back to a walk and dropped his reins. It was only the fourth time the horse had been ridden, and she deserved his full attention. The experience was overwhelming enough for her without him letting his focus wander away. He relaxed his body and reached forward to run soothing fingers through the chestnut mane in front of him. "You're okay, babe," he said. "You're doing a good job." He wiggled his fingers, digging in like another horse would if it were grooming the filly, and he felt her start to relax.

And that probably shouldn't have made him think of Evan, but it did. The way the man had just surrendered, had let his body become... what? Not a tool, not a toy.... Dan thought of Jeff's long, artistic fingers and smiled to himself. A canvas. That was what Evan had let himself become. A way for Dan and Jeff to express themselves: their desire, their love, their playfulness... everything they were. Dan let his mind drift, let himself remember the dazed, disconnected look on Evan's face as Dan had eased into him, the soft, breathy sounds he'd made. And Jeff had been right with them, his hands roaming all over both of their bodies, his lips warm and firm....

The filly danced a little, and Dan tried to call his mind back to business. There had been nothing remarkable about the night before; well, it had been remarkable, but not unusual. He and Evan and Jeff were pretty well established, and they'd created a lot of memories together. He remembered the way Jeff's whole body had tightened with the first sweep of Dan's tongue along the length of his cock, and smiled to himself. Nothing unusual. And that made it even sweeter.

He was trying to decide whether to give up or try to get some work done when he saw Robyn, one of the barn staff, waving at him from the far side of the arena. She had the barn's cordless phone in her hand. That was weird. He got personal calls to his cell, and it was hard to imagine a business call so important that Robyn would interrupt a training session. But maybe she had seen that he wasn't getting much done; he just hoped she hadn't realized *why* he was being less than productive.

He thought about trying to ride the filly over, but swung off her back instead. She probably would have been just fine, but there was no point in taking the chance. Pushing a horse too fast wasn't fair, and it wasn't good training.

He flipped the reins over the horse's neck and started across the arena. As he got closer, he saw Robyn's expression, and his stomach twisted just a little. He couldn't read her face very well, but she looked tense.

"What's up?" he asked, trying to sound casual. He doubted he could fool Robyn, but it was worth a try.

Robyn kept her hand over the mouthpiece even as she reached the phone toward him. "It's a woman." She frowned, as if trying to figure out the message. "Dan, she says she's your sister."

"Krista?" As if he had another sister. Jesus. It had been, what, fifteen years? Dan looked doubtfully at the phone. He honestly wasn't sure how he was feeling. He didn't know whether he wanted it to really be his sister, or whether he'd prefer that it was a hoax.

"Dan," Robyn prompted, "you should talk to her. She sounded pretty legit."

He obediently reached for the phone, and Robyn took the horse's reins without asking. She stood there, patting the filly's neck and watching him, as he took a few steps away and lifted the phone to his ear.

"Dan Wheeler," he said into the mouthpiece, trying to sound calm and businesslike.

There was no answer for quite a while, but then a tentative female voice said, "Danny?"

"Yeah, this is Dan. Who's calling, please?"

Another long pause. "Danny, it's Krista."

And Dan was at a loss. Was there some way to ask for proof of her identity without... well, without actually asking? Or, at least, without being an asshole about it? He decided to just be noncommittal and see where the conversation went. "Krista? It's been a long time."

"Yeah. It has."

Okay, she'd been the one to call *him*, so why was he expected to carry the conversation? He made a face at the wall then said, "Was it hard to find me? I've moved around quite a bit."

"I Googled you. I remembered you liked riding, so when I saw that there was a Dan Wheeler training horses, I looked for a photograph. And then I found some information about where you worked, and I got the phone number from a directory."

That was straightforward enough. Dan had been listening carefully to the voice as much as the words, and he was beginning to think that he recognized it. He could hear a little Texas, he was pretty sure, and something else as well. A tense, uncertain note, the same one she'd had so often in their childhood. Damn it. He didn't want to play this game, didn't want to get excited and then find out the whole thing was some stupid joke. “Krista? You remember the house on Forest Road? Do you remember the door to my room there?”

Another pause, and for a moment, Dan thought he’d called the stranger’s bluff and she was going to give up. But then the woman said, “You didn’t have a door. The asshole took it off its hinges after you wanted to keep it locked.”

Jesus. That was true. This was Krista. After so many years, he was talking to his sister. Dan’s mind raced. The last he’d heard, Krista had been running from the law, wanted for a string of armed robberies and other crimes. He leaned against the arena wall and slid down until he was sitting on the sandy floor. “Krista,” he said. “Krista, where are you? Are you okay?”

That was when she started to cry.

Evan was bored. Not even Chris, with his every-other-minute texted insults, could make this meeting anything but dull. So when his phone rang and he saw Dan’s name on the call display, he barely hesitated. “Sorry, guys,” he said as he stood up. “This is an important call. I need to take it.”

The meeting was in-company, so Evan was clearly the top-ranking person in the room. He could take a break whenever he felt like it. He briefly thought about sitting there and expecting everyone else to file out and leave him the room; he’d seen other people do it. But he’d always thought they were assholes, he remembered, and he headed for the door.

The call had already gone to voice mail by the time Evan was out of the room, so he listened to the brief message. “Evan, call me. It’s important.” Evan had known it was something big as soon as he’d seen Dan’s name; Dan texted him now and then, but he’d called Evan at work about three times in the two years they’d been seeing each other. If it was worth a phone call, it was worth Evan's time.

Chris poked his head out of the conference room. "You want me?"

"Maybe. It's Danny." Evan walked toward his office as he pressed Dan's call-back number. He turned to see Chris trailing behind him. "He sounded kinda stressed."

Chris shrugged. "Well, that's not exactly unheard of."

"He's been calm lately," Evan protested. Chris and Dan were best friends, but it was a strange, vaguely combative sort of friendship. Evan spent a lot of time keeping them from killing each other. Although he'd heard Chris claim that Evan and Dan were the ones who fought all the time, and Chris was the peacemaker. Obviously Chris was crazy, Evan concluded, and then Dan answered the phone.

"Evan. Are you at work?"

"Yeah. But I can come home if you need me. What's up?"

Dan sounded a bit dazed. "I just got a call from Krista. My sister."

Chris was watching Evan closely, waiting for a cue about whether his presence was required. "Dan," Evan said, "Chris is here. Can I put you on speaker?"

Evan gestured for Chris to shut the door as Dan said, "Yeah, okay."

"His sister called him," Evan said to Chris, and then he hit the speakerphone button. "Dan, did she say where she is? Is she okay?"

"She's a fugitive, Evan. She's not okay."

"What does she want, Danny?" Chris's voice was calm, and Evan was happy to let him take over. Chris was a lawyer, but he was also a semiprofessional Dan-wrangler, with a much longer history on the job than Evan had. "Did she say?"

"She's pregnant. She wants to turn herself in, I think. Or at least she wants to talk about it. She was pretty upset." Dan's voice was tense, and Evan wished they were in the same room so he could wrap himself around Dan's body and give him some support.

"Give me your phone," Evan said softly to Chris, who nodded and passed it over.

"We can help her, Danny," Chris said. "If she'll let us. But we need to do this right, need to be careful, or we could end up in shit for harboring a fugitive. We're going to need to get a criminal lawyer involved in this, for sure. Did she say where she is?"

"Not exactly. I gave her my cell number, and she's going to call me back later."

Evan looked down at the text he'd composed to Jeff. *It's Evan. Can you get to the barn? Dan needs you. I'm on my way.* He hit send. There were times when it was awkward, being in a threesome instead of a traditional couple. But sometimes it really helped to have a team.

Jeff pulled into the barn parking lot and saw Dan standing outside, leaning on a fence, looking at a group of horses grazing. Dan appeared calm enough, but Jeff doubted he actually was. Jeff had already been on his way to the barn when Evan had called him, so it hadn't been long since Dan had gotten the phone call. Not long enough to get any perspective on it all. Jeff figured this was going to be messy. Dan had always felt guilty for leaving his family, and for how things turned out with his sister, and the current situation would have thrown a lot of fuel on that fire.

"Hey, Dan," Jeff said as he stepped onto the carefully mown grass. He'd kept his voice low, and he'd been sure to speak from a good distance away, but Dan still whirled, his eyes wide and startled. Not a good sign. Jeff kept moving, slow and steady, and when he reached Dan, he leaned on the fence beside him and looked out at the horses. "Is that Winston? He's off stall rest?" Talking about horses was always a good way to calm Dan down.

"Uh... yeah." Jeff could practically see Dan working his brain around to the new topic of conversation. "The vet was out yesterday." Dan looked at the horse. "We aren't supposed to work him until there's another checkup, but he's okay to go outside."

"That's good news." Jeff edged over a little closer, so their hips and forearms were touching. "You doing okay? With the sister thing?"

"Dude, I'm not the one on the run from the cops. I'm doing fine."

Jeff nodded, slow and easy, ignoring the tension in Dan's voice. "Okay. Good. Evan's still on his way?"

Dan snorted. "Yeah. I told him not to, but he said if he didn't come home, he'd have to go back into the most boring meeting ever." He looked over at Jeff and rolled his eyes. It was amazing that Evan seemed to have recordbreakingly dull meetings almost every week. And useful that making fun of Evan helped Dan to relax.

"Chris isn't coming?" Jeff wasn't sure how to feel about that. He was envious of Chris sometimes, of his easy rapport with Dan. Everywhere but the bedroom, Jeff felt like he had to work for every confidence, fight for every smile; Chris showered Dan with insults, and Dan responded by sharing all his secrets and grinning like a lunatic. Then again, Chris didn't get to take Dan to bed, so maybe Jeff wasn't too displeased with his role in the whole thing.

"He's meeting with another lawyer. Someone who does a lot of criminal work. He says that we need to be careful, and be prepared." Dan sounded as if he was repeating the last part word for word.

Another thing to be jealous of; Chris actually had a useful function to perform. All Jeff could do was stand there and watch horses graze.

"Were you busy?" Dan asked. "You didn't need to come over. I'm fine. This is... it's weird, but it's not bad. It's good, really, as long as we can get her... I don't know. It's good if we can help her."

"And Chris is on the job with that," Jeff said. So, yeah, maybe he hadn't needed to come over. Maybe he was completely unnecessary. But he'd made the drive, so he'd stick around. "I was on my way, anyhow. I thought I might go for a ride, clear some cobwebs out before I started a new project." He felt like a sap, but he leaned over anyway and pressed a kiss to the spot just below Dan's ear. "I missed you."

"You saw me this morning," Dan said, but he didn't really sound like he was objecting.

"Yup," Jeff agreed easily. "I did. And now I'm seeing you again." He smiled. "And soon we'll see Evan."

"Yeah," Dan agreed. "It's... it's a weird situation. But we'll sort it out, right?" His voice was mostly confident. Mostly sure that his partners would be there for him. But, as always, there was that tiny trace of insecurity that threatened to break Jeff's heart.

"Absolutely," Jeff said firmly. He shuffled back and to the side, not far, just enough so that he could wrap his arms around Dan's warm shoulders. "We'll sort it out."

Chapter Two

Dan had been waiting for the phone to ring, but it still startled him when it did. He took a moment to look around Evan's living room before he answered. He needed a little time to collect himself, but it was also nice to be reminded that he had people on his side. Chris was there, looking calm and interested, as if this was all an intellectual challenge developed for his amusement. He was sitting on the sofa next to Susan, the criminal lawyer he'd recruited. Evan was in the wide doorway that led to the dining room, leaning against the wall, and Dan could tell that he wanted to be moving, wanted to be doing something. Evan wasn't a big fan of waiting. Jeff was standing behind Dan's chair, ready as always, and he reached a strong, steady hand down to grip Dan's shoulder.

"It's an opportunity, Dan," he said in his gravelly voice. "If you can get her to come in, we can help her get things straightened out."

"Straightened out," Dan repeated. He had no idea how straight things could hope to get, not with the long list of charges against Krista, but he also couldn't imagine her being on the run for the rest of her life. Surely there needed to be an end, eventually. Maybe it was time. He hit the button to answer the call. "Hi," he said.

"Hi, Danny." Krista sounded more in control than she had earlier. "It's me."

"Yeah. Look, Krista, before you say anything... I talked to a lawyer. She says that if you tell me where you are and I don't tell the police, I'm committing a crime. So don't tell me anything you don't want the cops to know, okay?" Dan really wasn't sure what he'd do if it came down to it. He wasn't sure if he'd betray his sister in order to follow the rules, in order to keep himself out of trouble. He didn't think so, but he didn't want to put it to the test.

"Oh. Okay." Krista sounded unsure. "Is this... I don't want to screw things up for you, Danny."

"No, it's okay. I want to help. We just need to be careful." He looked over to the couch. He wished Chris worked in criminal law, but he didn't, so Susan would just have to do. "The lawyer's here now, if you want to talk to her. I can give her the phone, or I can put you on speaker. But there's some other people here too. Friends. People you can trust."

"Danny, I just wanted to talk to you. I wanted *you* to help me."

It had been a long time, but Krista was still his baby sister. It hurt to say, "I can't. It's not that I don't want to, I just don't know enough. All I could do is get the lawyer here." And he hadn't even done that, really; Chris had. But Dan would pay for her, at least. "She seems nice, Krista." Dan didn't know where to go with this. He had a feeling he needed to keep Krista on the line; if she hung up, he really wasn't sure she'd call him back. "She seems smart. And she looks professional. She's younger than I thought she'd be." Dan had no idea why he'd started this; it was kind of nerve-racking to describe somebody while she was sitting there listening to him. But Krista hadn't hung up yet, so he kept going.

"She kind of reminds me of Mrs. Clayton. She was my second-grade teacher; you had her too, right?"

"Yeah." A pause. "Does she have the glasses?"

"No. Jesus, Krista, I wouldn't trust my baby sister to a lawyer wearing bright red glasses." He'd forgotten that feature of Mrs. Clayton's appearance. "I was thinking more of the hair. And her smile. Mrs. Clayton always had a nice smile."

"Yeah. She did." Dan could practically feel Krista's indecision, but finally she said, "Okay. Give the phone to her. I don't want to be on speaker."

"Okay," Dan agreed. "And, Krista—I'm glad you called me. I really want to help, okay? Don't...." He wasn't sure what he wanted to say. He thought of himself when he was younger, and how many chances at redemption he'd probably missed because he'd been too distrustful to see other people's good intentions. "We're family, Krista. I want to help."

She didn't respond, so he leaned over to pass the phone to the lawyer, and Jeff's hand slipped off his shoulder. Dan hadn't even realized that Jeff had still been touching him. But once the lawyer had the phone, he leaned back and Jeff's hand returned. "Good job, Dan," Jeff said. Dan brought his own hand up and twined his fingers through Jeff's. He'd done what he could, and he would stand by to do more, but he had the uncomfortable feeling that the whole thing was largely out of his control.

Evan moved as soon as he heard the front door open. It felt good to finally be active instead of just sitting there in the living room, listening to one side of a long and detailed conversation. At one point he'd gone and found a cell phone charger, in case the conversation kept going forever, but that was all he'd been able to do.

Now, though, he had a mission. He lifted a finger to his lips and shushed his sister before she'd even shut the door behind her. "Important phone call in the living room," he said quietly. "Keep it down."

"Keep *what* down?" Tatiana replied somewhat impatiently. "I haven't said a word."

"Okay, yeah, just keep it that way, okay?"

"This is nice, Evan." She sounded testy, but at least she was whispering. "'Welcome home, Tat. Hope you had a good trip, Tat. Come on in and tell us all about it, Tat....'" She raised an eyebrow at him and waited impatiently for him to respond to her prompts.

But Evan wasn't going to get sucked into that trap. Lord knew Tat had been a pain in the ass lately, full of independence and resentment for any limitations he tried to place on her behavior, but he absolutely had the trump card for this hand. And he was happy to play it. "Dan's sister called. She's talking to a lawyer, and they're trying to persuade her to turn herself in after a ten-year multistate crime spree. But, you're right, we should cut that off and have you tell us about your time in Sacramento. It's the state capital, after all."

Normally Tat would have something to say about his sarcasm, but the first part of his message had caught her attention, and she stared at him with her jaw literally dropped. "Dan's sister! Really?" She grabbed Evan's arm. "This is huge, Evan! Is she okay? Is *he* okay? Is Chris here? Is he handling it?"

"Slow down, brat. Chris is here, but there's another lawyer doing the talking. A criminal lawyer." He eased a little closer and dropped his voice even more. "This... don't get carried away, okay? It's not going to have a happy ending, Tat. Not the way you're thinking."

"If she turns herself in, though... that's like saying she's sorry, right? And Dan could help her. We could all help her. We could give her somewhere to live, and she could have a job...." Tat saw the expression on Evan's face, but she frowned angrily back at him. "It's rehabilitation, Evan! That's the point of the justice system, right? To get people to follow the rules. If she turns herself in, and agrees to follow the rules...."

Evan loved his sister. She was seventeen, sweet, and naïve

when she wasn't being rebellious and cynical, and she made him believe that anything was possible. But "possible" wasn't "probable," and he hated to see it when her optimism was crushed by reality. He spent a lot of his time with her just trying to soften that blow. "That'd be great, Tat. But it's not all about rehabilitation. There's supposed to be punishment too. That's what she's going to have to get through."

Tat looked unconvinced, but she didn't argue. Instead, she peered past Evan's shoulder, trying to get a look into the living room. "Can I go listen?" she asked.

Evan rolled his eyes. "Trust me—you don't want to. It's mostly Krista talking, and you can't hear that part, so everyone's just sitting in there, listening to the lawyer say 'Go on' every couple minutes, and trying to figure out the story." But Tat was like Evan; she couldn't just sit around while someone she cared about was having a hard time. And, just like him, if her energy wasn't given an outlet, it tended to get out of control. "Let's go make snacks," he suggested. "It's Tia's day off. We could make those mini-pita pizzas."

Evan had known that would get her attention. "Dan likes the Hawaiian ones," Tat agreed. "Do we have ham?" She led the way to the spacious country kitchen and they began to rummage through the fridge.

Evan thought about Dan and Krista, and he reached out and wrapped his hand around Tat's shoulder. He pulled her toward him, and she let herself be manhandled, then returned the hug. "We're going to help her, right?" she whispered.

"We're going to try," he agreed. He couldn't promise any more than that.

Jeff stretched his legs out and rested his feet on the coffee table. Dan was nestled in against his ribs, Evan was sitting on the floor, leaning back into the space between Jeff and Dan's legs, and everything was perfect. It was peaceful, and quiet, and safe.

Evan lasted about a minute before he started fidgeting, and Jeff smiled down at him. "You planning things down there?" he asked.

Evan spun around so quickly that he jammed his back into the coffee table, knocking the mini-pizza remnants onto the floor on the far side. "I think Susan's great," he said. When Evan had an idea, he spoke with his whole body, an evangelical zeal shining from his eyes. "But I think we need to be more aggressive on this one. I think we should get a whole dream team of lawyers. I can call down to LA, see who's hot down there, and we'd keep Susan on board, sure, but she needs help. This story hasn't gotten a lot of press, and if we can keep it that way, then there's no real pressure on the DA to be a hard ass. If we come on strong enough, we can push them right off balance, and get a really good deal. Or maybe she doesn't even want to confess—maybe we should be fighting for a not-guilty situation."

Dan didn't look convinced. "There's a lot of evidence, it sounds like. Video recordings and everything. And it's probably going to be a federal thing." Jeff tightened his arm just a little around Dan's shoulder, and Dan relaxed and leaned into him before saying, "That's what Susan said. Well, she said there's some California stuff too—the armed robberies were all down around LA. But they robbed two banks, and there's links to organized crime." Dan sounded tired, and Jeff wanted to help, somehow. But what the hell could he do? Dan said, "Maybe you're right. Maybe I should get more lawyers. I don't know. I can, I guess. But it's not going to just go away, Evan."

"What about the pregnancy?" Jeff asked. "How far along is she?"

"About six months, she thinks." Another sigh from Dan. "I guess maybe I should get ready for that. I mean, if she turns herself in... if she's in jail... she'll need someone to look after the baby. I don't know anything about the father, but...."

"Babies are excellent, Dan." Evan's hand rested gently on Dan's ankle. "We can get a nanny, but we can do a lot of it ourselves too. We can make it work."

"Don't get too far ahead of things," Jeff said. He'd never been able to understand how Evan could be as successful in the business world as he was. He'd been running his family's multinational company ever since his parents had died, and the business was doing very well. So Evan must have some sense of proportionality in that world. Maybe he just saved all of his sudden enthusiasms for his private life. "Don't go furnishing the baby's room or anything. We don't have any idea what's going to happen." And then the harder part. "And we don't know how long Krista's sentence will be. Or anything about her, or about what she has planned for herself. Do you really want to get attached to a baby and then have it taken away when its mother gets out of jail and decides to move?"

When Evan frowned, the resemblance to his sister was uncanny. How a six-foot-six man could look like a seventeen-year-old girl was a mystery, but Evan managed. "We can make it work, Jeff." Jeff smiled in spite of himself. Evan complained about having to be the heavy with Tat, having to try to keep her from being disappointed by life; Jeff never complained about playing the same role with Evan. Evan's passion kept Jeff young, and trying to control his enthusiasm made Jeff feel useful.

"Let's take it slow," Dan said. He leaned forward and stretched his hand out toward Evan's face, and Evan lifted himself up and shifted in. The kiss was gentle, and affectionate, and it made Jeff's smile soften. "Thank you, Evan." Then Dan turned to Jeff and twisted around until they could kiss, Dan's lips warm and sweet. Jeff knew he was probably imagining it, but he liked to think he could taste just a hint of Evan. "And thank you," Dan said.

“I haven’t done anything,” Jeff replied.

Dan didn’t say anything in response. He just snuggled in tighter and laced his fingers through Jeff’s. It was the only answer Jeff could ever imagine himself wanting, and he relaxed back into the cushions of the couch and let himself enjoy the moment.

Chapter Three

Dan wanted to ride. He wanted to be on a horse, his will combining with the horse's strength to turn them into one invincible creature. He wanted to be galloping over the hills behind the barn, feeling the thundering power of every stride, savoring the miracle that allowed his puny body to harness all that incredible energy.

Instead, he was stuck in his apartment, trying not to pace, waiting for a phone call. He felt like that was all he'd been doing for the last four days, ever since Krista had first contacted him. Sitting around, waiting for one damned call or another.

He was just checking his watch, wondering if it was too early to start drinking, when the phone finally rang. He answered it before it had a chance to ring a second time. "Hello?"

"Dan, it's Susan. We got the preliminary deal." The lawyer sounded exhausted, but still strong.

"Seriously? Damn, Susan, that's incredible. Evan's guys said it was a long shot."

"There's conditions. A lot of them. And you're involved, so I need to run it all by you."

"Yeah, okay. I mean... whatever it takes, I'll do it."

"You said that before, Dan, but I really need you to listen to the conditions and be sure you can live up to them. Okay?"

"Okay, yeah." Dan stood up and let himself move around the

room.

"We got the deal because she's pregnant, as far as I can figure. I made a strong argument, but really, we just got lucky to have a judge with a serious interest in child welfare. So the second she does anything to endanger the baby, this whole thing goes to hell."

"Susan, it's not like I'd let her endanger the baby anyhow."

"She's a grown woman, Dan, not a mobile incubator. She has her own interests, and you're not necessarily going to be able to control her." Dan still hadn't met up with Krista, but Susan had, and he wondered whether there was a warning in the lawyer's words. Krista had been strong-willed and impulsive as a child; maybe she hadn't calmed down all that much. But that didn't matter; she was family, and Dan would do what he could for her. He had to.

"Okay," he said meekly, and he waited for more.

"The deal only lasts until she gives birth, and it only lasts as long as she's cooperating *fully* with the investigation. We got her to a doctor, and apparently she's closer to seven months than to six. So for the next two months, Krista's full-time job is gestating and answering questions from federal and state investigators. If she is anything less than cooperative, the deal goes away. That's clear?"

"Okay, but they can't be abusive about it, right? I mean, they can't call her in the middle of the night, or keep her down at the police station for twenty hours straight or anything, right?"

"If anything like that happens, you call me, and I call the judge. Until we have the judge's instructions, we do *exactly* what the police want, in exactly the way they want it." Susan sighed. "Look, Dan, I've been working with Chris, and he's told me a bit about your background. We're going to get to that in a minute. But you need to be thinking of yourself as a solid citizen, here. You love the police. The police are your friends. They serve you and protect you. Okay? Dan?"

"So, I lie."

"Don't do it under oath. But in terms of your attitude, absolutely. Lie away." There was a note of something in her voice, but Dan wasn't sure whether it was humor or impatience. "Can you do that? Because if you can't, we need to find another arrangement."

"I can do it." He could. He wasn't the rebellious kid he'd been, and even back then, he'd never really *hated* the cops. They had been the enemy, sure, but it was nothing personal.

"Okay." She sounded like she believed him, and Dan had another flash of gratitude that Chris had found her. She was perfect for the job. She'd obviously managed to handle Krista, and she was tough enough to make Dan listen to her too. He needed that, and he forced himself to concentrate on her words before she noticed his distraction. "So, in short, Krista will be under house arrest. We didn't even ask for her to be released into your custody, since you have your own history of police trouble. So the house arrest will be supervised by an independent, licensed security company. She will not be allowed to leave the premises unless she's accompanied by law enforcement officers or by employees of the security company, and she can only leave for preapproved reasons. The judge has given us a list of allowable trips, and it's pretty short. Essentially, she can go to meetings with the police, meetings with her lawyers, and medical appointments. That's it."

This had been discussed earlier. Chris and Evan had conspired to keep the cost of the security company secret from Dan, but he knew it had to be astronomical. He never would have suggested such a thing, even if he'd known it was possible, but Evan liked to think big. And in this case, it seemed like the best solution. "And there's bail?"

"Two million dollars. Four hundred thousand of that is required as surety."

Damn it. Another favor from Evan. Dan hated it, but he

couldn't let his sister rot in jail because he was too proud to ask his lover for help. Couldn't let his niece or nephew come into the world behind bars, not if there was any way he could prevent it. "Yeah. Okay."

"If she violates the terms of this agreement, if she leaves—that money is gone, Dan. The full two million."

"Yeah. I get it." Dan had no idea how he'd ever make enough money to repay a debt that huge, but how could he refuse the deal? He was starting to feel trapped, and no amount of moving around the apartment was going to make that better.

"Okay, we're almost done," Susan said. Her cheerfulness sounded forced, as if she was fully aware of Dan's reaction to all this, but she charged on anyway. "Krista can't drink or do drugs, but hopefully that wouldn't be a problem anyway, since she's pregnant. She's subject to testing for any illicit substances at any time. And, Dan, the point of all this is that she is confessing to some pretty serious crimes. We're going to take the next two months to work out plea bargains with the feds and the state, and we'll do the best we can for her. There's a statute of limitations issue on some of the crimes, and evidentiary weaknesses on others, but quite a few of them are slam-dunk convictions. She's absolutely going to do time. She's asked me for an estimate, and I told her I really can't give her one, but... I'd be *shocked* if she was sentenced to less than ten years. I think twenty to thirty is more likely, between the federal and state charges. Now, hopefully she wouldn't serve her full sentence, but it's still a lot of time."

"Yeah. Okay." Dan tried to imagine spending that kind of time behind bars. He couldn't really wrap his head around it.

"Dan, I just want you to understand... right now, yes, Krista wants to turn herself in. She wants to stop running, and she wants to do what's best for her child. I truly believe that. But as the time gets closer, she's going to get spooked. She's going to be very, very tempted to run, and she's proven herself to be very good at that. We could go through a whole lot of trouble setting up a deal that she runs away from. And if she runs, it won't just be time that you've lost, it'll be a lot of money."

"So what am I supposed to do?" Dan really wanted to know the answer to the question.

But, of course, Susan didn't give it to him. "I don't know, Dan. I guess you need to look at how much you can afford to lose. When I told Krista the terms of the deal, she seemed to think it was impossible. The two million dollars threw her, but so did the private security, and she's not wrong. Those are two things that are beyond the reach of most Americans. My understanding is that they may not be out of *your* reach, but my understanding is far from complete, and even if you *can* reach them, it doesn't mean it's a good idea." She paused. "I'm sorry I'm not more use, Dan."

"I appreciate your honesty," he said, and he meant it. He needed all the information he could get, and he needed it straight up. "When do you need to know by? I mean—I don't have that kind of money. I need to talk to Evan."

"The government lawyers have given us until tomorrow morning. But, Dan—as I said, Krista is pretty well assuming that the deal isn't going to work. She's staying strong for now, but it's going to be a long night for her to worry about being pregnant in jail, giving birth in shackles... I think the sooner you decide, the better it would be. She's not in any sort of custody right now. I've got her in a hotel room, but if she gets scared, she's gone, and even if she comes back, she'll have blown any chance of a deal."

"Yeah, okay." Dan felt like he'd been saying that a lot. He supposed there wasn't much else for him *to* say. He was just absorbing information, trying to process it all somehow. Trying to figure out what the *fuck* to do about it all. "I'll talk to Evan and get back to you as soon as I can. Thanks." He ended the call and flopped down on the couch. He was suddenly exhausted, but his mind was racing, and he needed to calm down a little.

He wasn't too surprised to hear the knock on the door a minute or so later, and he didn't even bother to stand up. He just turned his head and waited. There were advantages to living in a small apartment, and one of them was that he could see pretty much the whole place from where he was sitting. He watched as the front door opened slowly and Evan's face peeked in. "Chris called me," he explained. "He said there's a deal, but that you'll need some help."

And Evan had come right over to offer it. After living with the man's generosity for two years, Dan really hadn't expected anything else. But just because Evan was offering, it didn't mean Dan should accept.

Evan flopped down on the couch next to Dan. Then he stood up and shifted over to the armchair. Proximity was good, but he wanted to be able to see Dan's face for this conversation. "So, Chris told me about the deal," he started. "And he told me that you were more or less going along with letting me pay for the security guys. Well, he said you were being a whiny bitch about it, but that we should ignore you."

"That sounds like Chris," Dan agreed tiredly. Evan wanted to wrap him up in blankets and put him to bed, but there was no time for that, not yet.

"He also said you needed four hundred thousand cash. And that if Krista booked out, you'd be on the hook for that plus one point six more." He waited for Dan's nod. "So, obviously you don't have that kind of money, and obviously I do." This time, he didn't wait. "But I don't want to lend it to you," he said.

"What?" Dan frowned. "I mean... yeah, okay." He stood up. He didn't seem angry, just confused, and Evan wasn't sure how to feel about that. How many times had he *encouraged* Dan to count on him, to take him for granted? And now Dan finally needed him, and it seemed like Evan was backing out, and Dan was just going to accept it? He didn't think he deserved better? Didn't think the *relationship* deserved better? It was frustrating.

And Evan didn't want to see any more of it, so he decided to clarify. "It doesn't make sense. If she sticks around, I'll get the money back, and it's not like I was going to charge you interest or anything. And if she doesn't stick around, you'd... I don't even know what you'd have to do to get that kind of cash. It'd be impossible. So I just want you to take the money. The four hundred thousand now, and the rest if she goes. I'll cover it. It's not a loan, it's just... yours."

And there was the expression on Dan's face, the wild, almost hunted look that Evan hadn't seen for a long time. It was the way Dan looked when he was feeling trapped in the relationship, intimidated by the closeness all three of them had worked so hard to build. It was a look Evan had hoped to never see again. "Evan, that's too much—" Dan started, but Evan cut him off.

"Don't say it, Dan. It's bullshit. If we were a traditional couple—one man, one woman—we'd probably be married by now. Unless you were being a pissy bitch about the ceremony, like you probably would be, but I bet we'd have fought through that, and my money would be yours." He stopped, and smiled. "Well, you'd probably have come up with some insane prenup, but I wouldn't have signed it, so you'd have been out of luck. You'd be rich." Evan stood up and took the two steps to stand in front of Dan. "I love you, Dan. You love me. We both love Jeff, and he loves us back. It's not traditional, but that doesn't mean it's less. Right?" He made his face strong, challenging Dan to disagree. He'd thought this out on the way over, and he knew he'd found the way past Dan's defenses. It was foolproof. Or at least he'd thought it was. Dan seemed to be trying pretty hard to find a loophole, though. Evan forced himself to wait quietly.

"It's not less," Dan finally said. "But...."

"But nothing." Evan smiled in what he hoped was a firm but kindly manner. "It's *our* money, okay? Yours and mine and Jeff's. And Jeff and I totally support your decision to spend some of *our* money on a member of *our* family. Okay?" He buckled one of his knees, let it shoot forward and jostle Dan's. "Okay?" he asked again.

"Evan—" Dan started to say, but then he stopped. He looked down at something... their knees? His feet? Evan wasn't sure, but he didn't really care, either, because when Dan looked back up, his face was calm. "Okay," he said. "Yeah. Thank—"

"Nope!" Evan interrupted. "No thanks necessary. It's no more than what you should expect."

Dan paused as if letting himself absorb that. Then he shook his head and smiled. "I was going to say, 'Thank you for getting me one of *our* beers, when you go to *our* fridge to get one for yourself.'"

Evan grinned. Dan could be stubborn, but he also had good common sense. And, Evan liked to think, he knew who to trust. "I see. I'll get on that." He leaned down and kissed Dan, and then leaned in a little further, letting their bodies connect. "Or maybe we could take a quick trip to *our* bedroom?"

Dan pulled away, but Evan could tell he wasn't going to stay away for long. "Too far," Dan said. He grinned as he raised an eyebrow and cast his eyes sideways. "Our wall is a lot closer."

Fuck, yeah. Evan's official story was that he worked out as a stress-reliever, but if he was being totally honest, he'd have to admit that *this* was why he worked out, so he could be strong enough to reach down and wrap his hands under Dan's ass, lift him without excessive strain, and pin his body against the wall with his feet barely touching the floor. Most of the time, Dan was dominant and controlling in bed, but sometimes... sometimes he wasn't. And Evan always wanted to be prepared for those times.

He caught both of Dan's wrists, lifted them over their

heads, and left one of his own hands up there, pinning Dan's wrists to the wall. His other hand roamed wherever it wanted to. Down over Dan's chest, just brushing over the growing hardness beneath his fly, up across his ribs, then back down to slide under the fabric of his shirt. Dan had less body hair than Jeff, just a light dusting on his chest, and his skin was soft and warm. Sometimes, Evan would spend hours on that skin, tracing patterns, kissing and nipping and exploring, but that wasn't what he was after right now.

He undid Dan's fly, slipped his hand inside to find the hot skin of Dan's swelling cock. "I'm going to fuck you," he said in Dan's ear.

"Yeah, that's the idea," Dan agreed. He seemed totally blasé, and even though Evan knew it was an act, he still felt the challenge. The dare. He tugged at Dan's jeans, his underwear, struggling to get the fabric out of the way, and he could feel Dan's lips curve into a grin against his cheek. Evan shifted his head and kissed Dan, hard and demanding, and Dan's lips curled again. He was happy to be getting to Evan, pleased to be the one who was still calm. Evan wrapped his hand around Dan's cock, tight, and ran his thumb up into the slit. Dan inhaled sharply, the first crack in his layer of control, and Evan jacked him roughly a few times, his hand confident and strong. He squeezed a little tighter, and Dan's head rolled back to meet the wall, his neck stretched and exposed. Vulnerable. Beautiful.

Evan kissed Dan's neck, then brought his hand down to quickly undo his own fly and worked his pants and underwear partway off. He pressed down on Dan's shoulder. "Get me wet," he instructed, and he released Dan's hands. Dan immediately fell to his knees and captured Evan's cock. Dan's mouth was perfect, his blowjobs literally staggering, but Evan wasn't going to let himself enjoy the sensations for long. At least, that was what he thought before Dan kissed the head of his cock, wet and sloppy, and then wrapped his lips around the shaft and eased down, down. He swallowed Evan's cock with steady determination. Evan was almost too well-endowed, and he'd never found anyone else who could take his full length so easily. He ran his fingers lovingly over Dan's cheeks, felt the motion beneath the skin as Dan's tongue worked its magic, soft and then hard, slow rolls mixed with quick flicks. The whole experience was making Evan almost crazy, almost out of control.

But not quite. "Lots of spit," he managed to say, and when Dan pulled off, he left his mouth loose, leaving a good coating of saliva behind. "Get up here. Turn around." Dan obeyed, no hesitation, no smart-ass comments, and that was the hottest thing so far. Evan spat on his own fingers, then eased them between Dan's ass cheeks. Dan canted his hips out, welcoming Evan, and it was almost too much. They'd struggled to get this far, but they'd made it to a place where Dan was comfortable like this, where he trusted Evan. It was a gift, and Evan needed to remember to appreciate it.

He eased his cock into place, worked his way inside, felt the muscles pulsing and then easing around him. He could feel Dan's body struggling to adjust, could tell when Dan's brain sent the orders to relax, and he leaned his head forward and kissed the back of Dan's neck. "You're perfect," he murmured, and then he sank the rest of the way in.

His hips started moving of their own accord, and Dan arched to meet every thrust, encouraging Evan to go harder, faster. Evan couldn't imagine himself ignoring that invitation. He eased one hand under Dan's shirt and splayed his fingers across Dan's chest, giving himself more control, and wrapped the other around Dan's throbbing cock. Dan's groan was Evan's reward, made even sweeter when Dan twisted his head around far enough that they could kiss, rough and sloppy. Every thrust of Evan's body drove the breath out of Dan's, and Evan found himself trying to inhale at just the right moment, trying to capture the air that had been in Dan's lungs and bring it into his own. He wanted to be closer, to be joined more tightly and completely than they ever had been.

He also wanted to get off, though, and after a while that took priority. Dan seemed to understand, and he shifted so he was braced on the wall by one arm, bent at the elbow with the forearm crossed in front of his face. That left his other hand free, and he used it to push Evan away from his cock. "Go harder," he ordered, and Evan straightened his body, braced himself, and complied. Eagerly.

He didn't last long after that. He tried to hold off, but then Dan came, his body arching and tense, his ass spasming around Evan's cock, and that was it. Two more rough, shuddering thrusts before he lost control, shooting his seed deep inside Dan's warm, pliant body.

Evan nuzzled his chin into the crook of Dan's neck, finding the spot that always made Dan squirm and laugh. "I love you, Danny."

"You get so fucking sappy after I let you top," Dan responded, but he didn't move away. "We should stick a spigot in you, drain it out, and boil up some syrup."

"If you stick your spigot in me, I wouldn't be the one topping anymore."

"Nice. You freak."

"You were the one who wanted to make syrup out of my sappiness," Evan protested, and he started to ease his body away. He didn't want to, but they couldn't stay like that forever. "You're going to call the lawyer? Tell her to go ahead?"

"Evan, two million dollars…." The post-fuck relaxation was instantly gone, and Dan's voice was back to being tense and unhappy.

"Only if she runs. If she does, she does, but hopefully she won't." Evan kissed Dan's neck. "She's family, Danny."

Dan nodded slowly, then eased around and bent over to pull up his jeans. "Yeah," he said, "she is. But I have no idea if she knows what that means."

Jeff looked at the pile of crap in his shopping basket and then looked over at Evan's cart. It had about ten times more items than Jeff had managed to find.

Evan caught his look. "It's polite," he protested. "Welcoming. And she's going to be stuck in the guest house for two months; she needs stuff to keep her busy."

"You're getting her a laptop *and* an iPad," Jeff said. "Speakers. Cordless keyboard." He leaned over Evan's cart and poked a little. "Xbox *and* Wii. Half a rack full of games. Seven million different controllers and accessories." He frowned. "What if she doesn't like games?"

"What if she doesn't like books? Your e-reader's going to be pretty useless then, isn't it?" Evan nodded smugly. "But my iPad will still be an excellent toy. There's something for *everyone* on the iPad."

Jeff had to admit that Evan had a point. Maybe Krista wouldn't be a reader. Dan wasn't, really. He only read about horses, and that could be considered work rather than pleasure. "Maybe I shouldn't get it," Jeff said. "Even if she *does* like to read, she can get books on the iPad, right?"

"Jeff!" Evan sounded genuinely disappointed. "She needs something with e-ink. She'll get eyestrain if she tries to read a whole book on a backlit screen."

"This is getting out of control," Jeff said. "What the hell are we doing, buying a million gifts for a stranger?"

"Come on, Jeff; they're not for her." Evan smiled softly. "They're for Dan. So he'll know that we care about the person he cares about."

Damn. Jeff should have been the one to say that. He reached his hand out and rested it on the back of Evan's neck. "Yeah. Okay. What else does Dan want us to buy for her?"

"Not baby stuff," Evan said. Jeff raised a questioning eyebrow as he brought his hand back to his side. Evan shook his head forbiddingly. "I promised Tat she could be in charge of that. She and your mom are going shopping tomorrow. I think Robyn's going too."

"What about maternity stuff? Like... I don't know. Clothes?"

"Tat's got dibs. But she said she wants to meet Krista first, get an idea of her coloring and her size. It sounded stupid to me—I'm pretty sure her coloring is like Dan's, and her size is going to be 'huge', right? She's seven months pregnant."

"So we're just in charge of toys?"

"Not baby toys. Tat would kill me. Just things to make the next two months better."

"Before she gets hauled off to jail." It was easy to get excited about the new member of their extended family, but hard to stay that way when Jeff remembered what was going to happen at the end of it all.

Evan sighed. "My guys say Susan's doing a killer job. They couldn't believe the deal she got for the next two months. But, yeah, they say there's no way she's getting away without serious time."

Jeff didn't really think this was the right place for the conversation, in the middle of a crowded electronics store, but he wasn't sure when they'd find another opportunity. "And we're prepared for that? I mean... the baby. If Dan gets custody of the baby... we're good with it?"

Evan looked shocked. "It's a *baby*, Jeff. Of course we're good with it! I know we haven't talked about it a lot, but... I want to be a dad someday. I was thinking we'd end up adopting, or doing some surrogate-mother thing, but this is so much easier! We're helping a kid, and helping ourselves."

"Careful, Evan." Jeff was back to being the voice of reason, the person in charge of crushing Evan's enthusiasm. Maybe he *was* getting a bit tired of the job. But there was no one else around to take care of it, and it absolutely had to be done. "We don't want to set up a situation where we're *hoping* Krista gets a long sentence. And if she gets a short sentence, she's going to want her kid back." And now the hardest part. "And in general, people raise their kids the way they were raised themselves, unless something comes along to break the pattern. Now, with Dan... I truly believe that the pattern is broken. Between Justin, and us, and just... I don't know, just Dan being *Dan*... I think he could be a great dad. But there's no guarantee that Krista's in the same boat." Jeff reached out again, his hand gentle on Evan's neck. "And we're going to have to turn that kid over to her, whether we think she's a great mom or not."

Evan didn't shrug Jeff's hand off, but he looked so mature, so strong that Jeff pulled it back on his own. This was business-Evan, and he didn't need guidance from Jeff or anyone else. "I've already thought about that," he said. "And the truth is she's got no money. I'm not saying we should be assholes about that. If she wants to stick around and be responsible and raise the kid near us and let us help out, then we can use the money to support her, and we can co-parent the kid. But if she's going to be irresponsible, if she's going to be a bad mother, then we can use the money to get in her way, or to pay her off. Either way, I'm confident that we can keep the kid nearby, at least. And probably with us."

"Jesus, Evan. Don't let Dan hear you talking that way." Jeff wasn't sure if *he* wanted to hear Evan talking that way.

Evan just rolled his eyes. "I'm not stupid, Jeff. Dan's... he's a romantic. An idealist. I know that. And I like that about him. I have no idea how he ended up that way, after everything he's been through, but I like it." He smiled at Jeff, calm and confident and powerful. "But I'm not. I'm the practical one. I'm the one who makes things happen. I'm the one who makes the world work for people like Dan."

It was true. They seemed the reverse, on the surface,

Evan with his enthusiasm and Dan with his cautious, almost suspicious approach, but underneath all that, Evan had it right. "And what am I?" Jeff asked softly. "How do I fit into your world order?" He said it lightly, almost jokingly, but he desperately wanted to hear Evan's answer. It was a question he'd been asking himself a lot lately.

Evan frowned at him as if the question was stupid. "You're *Jeff*," he said. But he seemed to sense that Jeff was hoping for more. "You're the glue that holds the idealist and the pragmatist together," he clarified. And then he reached out, the gesture unfamiliar to both of them, and he gripped the back of Jeff's neck and shook gently. "You're *Jeff*," he repeated softly.

"Can I help you with anything?" an efficient voice asked, and Jeff and Evan turned together to look at the uniformed salesman standing a few feet away. "Is there anything you're having trouble finding?"

Evan frowned thoughtfully. "Yeah. I think we need some kitchen stuff. Juicers, and steamers, and... I don't know. Healthy cooking stuff."

"Excellent," the salesman said with a smile. "We have an excellent selection of small appliances, right over here." He gestured gracefully, and Evan allowed himself to be guided. Jeff trailed along behind. He was *Jeff*. It seemed to mean something to Evan, but Jeff really wasn't sure what. He wasn't sure what it meant to himself, really. He looked at Evan, and thought about Dan, and wondered how Evan could even suggest that they needed extra glue to keep them together. At the start, sure, things had been a bit rocky. But they'd gotten over that, moved on, and now they were strong. Stable. Dan and Evan would stay together regardless of whether they had extra glue.

He caught up to Evan just in time to receive a big, enthusiastic grin. "A bread-maker," Evan announced. "Babies love fresh bread!"

"Babies love milk," Jeff corrected. "*You* love fresh bread. And you already have a bread-maker. And a housekeeper."

Evan ignored him and looked to his cart, then to the salesman. "I think I'll need another cart," he stage-whispered.

The salesman beamed. "I'll be right back," he said happily, and the shopping trip continued.

Chapter Four

Susan had been careful to keep Dan from finding out where Krista was staying. She'd said that she was protected by lawyer-client privilege, but there was nothing to keep him safe from prosecution, not if he knew where Krista was and withheld it from the police. He probably would have been willing to take the chance, but he hadn't really been in that much of a hurry to meet his sister. He was happy to have had a little time to prepare. He'd gone grocery shopping, given Evan's already immaculate guest house another quick cleaning, and done his best to calm the fuck down.

He checked the plate of cookies on the kitchen table and then opened the fridge and peered inside for the umpteenth time. If he needed another symbol of what a bad brother he was, the fridge was perfect. It was crammed full of every kind of food he could think of, most of which was going to rot before Krista had even a chance to eat it, all because he had no idea what she liked. He couldn't remember any food preferences from their shared childhood; he'd been so wrapped up in himself and his own stupid issues that he hadn't had any attention to spare for his sister. And he'd run away before he'd gotten a chance to know her any better.

He shut the fridge door and crossed to the coffeemaker. The Internet said that moderate caffeine was okay for pregnant women, but it hadn't been too clear on what "moderate" meant, so he'd bought decaf.

He heard a car door slam in front of the house and almost dropped the glass carafe. Obviously *he* didn't need any caffeine, either. He pressed the button to turn the coffeemaker on and wiped his hands on his jeans. A deep breath, and then he headed for the front hall. Another deep breath, and he opened the door.

There were a lot of people on the porch, and the only one he recognized was Susan. But he could figure out the rest. The people in navy uniforms were the security guards. And the pregnant woman was his sister. "Hi," he said, looking mostly at Susan. He couldn't believe he'd turned down Jeff and Evan when they'd offered to be there for this moment. He hadn't explained the relationship to Krista yet; he wasn't even sure she knew he was gay, although his relationship with Justin was pretty clear on the Internet, so even if she'd missed his orientation when they were younger, she'd probably figured it out by now. But he hadn't wanted to overwhelm her with too many people, especially when she wouldn't be clear on why they were there. He'd unfortunately forgotten the fact that he was socially ridiculous without their support.

But he didn't have to be, he remembered. Another deep breath and he let his face relax into a warm smile. "Krista," he said. He stepped out onto the porch, his arms carefully neutral; ready to hug if she wanted, ready to wrap around her shoulder more casually if she seemed cool. Her smile was almost as tentative as his had been, so he went for the shoulder-wrap, just a light squeeze, and then backed away. "It's really good to see you," he said, and he was pretty sure he meant it. "Come on in." He moved toward the door, and then looked toward Susan. "Do the guards need to be inside, or...?"

One of the guards stepped forward and held out his hand, and Dan stopped walking long enough to shake it. "I'm Ben Dumas. We need to take a quick sweep through the interior, but we've liaised with the Kaminski security team, and we can do the rest of our work from outside the house. We'll give you as much privacy as possible."

"Okay. That's great, thanks." Another warm smile, and Dan could feel his muscles warming up. He should have seen the need for this, should have been prepared, but he was getting in the game now. "Is there anything you need from me?"

"No, sir, I think we're fine. Thank you." Ben nodded efficiently, releasing Dan from the conversation.

Which wasn't exactly what Dan had been hoping for, but he went with it. He kept his mask on and turned to Susan and Krista. "Great. Come on in, then, and we'll get you settled." He paused and looked back at the car. "Do you have a bag or anything?"

Krista shook her head. She looked uncomfortable. "I'm traveling light."

"Okay." Dan wasn't sure whether it was appropriate for him to ask for details on all this, or whether he was supposed to be respecting her privacy. What the hell had she been doing for the last fifteen years, and how had she gotten to the place she was now? Or maybe he'd be just as happy if he didn't hear about all that. "Well, come on in. This is Evan's place, but he doesn't use it much, so he offered to let you stay here. A hell of a lot more comfortable than crowding in with me; I've got a one-bedroom."

"Evan," Krista started, then she glanced over at Susan before saying, "he's your boyfriend?"

Well, that was straightforward. "Yeah," Dan said. He'd explain Jeff later. He'd like to get a reaction on the homosexuality aspect before he introduced the threesome idea. "The kitchen's just through here. Are you hungry? There's food in the fridge—just a bit of everything, but you can make up a list for me when you're ready, and I can pick up whatever you need. And there's coffee."

Krista's head swiveled around as she looked at her new home. "This is his *guest* house?" she asked. "This is, like, the nicest place I've ever stayed. It's probably one of the nicest places I've ever *been*."

"Yeah." Dan had forgotten about that. He'd worked to keep himself from taking things for granted, at first, but at some point, he'd just let himself relax into Evan's world of casual wealth and immense privilege. "It's a pretty nice house. His parents had it built; I guess they used to have people living here full time, so, you know—it's not like it's just an extra bedroom or something."

"No kidding," Krista agreed. "Nice catch, man. Good to see one of us taking care of himself." Dan wasn't quite sure where to go with that, but apparently he wasn't expected to, because Krista was still going. "You said there was coffee?"

"It's decaf," he said, and it felt like an apology. "The Internet said—"

Krista groaned and put her hands over her ears. "I know, I know. Everything I eat goes into the baby. No smoking, no drinking, no drugs or any fun shit. God, I will be glad when this thing is out of me." She sounded sincere, but her hands shifted down to cradle her stomach in a loving, almost protective way. Dan wasn't sure what to make of the contrast.

Susan broke in politely. "Well, if you two are okay, I've got some paperwork to finish up." She turned to Krista. "You understand that you cannot leave the house unless you're going somewhere preapproved, right? I'll talk to the guards about letting you out on the porch—that doesn't seem like it's asking too much, and surely a little fresh air would be good for you. But otherwise, you're either going somewhere with the guards or the cops, or you're inside, right?" She tilted her head and gave a warning look. "We're getting a sweet deal, here. If you start pushing, it will absolutely fall apart. You understand that?"

Krista rolled her eyes, and Dan had a quick, vivid memory of her doing the same thing to their mother. "I understand," she said with a dramatic sigh. "I'll be good. I'm too fat to get anywhere, anyhow."

Susan didn't look totally satisfied, but she eventually nodded and turned to Dan. "Okay. If anything comes up, if you have any questions—give me a call. Otherwise, I'll be in touch in a few days to check in, okay?" And then she surprised Dan by leaning forward and pressing a quick kiss to Krista's cheek. "Be good," she urged, and she turned and left, her high heels clicking on the hardwood floor.

Dan kept his smile steady. "So, coffee? Or there's herbal tea, or milk, or juice."

"No sugar added in the juice, I hope. Who knows what problems *that* might cause." Krista's voice was bitingly sarcastic. She sank heavily into a chair at the kitchen table. "Coffee's fine, I guess." She frowned, then said, "Thank you."

Dan was already moving toward the coffeemaker. "No problem."

"I didn't just mean the coffee. I probably don't mean the coffee at all, if it tastes as crappy as most decaf. I meant... you know. Everything. The lawyer, and the house, and the guards. I get that your boyfriend is paying for it all, but thanks anyway."

"I'm paying for the lawyer," Dan said, and he immediately felt petty. Susan's fees were significant, but compared to the house and the twenty-four-hour guards, she was definitely a small expense. And Krista was *Dan's* sister—Dan's problem. "But, yeah, Evan's really generous."

"Have you guys been going out for long?"

"A couple years." Dan tried not to get distracted, tried not to think about Evan saying that if they'd been a straight couple, they'd have been married by now. It was too much, too big, and he had more immediate concerns. He set the mug of coffee in front of Krista. "Milk or sugar?"

"Both."

He found the fixings and they sat at the kitchen table and stared at their mugs. It shouldn't have been so hard to talk to his own flesh and blood. But it was. Dan thought about switching his social persona back on, but he decided against it. Krista was going to be in the guest house for two months, and, he assumed, in his life for a long time after that. He wanted their relationship to be truthful. And the truth was that he wasn't much good at small talk. Or talk in general, really.

She was the one who broke the silence. "Do you want to know about Dad?"

Interesting question, and he took a moment to think about it. "I don't know. He took off when we were kids, then he came back and turned his daughter into a bank robber. Is there anything you could tell me that would make up for that?"

Krista's eyes were calm and level as she took another sip of her coffee. Then she said, "What if I told you that *I* was the one who got *him* into robbing banks?"

"Is that true?"

Krista nodded. "Me and Scott—that's my husband—we'd been breaking into houses, mostly, but we hit a couple stores too. And then we started looking at a bank, and we needed a third. Dad was always short of cash, so he wasn't hard to convince."

"And where is he now? And Scott—where's he?"

"I have no idea." It was hard to hear an emotion in Krista's voice, but Dan tried anyway. Was she disappointed? Had she been abandoned? Or was she fine with the whole thing—had she left the men behind willingly? Or was she even telling the truth? Maybe she knew exactly where they were, but didn't trust her brother enough to share the information.

Dan didn't want to get into any of that. "Do they know about the baby? Your husband—does he know he's going to be a father?"

"He knows. But he's already a dad. He's got two kids with one ex, and one with another. But, you know—he's not really in any position to be much of a father. And his family's about as fucked up as he is." She cut her eyes down to her coffee, and when she looked back up, her face was sweet, almost innocent. It was unnerving, and for the first time, Dan wondered how it looked to other people when he donned his own mask. "But *you're* good with kids, right? You must be."

"What? Why?" Dan tried to understand where she was going. "Why would you think I'd be good with kids?"

"Just, you know...." Another sweet smile, but Dan wasn't finding it too compelling anymore. "Because you're gay. I don't believe in all that 'gays shouldn't be allowed to have kids' stuff. You're more sensitive, right? Gentler, or whatever. So you'd probably be really good dads."

"Jesus, Krista, that's a shitload of stereotypes all in one sentence."

"Look, Dan." Krista leaned forward intently. "We're family. Let me talk to you honestly." She apparently took his lack of objection as consent. "You've got a good thing going here. But how long's it going to last, really? I mean—how long before your boyfriend wants a newer, hotter model? He's always going to be rich, but you're not always going to be good-looking, right? We both know how men's eyes can wander, and how much they like novelty." She leaned back a little, apparently confident that she had made a convincing argument. "You need something to keep him interested, and to tie him to you. Something that he can't just walk away from when he gets bored. And what I'm saying is: a baby. I've got one, you need one." She smiled again, and it wasn't sweet anymore; she looked absolutely predatory. "Let's make a deal."

Dan had no idea how he would have responded, but it turned out that he didn't have to, at least not right away. There was a knock from the front hall, and then a familiar voice called out, "Hello? Dan? You here?"

Dan stood up quickly. "In the kitchen," he called. He wasn't sure if Evan's arrival was going to make things better or worse.

Evan knew he wasn't supposed to be there. Jeff had refused to come, saying that they needed to respect Dan's privacy, and Evan had gone along with that for as long as he could. But Jeff had plans for the afternoon, and as soon as he was out of the house, Evan had looked across the kitchen table to find Tat staring back at him. "We should at least say 'hi'," she'd suggested, and that had been all it took.

His bold curiosity had carried him right up onto the porch, had let him knock on the door, push it slightly open and call "hello." And then it had deserted him. Jeff had been right; this was an invasion of Dan's privacy. The guy hadn't seen his sister in more than a decade, and neither of them had been leading quiet lives; they had a right to get caught up. He winced before calling, "We're just going to leave some stuff out here, okay? Nothing important."

But he'd forgotten that Tat was at least as headstrong as he was. She tossed a scornful look his way and headed for the kitchen. Shit. This was absolutely Evan's fault. He followed along uncertainly.

"Hi, I'm Tatiana Kaminski," he heard her say, and as he rounded the corner he saw her advancing on the pregnant woman in the kitchen chair. Krista. Evan had been right that she would have the same coloring as Dan, but there wasn't much resemblance otherwise. Where Dan was lean and angular, Krista was rounded. She probably wasn't overweight, although it was hard to tell with the belly in the way, but she was soft, even in her face. Her eyes were familiar, though, green and quick, taking everything in.

"Hi, Tatiana," Krista said, and she extended her hand to take the one that was being offered. Then she looked over Tat's shoulder. "And you must be Evan." She struggled to her feet while Evan waited awkwardly. If it had been anyone else, he probably would have stepped forward, given her a hug, offered to help... something. But this was Dan's sister, and Dan was just standing there, watching. Evan didn't want to step on any more toes than he already had. And Krista made it up just fine, and held her hand out to Evan. "Thanks for letting me stay here. And paying for the lawyer and the guards and everything."

"Dan paid for the lawyer," Evan clarified. "And we're happy to have you here. Dan's...." Damn it, what was Dan? Obviously *Evan* knew what he was, but did Krista? What had been discussed so far, and why the hell hadn't Evan listened to Jeff and stayed the hell out of it all? "He's like part of the family. So you are too, by extension."

"Well, I like the sound of that!" Krista said. She looked over at Dan with an oddly meaningful expression and added, "I'm sure Dan really values the relationship."

That was a bit weird, but Evan let it pass. And Tat hadn't seemed to notice at all. She was staring at Krista's bulging abdomen with near-maniacal excitement. "Is everything going okay? With the baby? Do you know if it's a girl or a boy?"

Krista grinned. "Everything's good. Just went to the doctor and got all checked out, and he gave me a bunch of vitamins and stuff. It's going to be a beautiful, healthy baby." Another weird look at Dan, and Evan absolutely wanted to know what was going on there. "But I asked them not to tell me if it's a boy or a girl. I want to be surprised."

Tat nodded happily. "So no blue or pink yet—that's cool. I like babies in white clothes. I mean, we could get some yellow and green and stuff too, but we already got a bit in white—we kept the receipts, so we can return anything you don't like—and I think it'd be excellent to keep that as the base color for its wardrobe."

"Wow," Krista said. "I hadn't really gotten that far. I mean...." She looked at Dan again. "I'm not sure where the baby's going to be, after it's born."

That only slowed Tat down for a moment before she said, "Well, it'll need clothes wherever it is. I brought a few bags of stuff over, in case you wanted to look at it." She scowled at Dan. "And you probably want to sit on a comfier chair, right? There's good furniture in the living room—do you want to go in there?"

"Sure," Krista agreed, and she followed Tat without a second look at either of the men in the room.

Evan was left in the kitchen with Dan. "Sorry for busting in," he said. "Tat was pretty excited."

Dan nodded, but that never really meant too much, Evan had discovered. Dan would nod his head for practically any reason, totally without connection to actually accepting what was being said to him. The only way to be sure where you stood was to look him in the eyes, and right then, Dan's eyes were focused pretty intently on the doorway his sister had just passed through.

"You okay?" Evan asked. He waited, and finally Dan turned toward him and moved in. Dan was usually pretty good about reciprocating casual affection, but he didn't generally initiate it. Evan wasn't sure if this was a good or bad sign, but he opened his arms and let Dan step into them. Dan rested his forehead on Evan's shoulder.

"I'm okay," Dan said, his voice a little muffled. "It was just a bit weird."

"We'll sort it out," Evan promised. "We'll make it work."

"Yeah," Dan said, but Evan didn't believe him. He reached his fingers down to rest gently underneath Dan's chin, then lifted just enough to urge Dan to look up. Dan lifted his face before his eyes, but he finally looked at Evan, and Evan wasn't reassured by what he saw.

"It's going to work," he repeated, and he put all the conviction he could muster into his voice.

Dan smiled reluctantly. "If you say so."

"That's what I want to hear," Evan said, and he turned quickly, pulling Dan's head into the crook of his elbow and dragging him toward the living room. "Now let's go see what Tat's been spending all her money on."

Dan let himself be guided, and Evan tried to ignore the knot of worry forming in his stomach. What had made Dan so uncertain? And what could Evan do to make it better?

"So, everything's okay, then?" Jeff said. He was pulling his shirt back on and didn't bother to look at the doctor. Didn't bother, or couldn't make himself.

"I didn't say that," the doctor said, just as Jeff had been afraid he might. "I said I couldn't see the problem. But if you're having pain like that, as regularly as you are, then whether I can see it or not, there's something wrong. I'm going to refer you to a cardiologist, to rule out the most obvious, and the most serious, possibilities. When we get the results from that, we can talk about the next step."

"I was probably exaggerating things," Jeff said quickly. "It seemed like a problem, but—"

"Jeff, stop it. You've been my patient for almost twenty years, and this is the first time I've seen you outside of your yearly checkups. You're not a hypochondriac. You're experiencing a medical issue, and we've got a good team of people ready to help you with it." The doctor's voice was kind, but firm, and Jeff didn't try to argue with him.

But that didn't mean he couldn't deflect. "I'm forty-three," he said. "It's too early for it to be my heart, right? And I'm fit—I exercise and watch what I eat."

"High school athletes sometimes keel over with heart attacks." The doctor held up his hand before Jeff could respond.

"I don't think you're at risk for that. From the tests I could do here, everything seems fine. But you need to take this seriously. You're relatively young, and you're relatively fit, and those are both factors in your favor. But you're having chest pains. I want to know why."

Yeah. Jeff wanted to know why too. He finished buttoning his shirt and took the slip of paper the doctor offered him. "Dr. Lam works out of this office, so you can make an appointment at the front desk. There may even be something available today, if you're able to wait a while."

Jeff didn't want to do that. He wanted to get out of this place and forget all about it. He wanted to get back home and keep Evan and Tat from driving Dan crazy, and he wanted to meet Dan's sister and start trying to figure out how she was going to fit into their family. And apparently his preoccupation was clear on his face, because the doctor clucked disapprovingly.

"Jeff, you need to take this seriously. You came to see me; that was a good first step. Now you need to follow through." He paused, then added, "You need to take care of yourself so that you'll be in good enough condition to take care of everybody else." He smiled gently when Jeff looked at him in surprise. "I may only see you once a year, Jeff, but that doesn't mean I don't know you. Now, get out there and make an appointment. I'll follow up with Dr. Lam as soon as you've seen her. And, Jeff—if you can't get in to see her soon, I'm going to recommend a trip to the hospital to find another cardiologist. This isn't nothing."

Jeff nodded reluctantly and shuffled out the door. His heart was fine; he didn't need a cardiologist. But he thought of Evan's face, excited as he talked about Krista's baby, and he thought of Dan, stubborn and proud, working so hard to do the right thing. The doctor was right. Jeff needed to take care of himself so he could be sure he'd be around to take care of them. He found the end of the line for the receptionist and joined it, the referral slip clutched in his hands. He'd be okay. He had to be.

Chapter Five

"He's not one of the valuable ones," Dan explained. He looked over at Smokey, happily eating the carrot Krista had brought out to the porch, and thought how inadequate the words were. He tried to clarify. "I mean, he doesn't cost a lot. He was a gift, actually, so he didn't cost anything, except for five years of putting up with Chris's bullshit beforehand." He scratched the Quarter Horse's withers and looked over at his sister. He had no idea if this was making sense to her. "But he's mine. The other horses—some of them are great. They're all worth a lot of money, and they're talented athletes, and well-trained. But Smokey's mine. And he's well-trained too."

He looked down to see that Smokey had finished the carrot and had taken an experimental mouthful of the pink flowers that had been carefully planted along the porch's foundation. The horse was chewing thoughtfully, like a food expert savoring a new flavor, and Dan pushed him back a few steps. "Well-trained at some stuff," he clarified. "He's not, like, housebroken or anything." Dan couldn't really understand why it was so important to him that his sister appreciate his horse, but he couldn't deny that it was. He didn't want to stop talking, didn't want to give her the opportunity to speak and say something that would show that this was just one more area where she and he had nothing in common.

But when he dared to look back at Krista, she was smiling at the little cow horse on her lawn. "He's adorable," she said.

"Those videos you showed me… the eventers? They looked kinda scary. Too big, and, I don't know… too fancy. This one, though…." She reached her hand out, and Smokey politely raised his nose to sniff her fingers. Looking for more carrots, obviously, but willing to be petted if that was all she had to offer. "He's one of us, isn't he?"

Dan nodded slowly and let the relief wash over him. Krista understood. "Yeah. He's a tough little commoner. He's got a lot of heart, and he gets shit done."

"Can I get him another carrot? Or an apple?" Krista grinned. "Or I think I might have a few sugar-free candies somewhere in there."

"Evan gets carried away," Dan said, but he didn't feel the need to defend his boyfriend. Evan could take care of himself. "He sees something that sounds good, and he can't buy just a little."

"Well, the next option for candy that gross is to buy *none*," Krista said firmly. "I'm pregnant, not diabetic."

"He read an article," Dan said, and he smiled at Krista's snort. An article on folic acid had prompted Tia, the Kaminski housekeeper, to make spinach-stuffed ravioli and send it over. Krista had said it was surprisingly delicious, and the floodgates had opened. Robyn had read about calcium and how supplements weren't always enough, and had become an expert on all things dairy, despite her vegan leanings. Tat had set up "fruit of the week" programs from three different companies, because she'd read that a diverse diet was important. And Evan had found articles on babies being able to hear in the womb, and had somehow bought or had manufactured a huge set of "womb-phones," huge earphones designed to be strapped to the mother's belly. He'd sent along some Bach and Mozart to play, but Dan wasn't convinced that Evan wouldn't have found some way to introduce his own voice to the recordings, sending subliminal messages about living large and going for profit maximization.

Dan had been trying to avoid getting caught up in the hype. It was gratifying to see everyone so excited, so welcoming, but this was his sister. They had their own history together, abbreviated though it was, and hopefully they had some sort of a future together, as well. They were about more than gifts. And Krista was more than a baby-production machine to him.

She returned with an apple and a carrot, and fed them both to Smokey, laughing as the horse drooled apple juice all over her hand. "He just expects me to hold it for him?" she asked, waiting with her arm outstretched as Smokey chewed his second bite of apple.

"He's not wrong, is he? Some horses take the whole thing, but that's usually the ones that haven't gotten a lot of human affection. The ones that trust people, they've learned that they don't need to grab it all at once. And it's a lot easier for them to chew it a bite at a time."

Krista smiled affectionately at the horse. "So he's had a good life, then. Smokey's had people take care of him."

Dan nodded. "Yeah. He hasn't always been as spoiled as he's been the last few years, maybe, but he's always had it pretty good."

Krista's green eyes looked familiar to Dan as she turned and looked at him. "So maybe he's not really one of us after all," she said softly. She didn't wait for an answer, just went back to fussing over Smokey. Dan was glad she was willing to be distracted, because he really had no idea how to respond to what she'd said.

Evan liked to watch Dan. Doing pretty much anything, but especially doing things that really captured his attention and forced him to concentrate. Sex. Riding horses. And, strangely enough, cooking.

It had been almost sad, over the years, watching him get better in the kitchen. When Tia had first started teaching him to cook, every job had required his full focus; Evan could get turned on just watching Dan's frown as he chopped vegetables or stirred a pot of soup. Now, though, Dan was competent, almost expert, and he only had to concentrate for the more complicated stuff. Evan had considered trying to persuade him to take up cake decorating, or, if he was feeling more manly, leaving the kitchen and doing some wood carving. Or maybe he could make those miniature models, the ones that people used tweezers to put together. Evan didn't really care about the finished product, he just wanted to see Dan's frown of concentration, and the way he moved so gracefully and efficiently, as if his body was instinctively doing exactly what it was designed to do. But today he was trying something new in the kitchen, and he was looking just as focused as Evan liked.

It was unbelievably seductive, and Evan was glad Tat had stayed at a friend's house the night before. And he was glad that she'd chosen to live in a dorm when she went to college in the fall. It would be the best of both worlds; she was just moving to the city, so she'd still be close enough for him to keep an eye on, but she'd be far enough away that he could have the house to himself more often. Now if he could just figure out a way to get Jeff and Dan to agree to move in.

"How do you know when your butter is 'soft but not too soft'?" Dan groaned, and Evan remembered that for Dan, at least, this culinary adventure was not purely foreplay. "I should have waited for some time when Tia would be here." He looked over at Evan, perched on the breakfast bar stool, and shook his head in disgust. "You don't even know what I'm trying to make, do you?"

"It smells really good," Evan said supportively.

"That's the onions and the bacon. There's really nothing hard about caramelizing onions and frying up some bacon."

"I bet there's something hard somewhere else," Jeff said with a knowing smirk in Evan's direction. He was standing in the kitchen doorway, sweatpants slung low on his hips, thin T-shirt falling just right from his broad shoulders. His hair was still mussed from the pillow, and Evan really, really wanted to touch him. But that would just support his dig about Evan's little cooking fetish, and Evan didn't want to do that.

Dan frowned at both of them. "This is serious. I'm already using a speed-recipe, which is probably a bad idea. If we want these bastards to be edible, I really need to know how soft to make the goddamn butter."

"It's nice to see you've found a hobby that lets you relax and enjoy yourself," Jeff said as he eased himself onto the stool next to Evan's.

"They're going to be croissants, right?" Evan wanted to be supportive. "If you want, I can just go pick some up at the bakery, and we can slop the onions and bacon on top—it'd work."

"That's not what they're supposed to be," Dan said. "The onions and bacon are supposed to go inside." He frowned at Evan, and it was clear that he was trying not to admit to his own absurdity. "*Inside!*" he insisted.

"Well, this *is* serious," Jeff agreed. "Evan—get me some coffee. Dan—I think the butter's good right now. Go to it."

Evan was off his chair and moving toward the coffeemaker, but Dan just stared at Jeff. "You really have no idea what state the butter's in, do you?"

"None whatsoever," Jeff agreed easily.

"So you'll take full responsibility for any greasiness?" Dan raised an eyebrow challengingly. "*Full* responsibility?"

"You bet," Jeff said.

“Coffeeboy,” Dan barked. “Refill me while you’re at it. I have butter to spread.”

Evan did as he was told, and when he returned to his stool, Jeff rewarded his obedience by reaching a hand over and resting it on Evan’s thigh, a finger’s breadth away from his half-hard cock. Half-hard, but working its way up, if Jeff’s fingers kept moving like that. Evan shifted a little to give Jeff better access, but Jeff moved his hand just enough to maintain some distance. Evan’s cock twitched enthusiastically at the same time that he bit back a groan of frustration. More teasing from Jeff. The bastard was really good at it.

By the time Dan had finished whatever the hell he was doing, Evan was achingly hard, even though his cock had yet to be touched. Dan put a tray in the fridge and turned toward the breakfast bar. “That needs to chill for half an hour,” he said. Then he grinned. “And judging by how quiet you two have gotten, there’s something we could be doing with that time....”

“Get over here,” Evan practically gasped.

“Bedroom,” Dan said firmly. “Tat’s at a friend’s house, not out of town. She could come back at any minute.”

“It’s eight in the morning,” Evan objected. “She won’t be awake for hours.” Still, he appreciated the caution, and eased to his feet. He saw Dan grin at the bulge in his pajama bottoms and reached a hand down to cup himself. “While you were cooking something for us, we cooked up something for you,” he said. He tried to sound seductive, but there was no way *anyone* could carry off a line that cheesy, and he wasn’t hurt when Dan snorted a half laugh at him.

Then Dan’s expression changed, got sharp and almost dangerous, and Evan felt a chill go down his spine as his cock hardened even more. It was going to be one of *those* times, was it?

“Get your ass in the bedroom,” Dan said. His voice was quiet but firm, and Evan didn’t even think about objecting.

"Yes, sir," he agreed.

He started moving, but stopped abruptly when Jeff's hand clamped down on his shoulder. "Strip first," Jeff ordered. "I want you naked when you walk down that hallway."

Evan's arms were moving, pulling his shirt off over his head, before he was even aware of it. They had him well-conditioned, he guessed. And it wasn't like he ever really objected to getting naked. He shoved his pants down without any fanfare, taking his underwear with it, and then stepped back. He smiled a little to himself as he bent from the waist to scoop up the pile of clothes. He knew both Jeff and Dan were in position to get a good view. But he wasn't supposed to be in charge of this, so he didn't push his ideas any further. He just started walking, one hand wrapped around his cock, the other holding his laundry, and he knew damn well that Jeff and Dan were behind him.

He'd known they were there, but he hadn't known how close. And he hadn't realized that they were shedding their clothes too, not until two bare chests pressed up against the sides of his back, until two hot mouths found his neck. And then two strong hands reached forward, one from each side of his body, and tangled their fingers together, wrapping around his straining cock. He dropped his clothes as his hands clutched at the air, trying desperately to find control in a world that was spinning wildly, deliciously sideways.

"You want both of us, Evan?" Dan asked, and Evan knew exactly what he meant. They'd done it before, a couple times. It was intense, almost too much. Almost, but not quite. "You want us?" Dan's voice was rough and demanding, but Evan knew that there was no way Dan would go ahead if Evan was even a little hesitant.

"Fuck, yeah," Evan said.

"You're sure?" Jeff always had to be the careful one.

Evan turned in his direction, brought their lips together, and made the kiss deep and wet. "Absolutely," he said.

Dan's hand was already working down to Evan's ass. Just kneading the muscles, for now, but it was all part of the process. Maximum relaxation. Jeff smiled as he slid a finger into his own mouth, then pulled it out, slick and glistening. Evan stared at the finger as if it was hypnotizing him, following its slow descent until it was out of sight between his legs. Jeff's mouth followed his finger partway, but stopped at Evan's cock while his finger continued farther back. Evan knew what was coming, but he still gasped at the first wet touch against the sensitive skin of his hole. His body shuddered its acceptance as the finger eased inside, and Jeff's mouth rewarded him with firm suction and quick tongue flicks. The sensations were already almost overwhelming, but Evan knew that he was about to experience even more.

"Bed," Dan said, and Evan could tell he was speaking to Jeff because it sounded like a suggestion instead of an order.

Apparently Jeff agreed, because his mouth slipped away reluctantly, and his finger eased out of Evan's ass. "Me on the bottom?" Jeff asked as he started for the bed.

"Worked last time," Dan agreed. "Do you want to switch it up?" He was still next to Evan, still kissing his neck, running his hands all over his body, and when Jeff leaned back on the bed and wrapped his hand around his own cock, the combination of physical and visual stimulation was almost too much.

"Nope," Jeff said simply. He reached his free hand over to the bedside table and retrieved the bottle of lube. He squirted a little into his hand and ran that over his cock, smiling at Evan's expression.

"Okay," Dan said into Evan's ear, the proximity sending shivers down Evan's spine. "Let's go."

So they did. Evan let himself be guided over to the bed. He let himself be arranged, massaged, explored, and stimulated. He let his mind float away beyond rational thought, beyond anything but sensations and love and trust, and when Dan guided him over to straddle Jeff, he went willingly. When Jeff eased his cock between Evan's cheeks, found the hole and worked his way in, there was barely even a stretch, just a pleasant friction and fullness.

Evan let Jeff pull him forward, bending at the waist and finding Jeff's lips with his own. He wasn't surprised to feel Dan's slick finger playing over Jeff's cock, easing inside the ring of muscles to continue its exploration inside Evan's body. Another finger, and a third, and there was stretching now, absolutely. Evan let himself move, let his body adjust and start to enjoy the extreme sensations, and when he knew he was ready, he kissed Jeff deeply and then turned his head. "Do it, Danny," he said.

And Dan did. The first time they'd done this, there had been hesitation. Jeff had almost gone soft, he was so worried about hurting Evan, and Dan had pushed partway in only to pull out immediately and then start the whole process over again. Finally, Evan had convinced them that the tease was more painful than the stretch, and they'd gotten down to business. This time, Dan was confident. He was taking what he wanted, and Evan was happy to give it to him. He arched his back as Dan slid inside, breathed in an almost gasping breath at the stretch, and then braced himself.

He was dimly aware of Jeff, one hand on Evan's face, the other on Evan's cock, jacking him slow and firm in time with Dan's movements. But mostly, he was lost. It wasn't painful, it was just too much, too intense, and he felt like his world had simultaneously narrowed down to an incredibly bright point of pleasure and expanded to a diffuse, incomprehensibly large wash of sensation and brightness. He had no idea how long they were joined like that, no idea of the actual words that Jeff and Dan were saying in their quiet, husky voices. Even the orgasm that he could feel building seemed somehow inconsequential; it would release a tiny bit of the pressure building in his body, but not enough to make a difference. Evan didn't know what *would* make a difference. He didn't want the feeling to end, not ever, but at the same time, he needed it to. It was getting too intense, too extreme, and he wasn't sure his body could handle it for much longer.

He heard a new sound and realized that it was his own voice, high and strained. He wasn't saying words, wasn't trying to express anything. He heard the volume building, heard Jeff's words of what had to be encouragement, and then his orgasm washed over him, through him, and swept him away.

He came back to himself as he was being shifted gently to the side, snuggled in next to Jeff, whose body was almost as sweaty and spent as his own. "You okay, kid?" Jeff asked with a gentle kiss to Evan's temple.

"Fuck," Evan said. He was pretty sure there was more, but he didn't have the words.

Dan had been tidying up a little, and he pulled the blankets up over them all before sliding in on Evan's far side. "Yeah," he agreed. He kissed Evan's neck. "You get *two* croissants, after that."

"I don't know," Evan managed. He was feeling more like himself. "I heard they were maybe going to be greasy. The butter wasn't soft enough. That's what I heard."

"You heard *wrong*," Dan said with another kiss, this time to Evan's temple. "They're gonna be delicious."

"Okay," Evan agreed, and he snuggled in and let himself drift off to sleep.

"But she *wants* to go fast," Tat said, only a hint of a whine in her voice. "That's good for the cross-country, right?"

Jeff smiled at Dan's patient nod. "Yeah, it's good for the cross-country." Dan raised his eyebrows and tilted his head back far enough so he could see Tat, on her horse, from his spot on the ground. "But, Tat... are you currently *riding* her across the country?"

Tat rolled her eyes a little. Not enough to be insolent; as far as Jeff knew, she'd never tried that with Dan. And he'd never objected to her displays of independent thought. "No."

"So don't worry about what's good for cross-country. Worry about stadium jumping. And for that, I want her controlled. Maybe even relaxed." He reached up and gripped Tat's knee, shaking it gently. "Might help if her rider was a bit more relaxed," he suggested, and he looked pointedly at the reins. "If you keep pulling on her mouth, I'm going to make you ride her without using your hands."

Tat gave him another dirty look. "Just because *you* can do that doesn't mean that normal people can."

"Ride with your seat, Tat. All the time, not just for dressage." Dan stepped away and said, "I'm going to set up some trotting poles. You need to get her calmed down before you let her jump any more. Do the poles until she's bored of them, and if you're a very good girl, I'll set up an X at the end of them for a few rounds before you cool her out."

"Dan," Tat whined.

"Tat?" Dan's voice had just a hint of warning in it. Not heavy, but enough for Tat to hear, and she responded with another eye roll.

She leaned forward and patted the mare's neck. "Trotting poles will be fun, won't they?" she said. She scowled at Dan, smiled sweetly at Jeff, and headed back to work.

Jeff leaned his arms on the top rail of the fence as Dan ducked through and came to stand beside him. "She never pulls the 'it's my barn and I'll do what I want' trick?" Jeff asked.

"Not once," Dan said. He sounded proud. "She's a good kid. If the biggest fight I have with her is about rushing jumps...."

Jeff nodded. "Yeah. You're good with her."

Dan gave him a funny look. "You think so? I don't know. I just try to tell her what's going on. Why we're doing stuff."

"That's what's good. You treat her like an adult, right up to the point where she acts like a child." Then Jeff grinned. "Listen to me, talking like I know what I'm saying. I've never raised a damn kid."

"Even if you had, I wouldn't say it was enough to make you an expert." Dan shook his head, and Jeff was pretty sure he was thinking of somebody other than Tatiana. "Shit's complicated, man."

"Yeah." Jeff wasn't sure how to respond to that. Wasn't sure if it was respectful to start worrying about what to do with a baby that was not yet born, that might not be Dan's problem, and that Dan hadn't asked for any help with. "But you're smart. And you've got help—as much as you want."

Dan didn't shift away like Jeff had thought he might. There had been a time when any move toward intimacy, any expression that could be seen as acknowledging that their relationship was long-term and meaningful, had inspired Dan to look for escape routes. The behavior had faded, thankfully, but Jeff could still see it sometimes, when Dan was feeling stressed. Apparently he was okay for the time being, though. "Thanks." Dan looked out at Tat, dutifully taking the mare over the trotting poles, and then said, "Is it something... something you'd be okay with? If I had to look after the baby for a while?"

Jeff frowned. "Not on those terms. I mean, we're not talking a few weeks, Tex. If Krista asks you to help with the kid, that's going to be a multiyear commitment. Very long-term."

"Too long?" Dan asked, his voice carefully non-committal. "You'd be okay with something short-term, but you don't want a permanent change?"

Jeff turned to look straight at Dan. "No. That's not what I'd have a problem with. Long-term is fine; it's the 'had to look after the baby' that doesn't work for me." He shook his head. "That's not going to work, treating it like you're babysitting. Babies need to be loved, and they need to feel like they belong somewhere. They need a family, not a caregiver. If you take this baby, you need to think of it as a permanent commitment. A serious, life-changing relationship." He reached out and laid his hand along Dan's jawline, tilting his beautiful face just a little. "And I would be happy to be there for you as you go through that. But, no, I'm not interested in watching you fight to stay detached from a kid who's going to be desperate for your love."

Dan nodded slowly. "It's a lot," he said softly. "And it's not like... you know. Krista hasn't really asked. Not exactly. But she's made it clear that there's nobody else."

"It'd be better to put the baby up for full-scale adoption and let it find a family that will love it than to keep it around like it's an obligation or something."

Dan took a deep breath, and when he exhaled, there was a little quiver to it. "I just... it's scary. I don't know anything about being a dad." His smile was sharp. "Well, I have some ideas of what *not* to do. But other than that...."

"If it comes down to it, and you're willing to try, we'll make it work," Jeff promised. He ignored the twinge of pain in his chest. He'd been sure it was getting better, sure enough that he'd canceled his appointment with the cardiologist. This current pain was just... it was just a remnant. A pulled muscle or something. He smiled at Dan, and was rewarded with a smile in return. "We'll figure it out," he promised. And Dan seemed to believe him.

Chapter Six

"Do you remember the place on Dennison?" Krista asked as she dipped her cookie in her tall glass of milk. "The way it smelled?"

"Cat piss," Dan confirmed. "And it got even worse after Mom tried to clean it."

"She used ammonia!" Krista shook her head in amused disgust. "Like it didn't *already* smell like ammonia."

"Not a great housekeeper." They were getting onto dangerous ground here, and Dan wasn't sure how far he wanted to take it. Krista had been in the house for over a week, and they'd had lots of casual conversations, but nothing heavy. Dan thought maybe it would be a good idea to keep it that way.

Krista didn't seem to have the same sense of caution. "Not a great *mom*, really."

"She wasn't bad…."

"She let the asshole beat the crap out of you, Dan. He called you a fag, like, daily, and he'd slap me around too, when you weren't handy. And she never said a fucking word." Krista frowned at him. "Don't tell me that's the way a mom's supposed to act." Her hand was back on her stomach, cradling it protectively. The gesture had become familiar to Dan. And every time he saw it, he hoped that maybe he and Krista weren't as different as they seemed. He hoped that they had more than

Smokey in common, and that he'd somehow be able to build a real, meaningful relationship with her.

But the gesture didn't take away the sting of her words. "Mom did her best." The defense sounded weak, even to his own ears, and Krista was shaking her head before he was even finished.

"She could have done a hell of a lot better, if she'd remembered that it was her job to look after her kids instead of spending all her energy on her asshole of a husband." Then her face lost its stubbornness, and shifted into a crafty look. This expression was becoming just as familiar as the protective hand across the abdomen. "And I want better for my baby."

"Have you heard from Susan? She was meeting with the federal prosecutors today, right?" It wasn't exactly a change of topic, but Dan hoped that it would shake Krista off whatever path she was on.

"She hasn't called yet. But I talked to her last night, and she said there's no way I'm not doing time." Krista didn't seem too alarmed by the prospect; Dan couldn't tell if her calm was genuine or just bravado. "And like I said, I think you could really use a baby. It's... I don't mean to sound rude, Dan, but it's in everyone's best interest if you keep your boyfriend happy. I've been checking him out on the Internet, and that family is *rolling* in cash, right? And he's obviously generous." She waved her hand around the guest house. "He's a keeper, and you need to work at that relationship. You're not going to be pretty forever."

"Krista, if you want me to help you with the baby, you can just say that. You don't need to wrap it up like you're doing me a favor."

"A favor? Oh, no, my brother, I'm not talking about doing you a favor. I'm talking about making a deal."

This was what Dan was afraid of, and he'd been trying to avoid the topic for days. But she apparently wasn't going to let it go, so he took a deep swallow from his glass of milk, braced himself, and said, “What kind of deal?”

“I’ll sign full custody over to you. Or to you and Evan jointly. I don’t know the best way to play that. You’d probably want to check with a lawyer, see what the laws are like for gay adoption. For alimony or child support or whatever if you split up. Palimony, I guess it’d be. I don’t know. And I guess we’d have to look at your finances, in terms of what you’d be able to pay me. I get that you’d probably have trouble with a lump sum, but you could get him to give you, like, a monthly allowance, right? And you could just give a chunk of that to me.”

“You want to sell your baby to me?” On some level, Dan had known that she was leading up to this, but he still couldn’t make himself believe it in his core. “What about all that ‘a mom’s job is to look out for her kid’ stuff?”

“I *am* looking out for my kid,” she insisted, and for the first time there was a little heat in her voice. “I think you’d be a good dad. And I think Evan would be a good dad. So, what’s the problem?”

“What about Jeff?” Dan had mentioned Jeff a few times, but he hadn’t made the nature of the relationship crystal clear. It was a bit cheap to do it now, but he wanted to get a genuine read on how sincere Krista was about all this. “He’s part of the relationship too. All of us. A threesome. Polyamory. ‘Johnny has *Three* Daddies’.”

“Seriously?” Krista raised an eyebrow as she looked at him appraisingly, then tilted her glass and dunked her cookie again. “I guess you’d want to talk to the lawyer about *that* too. I mean... can three people even have custody of the same baby? I have no idea.”

“You haven’t even met Jeff, and you’re going to just give him your baby?”

“I’ve met Evan, and I know you. I don’t think either of you would be with an asshole.” She frowned, then smiled, quick and sharp. "Is Jeff rich too? That'd be excellent—you could probably play them off against each other. Maybe you should keep custody of the baby for yourself, and then if things go south, they can fight over you and the kid."

"Jesus, Krista! It's going to be a human being! A little... a little person. Not a tool for keeping people interested in me."

"It's easy to talk that way when you're young and good-looking, Dan. But ask yourself—how much of Mom's shit was because she was desperate to keep her man around? She hooked up with the asshole when she was looking good, and he treated her, and us, okay. But then she got sick, and less hot, and she didn't have anything to hold over him."

"*She* had kids! If your whole argument is that I need a kid to keep my man, then why didn't she have good luck with *two* kids?"

"Yeah, she had kids." Krista sounded like she couldn't quite believe how stupid Dan was. "But he didn't *want* kids. He could have gotten any woman knocked up if he wanted a kid. But your boys are gay. They're not likely to get anyone pregnant, right? And—well, I haven't met Jeff, but Evan definitely wants kids. He looks at my belly like it's a candy buffet. Plus, even if he decides he *doesn't* want the kid, in the long run, once you guys have been raising it together, I bet you'd be entitled to child support or something." She sat back and drained the milk from her glass, then shrugged. "Like I said, you should talk to a lawyer. But don't take too long—if you don't want to pay for the baby, I need to find someone who will."

Dan stood up abruptly, his hip jarring the table. "No. I'm not *buying* my niece or nephew. That's... it's not right, Krista. You shouldn't let—how can you give your baby to somebody just because they happen to be rich?"

"Don't preach at me." Krista shook her head in disgust. "You think it's *easy* being poor? Things were never all that bad, before you left. Sure, money was tight, but we got by. But when Mom got sick again, and the asshole lost his job... we didn't have *food* sometimes, Dan. That's not going to happen, not for my baby. So it's going to be raised by people who have enough money to raise a kid *and* have a little left over for the mom."

"'A little left over'? How much are you looking for, Krista? What's the price tag on your baby?"

She must have heard the sarcasm in his tone, but she ignored it. She leaned back in her chair, raised an eyebrow, and said, "Why don't you make me an offer?"

Dan had nothing to say, nothing that he wouldn't regret. So instead of speaking, he turned and headed for the door. He needed some fresh air to clear his head. Maybe things would make more sense from a distance.

Evan hesitated on the porch. He nodded to the uniformed security guard and thought about starting a conversation with him. He wasn't sure if he was doing the right thing, going to visit Krista like this, and maybe he needed to find an excuse to talk to somebody else instead.

But the door behind the screen was open, and there was movement beyond it, and then Krista appeared. "Evan?" She stepped forward and pushed the screen door open. "Hi. Do you want to come in?"

"I don't want to intrude," he said. He especially didn't want to intrude when he wasn't really sure what the hell he was doing there. Dan had been weird about Krista for the last few days, and Evan had decided to come down and see if he could figure out what was going on. But now that he was standing there, it seemed like a pretty bad idea. It seemed like him pushing his nose into Dan's business without an invitation. Again.

"No, it's not intruding." She stepped backward to make a path for him. "It's your house, after all."

"But it's your *home*," he said. He remembered having a similar conversation with Dan, just before Dan had moved out of the guest house. Maybe it was a Wheeler family tradition to be hyperaware of ownership.

"My home? My prison, more like it." But Krista didn't sound upset, just resigned. "I'm bored to tears. If you have some time to visit, that'd be great."

So Evan stepped inside and followed her back to the bright, airy kitchen. He'd asked his housekeeper to arrange for the place to be taken care of, but he wasn't sure if the cleaners had just been or if Krista was really tidy. He thought of Dan again, and wondered if compulsive stress-cleaning was another family trait.

"There's just decaf coffee, or juice, or milk." Krista opened the fridge and peered into it as if hoping something better had somehow appeared. "I really, really wish I could offer you a beer, but I think Dan's head would lift right off his pure little body if I suggested that he buy me some."

That didn't sound exactly like Dan, but maybe it was easier to be strict with someone else's diet. And obviously Dan was right, saying that Krista shouldn't be drinking. Evan was glad he'd never have to be pregnant. "Whatever you're having is fine."

"Milk on the rocks," she said, and Evan watched as she pulled two glasses down and filled them with ice.

"Dan drinks that too," he said. "I don't know if I've seen anyone else do it."

She grinned at him as she poured the milk. "We had a really crappy fridge growing up, with a kick-ass freezer. So if we wanted our milk really cold, we needed to add ice. I guess we both just got a taste for it."

It was strange to think of Dan, back then. Before he'd gotten in trouble, before he'd found Justin, before he'd lost Justin... and before he'd come to Evan and Jeff. Dan had been so many different people in his lifetime, and Evan only knew one of them. Krista knew another, and Evan decided that he was glad he'd come to visit her. Even if she couldn't explain Dan's current mood, she could still help explain *Dan*, as a whole. "You guys got along well?"

Krista made a face. "Not really. I mean, we were okay. But our house was never exactly peaceful. Not with our dad, and not with the asshole, later. So neither of us spent much time at home. We were never close, not like you and Tat."

"She said she's been coming over to visit."

"And bringing presents every time." Krista ran her hand down her gauzy maternity top. "It kinda sucks that everything's only going to fit while I'm fat. I bet this one outfit costs more than all the other clothes I own."

"Don't be too sure. Tat's a pretty good bargain hunter." That wasn't really true; Tat was an impulse buyer, just like Evan. But it seemed polite to pretend otherwise. And the fashion wasn't really what had caught his interest. "Your dad—he came back at some point? After Dan left?"

"Yeah," Krista confirmed. "I was still underage when my mom died, and the asshole had left when she was sick, so I was in foster care for a while. And then they got hold of Dad, somehow, and he got me out."

"And…." Evan wasn't quite sure how to keep the conversation moving. "The… the crime. It started right away, or were you a normal family for a while?"

She sighed. "I guess it started pretty much right away. But it was smaller stuff at first. He'd create a distraction, and I'd shoplift stuff. That sort of thing."

"You told Susan all that? I mean, how you were… I don't know, how you were raised to this life?"

"I told her," Krista agreed. "She said it might help." Krista shifted in her chair and ran her hand over her belly. "It makes it clear to me," she said softly, "how important it is for a baby to be raised in a loving, stable home."

Evan nodded. This was an interesting twist to the conversation. "I agree. It's something I've worked really hard to do with Tat."

"And from what I've seen, you've done a great job." Her fingers traced gently, absentmindedly over the stretched fabric of her blouse. "I talked to Dan about this baby—I'm not sure how he felt about it."

"I'm sure he wants to help out." Evan tried to make his voice comforting without sounding patronizing.

"I don't think...." Krista's hand fell away from her stomach. She reached for her glass of milk and took a long swallow. "I think I'm looking for something more than 'help'. Susan still isn't sure, but she says I'm going to go away for quite a while. I'm thinking... I'm thinking the baby needs a real family in the meantime. And then, when I get out, I can be the aunt, or whatever. That's what I think would be best."

Evan wasn't sure how to play this. He probably should have talked it over with Jeff and Dan first, but he didn't want to lose the opportunity now that it had presented itself. "I think... I mean, I can't say whether that's what's best. But if it's what you decide to do, I think Dan and I could absolutely give the baby a good home."

"Not Jeff too?"

"Oh." Of course Jeff. Jeff went without saying. But he hadn't known that Krista knew about that aspect of the relationship. "Yeah. Jeff too."

Krista smiled softly. "I really like that idea. There'd be so much love. Such a great environment to grow up in." She frowned and looked down at the table, and when she spoke, her voice was softer. "I just... I worry. I'm not as strong as I should be." Her laugh was bitter. "Obviously. Obviously I've made a lot of mistakes. I just worry that I might, you know... when I get out, I might forget all my good intentions. I'll be so lonely. I'll be lost, and broke, and... I don't know. I just worry. The custody stuff—it won't be totally secure, will it? Not with three dads. Scott—my husband—he'll be out of the picture. He didn't want the baby, and if he showed up around here, you could have him thrown in jail forever, probably. But Susan thinks I won't be in for that long. What if I come out and decide to make things bad for you? If I try to take the baby back?"

Well, Evan had a few suggestions to solve that problem, but he wasn't sure what the most tactful way to bring them up would be. "You wouldn't have to be lonely. You'd be the aunt, remember? We could find you somewhere to live, nearby. And a job, maybe."

"A job? Who the hell is going to want to hire me? No experience, and a felon. Yeah, I'll be a prize hire."

"I can find you work. Or, you know. If you're interested, we could set something up. A sort of trust account, maybe. I could deposit some money, and it would pay you a monthly income. And then, when the baby turned eighteen, you could have it all. You know—assuming that things had gone smoothly with the custody." Evan held his breath. Had that come out right? Had it been suitably vague, enough to sound like he wasn't trying to buy her off, while still making it clear that he was willing to throw money at the problem?

She didn't look offended, at least. She took a sip of her milk and then nodded slowly. "Yeah, maybe that would work. I mean---if I wasn't short of money, I think it'd be easier for me to be stable, and to build a new, real life for myself. And if there was enough in the pot... you know, enough for me to live off the installments, but still enough to be a reward if I made it to the kid's eighteenth birthday without doing something stupid... I think that might really work!" Her smile was bright and happy. "Wow, Evan, that's a great idea. I'm impressed."

This was happening a bit faster than Evan had planned. "Well, thanks. I'll need to talk to the lawyers, I guess." And now for the really tricky part. "And maybe it would be best if Dan didn't know *all* of the details. I mean, I'm not sure if he'd see it the same way we do."

"I don't know, Evan... I don't want to start lying to my brother."

"No, not lying! Just... you know. Don't bring it up. for now. And then once the baby's born, and he's seen it, and realizes how perfect it'll be... he lets me take care of stuff sometimes. You know, he'll... sometimes, he'll let me get him what he wants. Like paying for the guards, or putting up the money for your bail." The more Evan talked, the more convinced he was that he was doing the right thing. He'd need to get lawyers involved, and he'd absolutely need to figure out the best way to convince Dan. But he could do it. He smiled at Krista and raised his glass of milk. "Absolutely. We can figure something out."

She smiled back at him, and he was a little surprised by just how smoothly that conversation had gone. One more difference between Krista and her brother; nothing ever went that smoothly with Dan.

"Lower your right shoulder, just a little. Yeah, good." Jeff took a quick photo, then set the camera down and picked up his brush. He was using natural light for this series, and there were only a couple hours a day that really worked for what he was trying to do. Between his schedule and Dan's, it wasn't easy to coordinate times, so he absolutely wanted to get some painting done.

But he had a few other goals for the session as well. Dan was always calm when he was posing, and it was a good time to talk to him about difficult topics. Like.... "How are things going with Krista? It's been almost two weeks, now. You guys getting along?"

Jeff could see Dan making the effort to hold his pose instead of shrugging. He managed, and then said, "We're okay. I mean... you know. If we weren't related, I doubt we'd spend a lot of time together. But we *are* related, and she's a hell of a lot better than any other family member I've ever had."

Fair enough. Jeff mixed a bit more orange into his paint. "How's she feeling about going away? Susan hasn't got a deal sorted out yet, does she?"

"No, not yet." Dan kept his body still, but his eyes were moving around the room. Not quite frantic yet, but not entirely comfortable, either. Jeff needed to be careful about pushing him too much further. "And I can't really tell how she feels about prison. She sounds like she doesn't care, but that can't be right. I mean, she was on the run for ten years. You don't run that hard from something you're not worried about, right?"

"Maybe it wasn't *her* running. Maybe she was just following the men."

"Maybe. But she's not crazy. Jail *must* be scary for her. Even just having to leave the baby behind...."

And that was Jeff's opportunity. He felt manipulative, almost sleazy, but he needed to handle this situation. Evan had told him about the deal with Krista, and Jeff hadn't been impressed. He was pretty sure the whole thing was illegal, but he was confident Evan's lawyers could find a way around that. He wasn't sure whether it was immoral or not; it didn't really feel right, but it didn't feel totally wrong, either. The only part that he was sure about was that it was a terrible, terrible idea to go any further without getting Dan's agreement. If Evan had found some stranger's baby to adopt, that would be one thing. But this was Dan's sister's kid. He absolutely could not be left in the dark. And Evan had agreed with that, eventually. So Jeff had been assigned to figure out a way to bring Dan into the loop without making him explode. It wasn't an easy task.

"Has she talked to you about that, yet? About the baby? Gotten any closer to asking you to help take care of it?" Jeff tried to sound casual, but he really wasn't sure he succeeded. Luckily, Dan tended to be fairly clueless about reading people's emotions.

"Yeah, she talked to me." Dan didn't look happy. "She said I needed a baby in order to make a family, and I needed to make a family in order to keep my sugar-daddy sweet. It was a real brother-sister bonding conversation, for sure."

"Jesus." Jeff had wondered why Krista had approached Evan instead of Dan. He was beginning to get an unsettled feeling in his stomach, wondering whether Evan had actually been her second target. "So what did you say?"

"I said we could talk about me taking care of her kid, if she wanted, but I didn't need to have it presented to me like she was doing me a favor. And then she said she wasn't looking to *give* the kid away."

"And what did you say?" Jeff was pretty sure he didn't want to hear the answer.

"I told her to forget it. There's no way I'm going to buy a human being." Dan broke his pose long enough to shake his head in disgust. "I mean—if Evan gets tired of me, then fuck him. I'm not going to try to trap him with some baby I don't even want." Dan glanced over at Jeff with a quick grin. "Same goes for you, Stevens. Anytime you want to go, there's the door."

"That'd leave you in my house, with me on the street, Tex. I don't see the need to figure out the details of either of us leaving the other, but if it comes down to it, you're the one going out the door." Jeff had a quick flash of the doctor's appointment he'd canceled, the one he'd forgotten about the week before, the rescheduling calls he'd been avoiding, and he wondered whether his will was up to date, and where it was; he wondered how having a baby would be affected by that. But he kept his voice light; his job here was to deal with Dan. "You're not getting my house, buddy."

"*Palimony*," Dan spat out. "That was another of her sales points. If Evan dumped me after we'd been raising her baby together, I could sue for palimony. She's...." He trailed off and looked at Jeff guiltily. "She's practically me. Who I used to be. I mean, she's a bit more aggressive about it, but...."

"So there's hope, then," Jeff said quickly. "You've changed, so she can too." And, really, Dan's estimation of his sister's moral strength wasn't the most worrying part of this conversation. "Did you mean it, when you said you didn't even want the baby? We talked about that, and it sounded like you were thinking about it."

Dan frowned. It was a good thing Jeff wasn't trying to paint his face. But really, Jeff was no longer doing any real painting. He was just standing there with a brush in his hand, waiting to hear how much trouble he was about to deal with.

"I don't know," Dan finally said. "I mean, it's not something I ever really *wanted*. I never really thought about it, really, not until all this. Evan's all crazy about the idea, but I don't know. It would be hard. Evan thinks you can solve every damn problem with money, but if I *did* have a kid, I wouldn't want it raised by a nanny. And what if the baby has something wrong with it? I mean... what's the right word? What are we supposed to say? Not 'handicapped' anymore, right?"

"'Special needs', I think." Jeff set his brush down and walked over to stand next to Dan.

"Yeah, okay. What if the kid has special needs? Like, more special than every other damn kid, 'cause it's not like any of them are exactly normal. Look at Taylor and Owen. *Technically*, Owen's a regular kid, but does the little bastard *ever* sit still?"

"Owen's four, Dan. He'll calm down." Jeff tried to sound certain, but he remembered the last time Dan's old friend had brought his son over to the house. It had been a good thing Tat had been around to babysit, because the little guy'd had all the men hopping, trying to keep him out of trouble. "And we'd have a baby-proofed house, I guess. If it was our baby." But that was another issue to be dealt with. "Or your baby. I don't know how it would work, legally. Have you talked to Chris? I expect Evan's got a team of lawyers looking at the issue from every angle?"

"I have absolutely stopped talking to Chris about any of Evan's shit. He doesn't just say 'Sorry, client confidentiality, can't talk about it.' That would be—well, it'd be annoying, but I could handle it. But the fucker just rubs my nose in it. 'Oh, sorry, Danny, I don't think you're trusted with this information. It was wrong of me to even mention it.'" Dan leaned his head into Jeff's neck. "He's an asshole."

"Well, maybe we should talk to Evan about it. See where everyone's at."

"That's always your answer." Dan kissed gently in just the right spot to make Jeff's toes curl inside his shoes.

"Is it ever a bad idea? I mean, you're busy, Evan's busy, I'm... well, I'm more flexible than you guys, right now, but I do have stuff to do. I don't think the three of us have been in the same room for more than a quick meal or a quick fuck in, what, a week or two?" Jeff tried to ignore Dan's gentle kisses, tried to think back, and was appalled to realize that it had been at least that long. "We always do this. We're really good about communication when we have nothing important to talk about, but when something comes up, we get busy and lose track of each other. When we should be talking the most, we talk the least."

"We are deeply flawed," Dan agreed, and he slid off his stool and shuffled around to stand in front of Jeff. His shirt was already off, for the posing, and his eyes were bright green in the sunlight. He was absolutely beautiful, and when he leaned in and found Jeff's lips, there was no thought of resistance. Painting could wait, and so could the rest of the conversation.

Dan's fingers were warm as he slid his hands underneath

Jeff's ragged T-shirt. Jeff raised his arms and let Dan pull the shirt off, then brought his hands back down to rest on Dan's waist while they kissed, deep and wet. This was where their modeling sessions ended up, nine times out of ten, and even if Jeff's portraits of Dan hadn't become his signature paintings, he'd have kept painting them just for this. Dan was sweeter in the studio, less concerned about control. It was like he'd bend himself to Jeff's will while he posed, and then didn't shake the attitude off for a while.

Jeff forced himself away from Dan's lips and hands, and Dan reluctantly let him go. "Undress for me," Jeff said, and he undid the button of his own jeans before sitting down on the couch to watch. "Go slow."

Dan did as he was told, and it was as perfect as Jeff had anticipated. He wished Dan had been wearing more clothes, really, because he only had jeans and underwear to strip out of. Not even a pair of socks. But Dan did the best he could with what he had, a slow, sexy shimmy to edge the jeans off his hips, running his hands over the fabric of his underwear and then dipping inside to wrap around his hardening cock, staring at Jeff the whole time, his face calm, his eyes bright and wide. This wasn't the first time Jeff had asked Dan to strip for him, and every time, Jeff thought maybe he should give up the painting and become a filmmaker. It seemed wasteful, almost sacrilegious to hoard all this beauty for himself. Then he thought about letting anyone else see the film and realized that he would never be able to stand it. He could barely manage to let go of his portraits of Dan.

They were both fully hard by the time Dan's underwear hit the floor, and Jeff smiled lazily as he said, "Come over here." He nodded down at his straining fly. "Give me a hand with this, will you?"

"Just a hand?"

Damn it, Dan's voice was just as seductive as the rest of him.

"Your call. What do you think I'd like best?"

Dan dropped to his knees between Jeff's wide-spread legs. "You like my mouth." He reached for Jeff's fly, but just ran his fingers thoughtfully over the metal teeth. "And you like my ass." He raised a playful eyebrow. "As I recall, you've liked my armpit on occasion... and between my thighs...."

Jesus, Jeff did not need to hear a replay of their previous encounters, not if he wanted to keep any sort of control over the current situation. Over himself. "Do you want me to pick? I'll give you a hint—I'm feeling a bit more traditional today. Probably not looking at your armpit."

Dan grinned, and his fingers deftly pulled Jeff's zipper down. Jeff's cock was already halfway through the fly of his underwear, and Dan freed it the rest of the way before leaning in and giving the head a long, thoughtful lick. "How about what *I* want?" Then he grinned. "Damn, I win, don't I? *That's* what you like best... giving other people what they want." He kept his hand on Jeff's cock as he straightened and brought their faces level. "And I want to kiss you while you're inside me. I want your fingers in me, and then your cock, stretching me wide, fucking me deep...."

That was as far as he got before Jeff couldn't control himself any longer. He surged forward, caught one arm around the back of Dan's head and pulled him in for a hard, sloppy kiss. He could feel Dan's smile, but he kissed through it, his hands slipping down over Dan's bare ass and pulling him in closer, tighter. "Take my pants off," he said, and Dan got to work. There was a bottle of lube on the end table; after all, this outcome hadn't been completely unforeseen. Jeff reached for it as he lifted his hips to have his clothes pulled off, and by the time Dan was back, Jeff's fingers were slippery.

Dan grinned and eased his way onto Jeff's lap. One hand braced on Jeff's shoulder, the other wrapped around their cocks, and he started moving, slow and easy. His kisses were deep and almost sleepy, but that all changed when Jeff got his fingers in place and pressed two inside. “Oh, yeah,” Dan groaned into Jeff’s mouth, and he groaned again when Jeff found the right spot and curled his fingers into it. Jeff was tempted to just keep it like this; he could work Danny up, bring him back down, work him up again, and again, and finally push him right over the edge, and it would be perfect. He’d done it many times, and he fully planned to do it many more. Watching Dan lose control was one of the sexiest things Jeff could imagine. But it wasn’t what Dan had said he wanted, and when it came down to it, Dan was right. The most important thing for Jeff was to make Dan happy.

So he worked his fingers a little longer, made Dan squirm and let himself enjoy it, and then he slipped his hand free and guided Dan up higher on his knees. They stared into each other’s eyes as Dan lowered himself onto Jeff’s straining cock, slow and easy. When Dan was all the way down, he closed his eyes for a moment as if memorizing the sensation, then leaned forward to kiss Jeff before starting to move. He kept it slow. Jeff wasn’t sure if this was because Dan was trying to please him, or because Dan had finally come to believe Jeff’s philosophy that slower was often better. He didn’t care all that much, really. He just rested his head against the back of the couch and gave in to the sensations. Dan wrapped around his cock, tight and hot. Dan’s cock brushing against Jeff’s stomach, Dan’s fingers tracing over Jeff’s skin, Dan’s lips on Jeff’s mouth, then his neck, then back to his lips. Jeff brought his hand down to wrap loosely around Dan’s cock, but other than that, he was passive. This was Dan’s ride.

And it went on for a long time. Jeff couldn’t even guess how long. He knew Dan had taken a break to relube at some point, and that wasn’t usually necessary. But otherwise, he had no idea. He finally felt Dan’s rhythm begin to change, felt the slow, easy waves of his body gradually intensify, as if the tide was coming in. Dan pulled his lips away from Jeff’s and looked down at him, eyes still wide, still impossibly green, and Jeff smiled. “You’re beautiful,” he said softly.

“You too,” Dan said, and he rocked a little harder, a little deeper with each thrust. Jeff could feel his own body shaking off its passivity, and his hips started moving on their own, rising to meet Dan, pushing to get further inside. “I love you,” Dan said.

“Yeah,” Jeff agreed, but he couldn’t really say what he was agreeing to, not right then. Not with Dan squeezing him tighter, riding him harder and faster, their skin slapping in time with their movement, their breath coming in short, shallow gasps. Jeff felt his orgasm building and tried to hold it off, but when he saw how far the flush had spread down over Dan’s chest, he knew he didn’t have to worry. Dan was even closer to the edge than he was. And sure enough, as Jeff watched, fascinated, Dan’s eyes drifted shut, his body arched and spasmed, and the cock in Jeff’s hand jerked and shot come onto Jeff’s chest. It was so perfect, so mesmerizing, that Jeff barely realized his own body was following along until his eyes couldn’t focus on Dan anymore, couldn’t see anything but bright whiteness, and the ecstasy that washed through his body was all the sweeter because he felt like he was sharing it.

By the time Jeff’s eyes were working again, Dan was smiling at him. “You’ve got to admit—there’s a good reason we never seem to talk anymore.” Dan kissed Jeff gently. “It’s not like we’re not putting our time together to good use.”

“Talking would be good too,” Jeff managed to say. He thought again about the missed doctor’s appointment, and wondered what Dan and Evan would do without him around. Would they ever talk? Would they deal with their issues, or push them away until they built up into a pile that would crush the relationship? Damn it. He really should have gone to the doctor. He let his fingers trace over Dan’s cheek and down to his lips. He was just afraid of hearing what the doctor would say. He was afraid of having so much and then being told he was going to lose it.

Chapter Seven

Ginger was having one of her days. Chris's mare was a talented, athletic animal, but there was pretty clearly something wrong with her brain. Dan liked to think it was part of what made her such a good match for her owner.

"It's a *leaf*, you psycho," Chris said, pushing the horse forward with his hips. "We are not going to play your stupid games today."

"Don't listen to him, Ginger," Dan advised. "It's obviously a landmine. If you step on it, your legs will be blown right off."

"Don't encourage her."

"Stop being stubborn, Chris. I can take Smokey ahead, and she'll follow him." This was always a touchy area. Dan was a professional horse trainer, but it wasn't like he had any special education in the field, and Chris had been riding all his life. So, if they were dealing with the eventers, Chris would acknowledge Dan's expertise. But in any other area of riding....

"I know what I'm doing," Chris insisted. "I want to be able to ride alone sometimes. She needs to trust her rider, and do what she's told. We can't use Smokey as a crutch all the time."

"You've been riding her for five years, Chris. If she doesn't trust you yet, she's not going to change her mind because you drive her over a damn leaf."

"It's a *leaf*." Pure Chris. He was a logical person who built his life on rational decisions, and he was alternately confused, amused, and frustrated by those who didn't. Including animals.

The path was wide enough for Dan to move Smokey up next to Chris and the mare. He gave Smokey a loose rein, and the Quarter Horse leaned out to sniff at Ginger's muzzle, then extended his head down to the ground, looking for grass. "See, Ginger?" Dan said. "Nothing to be worried about. You trust old Smokey, don't you?"

But Smokey snorted a little, and the current of air lifted the side of the leaf, and that was it for Ginger. She reared, and when Chris got her down on the ground, she started bucking before he could get her turned. Then she charged forward, jumping over the leaf like it was the Grand Canyon, and headed down the trail at full speed.

Dan wasn't sure whether to laugh, be concerned for Chris, or be concerned for Ginger. There really was something wrong with that mare's brain. "What do you think, Smokey?" he asked, and the horse twitched his ears in the direction Chris and Ginger had taken. "You want to go after them?" Dan ignored the small, barely there churning in his stomach. He had to. If he gave in to it every time it appeared, he wouldn't be able to do his job. Justin had died from a riding accident—that was true. Riding could be dangerous—that was true too. But it just wouldn't work if Dan got upset every time something went wrong with a horse and rider. He couldn't let it happen. So he ignored the churning, put the doubts out of his mind, and kept his voice light. "Okay, Smokey. You can go find them." He shifted his weight enough to let the horse know he could go forward. "Let's take it slow, though. But not too slow. Let's try a jog," he decided, and as soon as he said the words, Smokey started his slow trot. Dan knew he'd squeezed just a little, tensed his body that tiny bit that let the horse know he was looking for a change, but it was so subtle, so slight, that it was really easier to believe the horse understood English than to believe he'd read the body language. Of course, Smokey was just as sensitive when Dan said *nothing* out loud, but there was an explanation for that too. "You're psychic, right, Smokes? And Ginger's just psy*cho*."

Smokey twitched his ears but didn't otherwise respond. Typical.

They didn't have far to go before they saw Ginger and Chris. Just as he'd ignored the earlier tension, Dan tried not to notice the way his stomach relaxed at the sight of Chris still safely on Ginger's back. They didn't look too good otherwise, though; they were standing in a patch of greenery off the side of the path, Ginger staring down at the plants around her as if they were snakes about to twine up her legs. Chris looked disgusted.

"I swear, I think the crazy bitch found a patch of poison oak to stand in," he said as Dan got closer.

Dan squinted at the plants. He'd never noticed them before, but… it wasn't completely impossible that they were poison oak. "It shouldn't affect her," he said. "But, yeah, maybe. You should probably wear gloves and wash her down when you get back to the barn."

"When the hell is *that* going to be?" Chris asked plaintively. "She's completely mental today. Did you slip acid into her feed or something?"

Dan had a response ready, one that mentioned Chris's habit of ignoring the horse for weeks on end and then expecting her to be completely calm about being ridden, but his phone rang, distracting him. He looked at the call display then pressed the button to answer. "Hey, Evan. What's up?"

"Is Tat with you?" Evan sounded tense, so Dan didn't try to chat.

"No. I haven't seen her all day. Wasn't she going into the city with friends?"

"She did. And then we don't know what happened. She went to the bathroom and didn't come back."

"What do you mean? How long ago? Maybe she just lost

track of her friends—they're kids, they're a bit flaky...."

"She had a security guy with her. He was waiting for her at the end of the hall, and she just...." Evan took a deep breath as if trying to calm himself. "He waited, and then he went in to look for her. That took a while, because he had to knock and wait and whatever, but he searched the bathroom, and she wasn't there. But there was another way out, down the hall in the other direction."

"Evan, she probably just ditched the guy. You know how she feels about security. Why did she have someone with her, anyway? I thought that was just for events where people could predict where she was going." Dan had Smokey turned and headed back for the barn as he spoke, and he was dimly aware that Ginger was following obediently behind him.

"We... you know. Lately, the security guys thought it would be good to have a bit more contact. Just in case."

"In case...." And then it hit him. "In case my sister's a kidnapper?" It didn't make sense, but Dan couldn't think of what else Evan could be saying. "Is that... Evan, it was *your* idea to have her stay on the property. I could have found a place for her somewhere else."

"No, it was my idea. Absolutely. I'm fine with it. But you know how paranoid the security guys are."

"Shit." Dan wasn't sure what else to say. "You should have told me that, Evan. But, okay, that doesn't change anything right now. Tat still could have just ditched the guy. She hates security, and she likes Krista, so she wouldn't think it was necessary...."

"Yeah." Evan sounded like he was trying to convince himself. "That's what we're hoping. I just... I was really hoping she was with you."

"I'm sorry," Dan said. "You've tried her cell?"

"Yeah, of course. Goes straight to voice mail."

"Okay, yeah. Look, Evan, I'm ten minutes from the barn, and I'll ditch Smokey and be at the house in fifteen, okay? She'll probably already be there, and we can yell at her together. You've called Jeff?"

"I left a message. I don't know where he is."

Jeff wasn't great about answering his phone, so there was nothing to be alarmed about there. Still, it was one more person Dan loved who was unaccounted for, and he really didn't need the extra stress. "Okay. It's going to be fine. She's fine. But I'll be there soon, okay?"

"Yeah. Thanks, Danny."

Dan shoved his phone back in his jacket pocket and looked over at Chris. "Tat's missing again; Evan's freaking out. Again." Dan asked Smokey to jog, and Ginger followed suit without complaint, trotting up beside Smokey like a perfect trail horse. "Did you know they had extra security on her? Because of Krista?"

Chris looked uncomfortable, then nodded. "Yeah. Evan said it wasn't necessary, but you know how the security guys are."

"Yeah, and I know who their boss is too. It's not like they can *make* Evan do something he doesn't want to do."

"Take care of his sister? Yeah, Dan, I think it's pretty fair to say that Evan wants his sister to be safe. I don't think that's a bad thing."

"So why didn't anyone mention it to me? If it's all so logical and straightforward, why didn't anyone tell me about it?" Dan was tired of this dynamic.

"Because the *extra security* is logical; *you*, not so much." For once, Chris didn't sound like he was making fun of Dan. Instead, he sounded sympathetic, as if he were breaking a hard truth to someone too stupid to see it, and that made the whole thing much harder to take.

"Yeah, fine," Dan said, and he was pretty sure he hadn't done anything to ask for it, but he didn't object when Smokey broke into a lope. He edged over so he was in the middle of the trail, no room for Chris to get beside him on either side, and he headed for the barn. The primary concern was finding Tat; after that, Dan could talk to Evan about the secrecy.

Evan resisted the urge to slam his cell phone onto the table when he heard Tat's cheerful voice on the other end of the line, advising him that she was unable to take his call and suggesting that he leave a message. He'd already left four messages, with increasing levels of irritation and then fear. Where the hell was she?

"She's seventeen," Dan said from beside him. "She's a bit rebellious, but she's tough and smart. She'll be fine." Dan's hand was on Evan's, trying to calm him down. It had worked when Dan had first arrived, but it wasn't doing much anymore. It had been five hours since the security guard had lost track of Tat, almost four since Evan had gotten the call to let him know she was missing. Four hours of going crazy, and no amount of hand-holding was going to make that acceptable.

"Without a ransom demand, kidnapping seems unlikely," Bill Albanese said. He was Evan's head of security, and he was a man who believed in staying calm in all circumstances. Normally, Evan appreciated that about him. But not in this case.

"So maybe she just got picked up by a *regular* psychopath. Someone who hurts girls for fun instead of money." Evan pulled his hand away from Dan's and stood up. He needed to move. He could feel Bill looking over at Dan, looking for guidance on how to deal with this, and it made Evan crazy. He didn't want to be *handled*, he wanted to have his sister back. He loved her, of course, but she was also his responsibility. It was his job to look after her, and he wasn't doing it right.

He saw Dan stand as well, but was glad that he didn't

try to get any closer. Evan's whole body was vibrating with frustration, with an urge to do something, anything. He really didn't want Dan getting too close to that energy level. "The cops are 'looking into it'?" he said to Bill. "What the fuck does that mean? Are they taking this seriously, Bill?"

"Not as seriously as the first time we called and reported her missing, years ago. Each time we call, their response is a little less intense." Bill shrugged regretfully. "At this point, I think they're thanking us for the information, and waiting for us to call back after twenty-four hours to escalate the alert. Or more likely, for us to call back and say she's turned up safe and sound."

"What about that girl from the debate team?" Dan asked suddenly. They'd been calling all of Tat's friends, trying to find any trace of her, but Dan was right; they hadn't called the debate girl.

"What the hell was her name?" Evan frowned in concentration.

"I think she was only here once. Something Spanish, right?" Dan looked up at the ceiling as if hoping it was written there. "Adele, maybe?"

Evan nodded his head toward Bill. "Call the school, find an Adele on the debate team."

"Adelia, maybe," Dan added. "Last name maybe started with an M?"

Evan felt like he should have been taking notes on Tat's life. Sure, it was important for her to develop her independence, but not like this. Not with him hunting around desperately trying to find traces of her activities, her acquaintances. He should just *know* these things, like he had when she was younger.

"Andrew—get on that, please," Bill said. "The school will be closed, but the headmaster's name is listed on the client sheet." Then Bill turned back to Evan. "I'm still optimistic that this is a noncriminal situation. But in the interest of covering all our bases.... You have a known felon living on your property. Your sister has been in almost daily contact with her. I know you called down to check whether Tat was there, whether she'd been seen, and I know you were satisfied with the answer you got." Bill looked toward Dan apologetically, but when his eyes returned to Evan's they were firm and resolved. Another reason Evan valued the man, but he was pretty sure he didn't want to hear what Bill was about to say. "In the absence of any other leads, we should be questioning your guest more closely. I certainly hope that she's innocent, but we need to be thorough."

Evan had no idea what to do. He turned to look at Dan, who wasn't returning his gaze. Instead, Dan was staring directly at Bill. He didn't look defiant or angry, though. Instead, he looked almost sad. "Just like you had to be thorough with me, when I moved out here," he said. There was a pause, then Dan shook his head as if clearing it of bad thoughts. "Let me talk to her first. Let her know what's coming. I won't...." He raised his hands helplessly. "I was going to say I wouldn't give anything away, but there's nothing *to* give away. We don't know anything, right?"

"If she *is* involved, assuming there's something to be involved in, even telling her we don't know anything is telling her something." Bill and Dan had gotten off to a rocky start back when Dan had first arrived and had been under suspicion, but in the years since they'd developed a mutually respectful relationship. Evan listened carefully to see if that relationship would stand up to this challenge. "How about if you go down and talk to her, tell her we're coming, and that's about it? Don't mention the specific situation, don't give her any facts or background. Does that work?"

Dan nodded. "Yeah. I can do that." He patted his pocket to check that his phone was still there. "And you'll call me when you hear from Tat, so I don't have to worry about all this anymore."

“Absolutely,” Evan agreed. “I’ll call as soon as I hear.” He watched Dan heading for the door, and tried to keep his optimistic smile fixed on his face. Tat would call. She’d call soon.

She had to.

Jeff tried not to feel guilty for the sense of relief he’d gotten when he listened to Evan’s message. “Family emergency,” he’d said to the receptionist, holding up his cell phone as if it somehow provided proof. “I’ll call to reschedule.”

It was the third appointment he’d blown off, but he’d been there, this time. He’d been going to do it. It wasn’t his fault Tat had gone missing. And it wasn’t like he could just ignore the fact that she had.

He’d never ignored it before, after all. And there had been several similar situations in the past. Typical, careless kid stuff, forgetting to charge her cell, forgetting to call home to say she was going somewhere with friends… forgetting to act like a complete grown-up, really. It was nothing that families all over the country weren’t going through, but the alarm level was raised substantially by combining an overprotective older brother with a security team that believed kidnapping was a real, significant threat.

No, not something to be ignored, but not something to panic over, either. Jeff turned into the long driveway of the Kaminski estate and tried to ignore the pain in his chest. It wasn’t a constant thing, but he didn’t think it was getting any better. Maybe it was getting a little worse, he decided as he tried to draw a deep breath and almost doubled over from the shock of pain. But he could manage it. He didn’t really need to breathe all that deeply, most of the time. He’d go to the doctor; he would. But he had things to take care of first.

He had another quick stab of pain as he hit the brakes to avoid a collision with Dan's truck. Dan wasn't going that fast, but he was clearly lost in thought, not even looking to the side as he pulled into the road that led to the guest house. Krista's house, Jeff realized, and he wondered just how that was going to play into the current Tat drama. Probably not going to be smooth, he decided, and he turned the wheel and aimed his car to follow Dan. Evan would have his entire entourage around him; Dan might need a little support.

And so might Krista, Jeff decided. He hadn't met her yet, and this wasn't the best time for it, but maybe this was just one more thing for him to take care of. He needed to make sure everybody was all sorted out before he heard what the doctor had to tell him.

Chapter Eight

Dan was gathering his courage for the upcoming conversation when he heard a noise behind him and turned to see Jeff's car pulling in. Jeff. That was perfect. Jeff would make everything better. Dan took a few steps toward the car and tried to smile as Jeff climbed slowly out. Too slowly.

"You okay, Jeff? You're looking a bit creaky."

"Oh, yeah," Jeff said. "I worked out too hard yesterday, maybe."

"Getting old, man. You need to take better care of yourself."

"Yeah, that's on my to-do list."

Jeff was close enough now for Dan to touch, and he reached his hand out to wrap around Jeff's neck. It felt so good to have warm, solid skin under his fingers. "You've heard from Evan?"

Jeff nodded. "Heard Tat was missing again. Saw you coming over here, and I put two and two together. How crazy is he?"

"He's tense, but he's being pretty good. Bill Albanese is there, and he's always calm. But he's the one who really wants to talk to Krista. He says there's no evidence of any crime, but if there *is* a crime, he knows where he wants to start looking."

Jeff looked like he wasn't surprised by any of that. "And you're here to...?"

"Let her know what's coming. They kind of blindsided me,

back when I was public enemy number one. I just wanted to let her know... I don't know. I guess I wanted her to know that even though it totally *feels* personal, it really isn't."

Jeff's hand gently gripped the waistband of Dan's jeans, his knuckles just brushing Dan's belly button. It felt familiar, and comforting. It made Dan feel like he was owned by somebody. Claimed, and valued. Not adrift, not a temporary part of Jeff's life. He was *Jeff's*, and he was Evan's, and whatever was happening, he just needed to remember that.

"You ready to go in, then? You want me to go with you?" Jeff smiled gently. "Or it's fine if you want to do it alone. She doesn't even know me."

"And it's time that changed," Dan decided. He reached down and gripped Jeff's fingers. "Come meet my sister, Jeff. She's a mercenary pain in the ass, but, you know—she's family."

That was what Dan needed to remember, he decided as he nodded to the security guards and headed for the front door. Tat was family, but so was Krista. Evan's security guys would do what needed to be done to protect one of them, but that didn't give them the right to walk all over the other. Dan would make it clear to Krista that it wasn't personal, but he'd also be sure to let her know that she had the right to be upset about it.

He knocked on the screen door and heard Krista bellow, "Come in," from somewhere inside. She was probably sitting down in the living room. She'd found one chair in there that was comfortable for her while she was in it, but that she had a hell of a lot of trouble getting out of. She'd joked about getting a catheter so she wouldn't need to stand for bathroom breaks; she definitely wasn't going to struggle to her feet just to answer the door.

"Hi, Krista," Dan called. "It's me. With Jeff."

"Living room," she replied, and Dan grinned. He'd been right.

"She's probably stuck in her chair," he said softly to Jeff, then led the way in to find her. “Hey,” he said. “Krista, this is Jeff. Jeff, Krista.” He supposed he should probably do some sort of little anecdote-based introduction, but he didn’t feel up to it. They’d both heard plenty about the other, and he wasn’t going to pretend they hadn’t.

“Hi, Jeff. Good to meet you.” Krista turned to look at Dan. “You heard from Tat yet?”

“No.” He sat down on the edge of the nearby couch, and Jeff found his own seat in an armchair. “The security guys are taking it a bit more seriously, since she’s been missing for a while.”

“They started blaming me yet?” Krista’s look was level, and Dan couldn’t be sure exactly how she was feeling.

“Not exactly,” he said carefully. “But they do want to ask you some questions. And I said I’d come down and let you know that it’s just… I don’t know, exactly. I guess that it’s par for the course? They gave me a pretty hard time when I first moved out. They didn’t even want me living on the property.”

“Were you under armed guard the whole time?” Krista raised an eyebrow. “’Cause I am. What the hell do they think I could have done with a whole team of security guys watching me all the time?”

“That’s probably why they were okay with you living here,” Dan acknowledged.

Jeff finally spoke, his voice rumbling and calm. “But ‘okay’ is a relative term with these guys. My mother’s seventy-two years old, pillar of the community, and they still did a thorough background check on her when she moved down and started spending time with Tat. They’re paid to be hypervigilant. It’s their job.”

“It’s nothing personal,” Dan said.

“It feels a little personal,” Krista responded, but she didn’t really seem that upset. Dan remembered his own reaction when he’d been under suspicion, and wasn’t sure whether Krista was calmer than he was or just a better actor. She saw his look and shrugged. "Danny, I'm on my way to jail. I committed a *lot* of crimes. They'd be stupid *not* to look at me for something like this. I mean, I have no idea how they think I managed to do whatever they think I've done, but being treated like a criminal is kind of fair, when you're a criminal." She braced her hands on the side of her chair. "But I have no idea what the manners are for something like this. Am I supposed to, like, offer them refreshments? I could give them coffee, but it's the damn decaf, so I don't think that'd make them like me too much."

This was a lot easier than Dan had expected. "Stay put. I can put a pot of coffee on, if you want. But, no, I don't think you're expected to act like a hostess. Just tell them the truth and get them out of your hair. If you want Susan here, I can give her a call, but I think Evan's guys are pretty used to handling confidential stuff. If you tell them something, they aren't going to go running to the cops about it, not unless it's related to finding Tat."

"Okay, then." Krista leaned back in her chair and stretched like a cat. A very, very pregnant cat. "Bring them on, then, Dan-O. No worries."

It was nice that Krista had no concerns, Dan thought. He wasn't sure he could say the same for himself. There was nothing about this situation that he liked.

Evan stood in the hallway of the guest house, checking his call display and listening to Krista chat with the security team. She seemed totally calm, totally unconcerned about the entire process. The exact opposite of Dan's reaction when he went through this process years ago. And Dan had been innocent. So did that mean that Krista was guilty? Evan looked down the hallway to the kitchen, where Dan was helping Jeff make sandwiches. Krista was just a calmer person, probably. There was no reason to believe she'd done anything to hurt Tat.

He looked at his phone again. Still no call. Where the hell was his baby sister? If Krista knew anything about this....

Evan had invited the woman onto his property, so intent on doing what *Dan* would think was the right thing that he'd ignored his own instincts. He'd said it himself; Dan was the romantic, and Evan was the practical one. Evan was the one who got things done, and took care of the people he cared about. So what did he do when he cared about two different people, when taking care of Dan got in the way of taking care of Tat?

Dan was a grown man. Tat was a child. She *had* to be his priority, and Dan would understand that, surely. Eventually, at least. Evan looked at his watch, then took one more look at the empty screen on his phone before stepping into the living room.

Then he said, "I'm sorry for the inconvenience, Krista, but I need to ask you to return the computer stuff that I lent to you. The laptop, and the iPad." He tried to think of what else there might be that would have evidence on it. He could call the phone company and get the records for the guest house landline. Krista hadn't had a cell phone with her when she'd arrived, so she still wouldn't have one, unless Dan had bought one for her. And Evan didn't think Dan had. What else, where else might there be evidence, where else should he be looking....

"Mr. Kaminski? You want us to retrieve her computer?" Bill looked a bit surprised, and that wasn't good. Evan wondered whether Bill was taking this whole thing seriously enough. Tat had been missing for six hours. She was gone, it was Evan's fault, and the people Evan paid to take care of all this were having a damn tea party with the prime suspect. The only suspect. Because if Krista wasn't involved, then they had no clues. No idea whatsoever of where Tat was, or who had her, or why they wanted her. No idea of how to get her back.

He forced a tight smile onto his face, for Dan's sake, although

Dan was still in the kitchen, so unconcerned about the whole thing that he was making snacks. "Yes, please," he said tightly. "And the iPad." He turned his smile toward Krista. "Just as a precaution."

"They're yours," she said coolly. "The iPad's upstairs in the bedroom, I think. The laptop's in the kitchen."

In the kitchen. With Dan. Who was absolutely unlikely to be as calm about this as Krista was being. But Evan couldn't worry about that, not while Tat was missing. He watched as one of the security team headed upstairs to retrieve the iPad, then followed another into the kitchen. The man was unplugging the laptop by the time Evan arrived.

"What's going on?" Dan asked. He was clearly talking to Evan, not the security guard.

"We're going to take a look at the computer stuff. Just to make sure." Evan tried to sound neutral and forced himself not to look at his watch again. Where the hell was Tat?

"To make sure of what?" Dan asked. "Did Krista say this was okay?"

"She said the computer's *mine*, Dan. Which it is. I loaned it to her, and now I'm taking it back. She doesn't need to say it's okay."

Dan stared at him like he was trying to figure the situation out. Evan wanted to care. He wanted to explain, and soothe, and maybe even apologize, but there was no room in his brain. All his energy was going toward keeping himself from panicking, and he couldn't get into a discussion with Dan, not right then. Not until his sister was back safely.

"There's no reason to think this is any different from any of the other times Tat's taken a break, Evan." Dan sounded like he was trying to control himself. "You're throwing your weight around, accusing people of crimes that haven't even been committed, and you should *stop*."

"It's natural to be worried, Evan," Jeff started, but Evan put his hands up in front of himself, warding them off.

"Could you two please not tell me how I should feel, or how I should be acting? Jeff, you don't have a sister, or a kid, or anything else that would let you know how I'm feeling. And, yeah, Dan, you *technically* have a sister, but you obviously don't care about her like I care about Tat, or you never would have left her behind with your criminal father." Evan knew he was way over any line that had ever been drawn, but it felt good to be able to let go of some of the tension. Then he saw the look on Dan's face, and it didn't feel so good anymore.

But Dan didn't say a word. He just stood there, his eyes cold and hostile. Evan watched the security guard ease past with the computer in his arms, and he knew he had to follow. He had to get his guys on the job, had to help them search for evidence. He had to get Tatiana back home where she belonged. "We'll talk about this later," he said to Dan.

"Go fuck yourself, Evan," Dan replied, his voice as cold as his eyes. He looked down at the platter of sandwiches he'd been working on, then turned his head toward Jeff. "You can handle the distribution, right? And you can give me a call when Tat shows up?" He turned to Evan and said, "Not that I care about that, of course." And then he was gone, down the hallway toward the front door.

Evan turned to Jeff. "I do not have time for his hypersensitive bullshit."

"I guess you'd better get back to whatever you're doing, then," Jeff said. He sounded only slightly warmer than Dan had.

Fuck. Everything was going to hell. But Evan couldn't worry about that. Once Tat was home, he'd fix things. Until that happened, though, he had other priorities.

Jeff watched Evan as he headed back to the living room, and tried not to think about what had just happened. He tried to stay calm and take even, shallow breaths, but he could feel the pain building in his chest. He fumbled with a glass, managed not to do more than gasp when lifting his arms made it feel like there was a knife in his chest, and braced his wrist against the side of the sink to keep the glass from shaking while he filled it with water. He had aspirins; they were supposed to be good for his heart. They wouldn't do much for pain like this, but....

Jesus Christ, he could barely breathe. He bent at the waist instead of lifting the glass to his lips, and that helped. He leaned forward a little more, took a sip of water, and tried to control his breathing. This couldn't happen. Not now, when Dan and Evan needed him, when Tat might be in trouble. There was too much he needed to do.

He rested his forehead against the cool stainless steel of the sink and tried to will the pain away. He could only be grateful that Evan and Dan had left before they'd seen his weakness.

"Jeff?" A new but familiar voice, and Jeff managed to turn his head far enough to see Krista, hand on her belly, standing in the kitchen doorway. She was looking at him with a detached, almost amused expression. "You okay?"

Jeff could do it. He had to. He forced a smile onto his face and shifted his body to the side so he could still lean on the counter without having his ass pointed straight at Dan's sister. "I'm fine. Just...."

"You're gray," she said matter-of-factly. "Something hurts, right?" She raised an eyebrow when she saw his expression. "I've been on the run for ten years. Off the grid. No hospitals, no doctors. I know what pain looks like." She crossed the floor toward him and rested a warm, surprisingly gentle hand on his shoulder. "Your back?"

"No." He had no idea what he was doing, being honest with this woman. He should have just gone along with her, said he'd put his back out, said it would be fine.... "There's something in my chest."

"Like a heart attack? You want me to call 911?" She grinned. "That'd be fun, to have an ambulance show up in the middle of this circus. Evan's head would lift right off his body, I bet."

Jeff was glad he was providing some amusement for this woman. "I don't think it's a heart attack. It's been happening for a while now."

"And you haven't gotten it checked out? Tsk tsk." She still seemed pretty damn casual about the whole thing, and Jeff couldn't decide whether he was relieved or annoyed. "Do you want me to do something?"

"I don't think so. It should go away."

"I could bring you a chair."

Jeff felt an almost physical wave of relief at the thought of being able to slump down, to stop trying to support himself. "Yeah," he said. "That'd be good."

So she pulled one of the kitchen chairs away from the table and maneuvered it around behind him, then pressed it gently into the back of his knees and let him collapse into it. There was pain when he moved, but then he was sitting, and everything seemed much better.

Krista smiled at him in a self-satisfied way, as if she was pleased to have solved the puzzle. "And you think it should go away pretty fast?" she asked.

"Usually does."

"I just came in to look for sandwiches. I hadn't had lunch yet, when all this started." She nodded her head in the direction of the food Dan and Jeff had been working on. "So I'll just grab one of those. I can eat it in here, and then if you pass out or something, I can get help. Okay?"

"Okay," Jeff agreed. And he was surprised to find that it

was. He couldn't imagine the drama that would have ensued if Dan or, God forbid, Evan had found him like that. But Krista seemed to be taking it in stride. She got her sandwich and started eating, and he sat and rested, and he thought about her words. *I know what pain looks like.* It was sad, that she had such a familiarity with the uglier aspects of life. Sad that she'd had to face them without any of the supports that Jeff had always taken for granted. But right then, if he let himself be selfish, he was glad that she'd been made tough. It made things a lot easier for him.

Chapter Nine

"Susan, it's Dan Wheeler. I need to talk to you. As soon as possible. Please call me back." Dan hung up and stared out the windshield of his truck. He was parked by the barn, and he could see Robyn leading one of the young Hanoverians out to the pasture. The horse was dancing a little, and Dan tried to focus on that. He tried to find the animal's strength and borrow just a little of it. He thought about getting out of the truck and going to find Smokey, but he didn't think he could manage it without running into somebody, and he really didn't feel ready for small talk.

He pulled his phone out again and found Chris's number. Chris had been sent to help track down possible friends of Tat's, but he answered after the first ring. "Is she back yet?"

"No, not yet." Dan remembered too late that he was kind of pissed off at Chris, but he couldn't be mad at everyone all at once, and Evan had definitely surged into the lead of the asshole race. "What do you know about Krista's deal? Does she have to stay in the guest house, or could I find somewhere else for her if it isn't working out there?"

There was a pause before Chris said, "You'd have to go back to the judge for any change in the deal, including a new address. Hopefully it'd be fine, but there's always a risk that he won't like it. Or that he'll come to his senses and realize he was way too generous the first time around." Another pause, then Chris said, "Why? What isn't working out?"

"Evan's panicking about Tat, and he's being an asshole." It sounded petty, Dan realized. Sounded like he was being a drama queen, making this crisis about himself, instead of about Tat. Or Evan, or Krista, or any of the other people more directly involved than he was. But he hadn't been looking for trouble, he was sure of that. "He talks a good game, you know? About helping out, and his stuff is really 'our' stuff, and all that shit. But as soon as the chips are down... well, they're all his chips. He was letting us play with them, but they're going home with *him*." Dan remembered Evan's speech about how he wasn't loaning Dan the money for Krista's bail, he was just using some of *their* money to help *their* family. That hadn't lasted long, and Dan felt like an idiot for having believed it. What the hell had happened to him? When had he gotten so soft, that a little talk about some hypothetical, impossible marriage had made him forget the reality of the situation? "So I thought it'd be easier if I found somewhere else for Krista."

"Easier for Krista, or for you? 'Cause it sounds like *Krista*'s pretty comfortable where she is, Danny. If you pull her out of there, you probably shouldn't be going around talking about *Evan* taking his toys and going home."

Well, that was an interesting development. Apparently Dan *didn't* have to abandon his anger with one person in order to be angry at another. "Thanks for your help, Chris."

"Give me a break, Dan. What do you want me to say?"

"Nothing. I think I've got the picture. Evan's a prince, and whatever he does is fine by you. I'm a hysterical idiot who can't be trusted with basic information, and who has temper tantrums and blames other people. I get it."

"Okay, Danny, that's not really what I think. But you've got to admit, your current behavior isn't doing a lot to—"

Dan hadn't really planned to hang up, but he wasn't sorry that he'd done it. Maybe Chris was right, and Dan was out of line. He thought of Evan saying that Dan obviously had never really cared about Krista, and he felt the familiar guilt. It wasn't like Dan had ever given Evan a reason to believe otherwise. What had Dan ever done to look after his family? Evan was responsible for a teenage girl; Dan could barely look after himself. Yeah, Evan was throwing his weight around, and yeah, it rubbed Dan the wrong way. But maybe Evan had a right to act like he did; he was the responsible adult, after all.

But that didn't mean that Dan had to like it. And it didn't mean that he couldn't protect himself. If taking favors from Evan meant that Dan had to put up with Evan's shit, then Dan really didn't want to take favors from Evan. The trapped sensation that he'd felt when Krista had first shown up was back, stronger than ever. He was already struggling to pay the legal fees; how the hell was he supposed to pay for somewhere else for Krista to stay, and for the guards that would have to supervise her? She could move into his apartment, he supposed. A single guard could keep an eye on the one exit, so that would cut down on costs, and it wouldn't kill Dan to sleep on the couch for a month or so. Or maybe he could stay at Jeff's.

Or maybe at Evan's. Dan really wasn't sure how big a deal this fight was. It felt pretty huge right then, but maybe that would fade. But, no, he still needed to keep some distance. He'd let himself get sucked in to Evan's world of favors, but as Evan had made all too clear, when he loaned something, it wasn't permanent. He could and would take it back when it pleased him. So Dan wouldn't accept the loans or the favors, and sleeping in Evan's bed, eating his food, feeling at home in his luxurious house—that was all a favor. It was something that Evan could take away whenever he wanted to, but he couldn't do that if Dan never accepted it.

He loved Evan. He knew that was real, and strong. But the guy was not easy to live with, and Dan needed to make some changes. He had no idea how Evan would react to them, but Dan was pretty sure he wasn't going to let that become his problem.

Evan's phone rang. He looked at the display and jerked the phone to the side of his head. "Tat?" He needed it to be her. Needed her to be safe. But what if it was just somebody else with her phone....

"Hi, Evan." Tat's voice was clear and calm. "I'm sorry if you were worried. I'm fine."

Evan couldn't even name his emotion. Was it possible to be completely enraged at the same time that he wanted to collapse with relief and love? "Tat? Where are you?" he managed.

"We went hiking. In a canyon. I guess my cell didn't get coverage there." She still sounded calm, and Evan realized she had probably practiced all this. Hell, maybe she'd planned the entire drama.

He wasn't sure where to begin shoveling through that pile of bullshit. "You ditched your security, Tat. You *knew* I'd be worried." His voice was reasonably level, but his legs were trembling, and he sank into the nearest chair without being aware that he was moving.

"The security was completely unnecessary, Evan." Tat sounded a little less rehearsed, a little less mature, and it was strangely comforting to hear her being testy. "I was with friends, and we weren't going anywhere that anyone would have known about."

Evan couldn't have this conversation. "Where are you, Tat? I'm sending a security team to pick you up, right now."

"No, Evan. I'm fine. I'll be home in a bit. Like I said, I'm sorry you were worried." And then she hung up. She had apparently made the statement of independence that she had intended, and that was it. He pulled the phone away from his ear and stared at it in disbelief. He was tempted to call her back, but he was pretty sure she wouldn't answer.

He realized that he had quite an audience, and raised his eyes to find Jeff looking a little pale but smiling anyway. He'd been sitting quietly on the couch since he'd come in with the sandwiches, watching and waiting along with Evan. It had felt good to have his support, even if it reminded Evan a little too much of Dan's departure. "She's okay," Jeff said softly.

"She's fucking *dead*," Evan corrected. He jerked upright, his energy back, and turned to Bill. "Sorry for the false alarm." Then past Bill to look at Krista, still sitting in her armchair, serene as the Mona Lisa amid all the chaos. He had felt like a fool talking to Bill, but he felt like something much worse when he looked at Dan's sister. "I'm sorry for bothering you. I'll get the laptop and iPad back. Sorry." Obviously the words weren't enough, but they were all he had.

"Don't worry about it. I don't really need them," she said calmly.

"No, I'll get them. If you're not enjoying them, maybe there's some software you'd like, games or movies or something...."

"No, I'm fine. You hang onto them. I appreciate the thought, though."

Evan wasn't sure how to take this. Was Krista just as angry as Dan, but hiding it better? Was this her version of Dan's mask, a calm exterior to shut out people who didn't deserve access to the insides? "I really am sorry," he tried again. He realized just how much he had to lose if Krista decided to stay angry at him. He couldn't discuss it with all the people in the room, but he hoped he could get a message across anyway. "I guess I'm a bit overprotective. You know—of kids under my care. I really... I guess it's not fun for everyone else, but I take my responsibilities very seriously." *And I'd take good care of your baby*, he tried to say with his eyes.

"Okay," Krista agreed blandly. There was no sign of her receiving his message, and no sign that she cared. She turned her head toward Bill. "Could I impose on you to help me up? I'm pretty tired, and I think I'll go have a nap."

"Of course," Evan said, stepping toward the door. "We'll get out of your hair."

"It's your house, Evan," she said calmly. "Obviously you can stay as long as you want." She headed for the stairs. "I'm a sound sleeper; I'm sure I'll be fine."

"No, it's...." Evan stopped. He looked around the room, saw the security personnel, the half-eaten sandwiches and empty coffee cups, and realized that he'd made himself and his team completely at home. He hadn't even thought about it; it was his guest house, and she was a suspect in his sister's disappearance. But now that Tat was safe, Krista was back to being a guest, and he really hadn't treated her well. "We can tidy up before we go," he tried.

"Whatever you think is best," she replied, and she started up the stairs, slow and tired-looking. Evan needed to make this up to her, he decided. And he needed to make it up to Dan, as well. He wasn't sure which apology would be more challenging.

Jeff had thought about driving himself to the emergency room, but the pain had started to fade shortly after Krista had gotten him the chair, and he decided that he could stick around. Then, after the crisis was resolved, he could have gotten some attention, but he really just wanted to go to bed. He'd have a couple glasses of bourbon first, he figured, and that would take the edge off. And he would go to the doctor the next day. He would. Standing on the sidelines watching Evan and Dan fight had made it clear that he was no good to them as he was, so he'd have to get himself fixed. Or, if the news was bad, he'd have to start figuring out how they'd get along without him. Either way, the time for indecision was over. He was tired, but determined.

He saw the truck in his driveway as he pulled in and looked over to see Chris sitting on his porch. Chris. Young, healthy Chris, with a good head on his shoulders, who got along with both Dan and Evan… maybe Chris was a resource Jeff needed to be keeping in mind. If he couldn't be around, maybe Chris was a reasonable substitute. He tried not to think about Chris's recent experimentation with bisexuality. He refused to let himself consider Chris replacing him in bed. There was nothing Jeff could do about the possibility, and that meant he had no reason to torture himself thinking about it.

"Hey," Jeff said as he climbed out of his car. "What's up?"

"Jesus, Jeff, what's up with *you*? You look like you got hit by a train." Chris stepped off the porch, skipping three steps and landing easily. Jeff tried not to hate him. And he tried not to think what it meant, that he'd been able to hide his illness from the two people who were supposed to be closest to him, when Chris had seen it at a glance. It was because Evan and Dan hadn't seen him at his worst, he told himself. At least, they hadn't seen him at his worst when they weren't in the middle of their own dramas.

"I'm not feeling too good," he admitted. There was no point in trying to deny it.

Chris gave him an appraising look. "What kind of not good? Do you want me to drive you to the doctor? 'Cause I'm serious, man, you look terrible. All gray and nasty."

"Thanks, Chris," Jeff said dryly. "Always good to hear. But, yeah, I just want to sit down. And maybe have a drink."

"Do you want me to call Danny? Or Evan?"

"No, I'm fine." Jeff dragged himself up onto the porch and sank down in one of the Adirondack chairs. It felt like something was pulling when he moved, as if there was something in his chest that was tied too tightly to something else, but when he was still, he was okay. He still had his keys in his hand, and he lifted his arm a few inches and showed them to Chris. "Any chance of you going on a Turkey hunt?"

Chris still looked skeptical. "Are you sure it's a good idea for you to be drinking?"

"I'm absolutely positive," Jeff said, and apparently his voice was persuasive, because Chris took the keys and unlocked the door. Lou, Jeff's dog, bounced out to greet them both, and at least Jeff didn't have to worry about her. She spent half her time at Evan's anyway; she'd be fine there if he couldn't take care of her anymore. He let his fingers rub through the soft fur of her ears, and for the first time wondered why Chris was at his house, waiting for him.

Then he didn't care, for a while, because Chris returned with two glasses of ice and a bottle of beautiful brown liquid. Chris poured for them both, handed Jeff a glass, and sank into the neighboring Adirondack chair. He raised his glass in a gentle toast, which Jeff managed to return, and they sat quietly for a while, enjoying their drinks and the oncoming dusk.

Chris was the one to break the silence. "So, I came over here for a reason. It seemed like a good idea at the time."

"Yeah? Don't leave me in suspense."

Chris sighed, then took another sip of his drink. "Well, it wasn't exactly a *good* reason, maybe. I mean, I was framing it in my head as 'asking for advice', but now that I think about it, maybe it's more like 'bitching'."

"Bitching's good too."

"Yeah? Well, then, I've got a bellyful of 'good' to share with you." Chris grinned quickly, then leaned forward and braced his elbows on his knees, looking intently at Jeff. "I just... it occurred to me that you're probably the only other person who really understands how it feels. Being stuck between Dan and Evan all the time, I mean."

Jeff wasn't sure how to take that. "You feel stuck between them?"

"You don't?" Chris sounded incredulous. "When they get along, it's fine, but as soon as there's even a little bit of tension, they both try to get me on their side, and neither one of them seems to realize that I'm getting pulled in two directions. I mean... I *work* for Evan. He's my boss. *And* he's my friend. But Danny's... I don't know, he's *Danny*. He's...." Chris faded out. "You know," he finished lamely.

And Jeff was surprised to find that he *did* know. Not just about Danny being Danny, but also about being caught in the middle. "Evan's so bullheaded, once he decides that something's right. And Dan's just as stubborn in the opposite direction. Neither one of them is any good at seeing things from the other's perspective."

"Exactly," Chris said triumphantly. "They're usually good, but when they get going, they're like little kids. *Annoying* little kids, not the cute, well-behaved kind."

And that was another reminder. "Evan wants to adopt Krista's baby," Jeff said. He was sure Chris already knew, but it wasn't something Jeff thought had been discussed enough.

"And Dan doesn't," Chris agreed.

"Is that for sure? I heard him say he'd step in if she needed him. It sounded like maybe he wasn't totally against the idea in principle."

"But he doesn't like the terms of her deal. Yeah."

"It *is* problematic. Buying a baby...." Jeff wasn't sure how he felt about it himself.

"But from Evan's perspective, it's... I don't know. Money doesn't mean the same to him that it does to Danny." Chris sounded like he'd given this some thought. "For him, it's like air, or something. If Krista wants money, and he *has* money, why not pass it along? Everyone's happy."

"Except Dan."

"What about you? Are you looking to be a daddy?"

Jeff wondered why he'd never asked himself that question. He wondered why Evan and Dan didn't seem to have asked it either. "I don't know." Would a baby be just one more responsibility that he'd be unable to fulfill if things didn't go well at the doctor's? "It's complicated. With three of us, especially. I mean, Tat was old enough to sort of understand, and we've kept it pretty quiet, in general. A little baby… that would be a lot trickier. And a much longer commitment."

They sat silently for a while, each thinking his own thoughts and sipping his own drink. Then Chris said, "For what it's worth, I think you'd be a great dad." Then he frowned. "Unless you… unless you spoiled the kid. I don't mean with stuff. That'll be Evan, for sure. But the way you act with Dan and Evan, acting as if they're the only important things… that's great when a kid's a baby, but I wonder…." He took a thoughtful sip of his drink, and didn't seem inclined to finish the thought.

But Jeff was pretty sure he wanted to hear the rest of the sentence. "You wonder what?"

Chris looked apologetic, but at least he continued. "I wonder if that's part of the reason Evan and Danny act so childish sometimes. I don't mean just you. Maybe I'm part of it too. You and I both drop all our own shit the second either of them sneezes. I wonder if they act like they're the centers of the universe because *we* act like they are too." He shrugged. "And I wonder if the same thing might happen with a kid. Is there a way to make someone feel totally secure and totally loved without teaching them to take other people for granted?"

Jeff drained his glass and wordlessly extended it for a refill. He didn't say anything in response to Chris's question, but he definitely thought about it. And again, they sat there quietly, drinking, and they watched as the night fell.

Chapter Ten

It had been Chris who'd left a message on Dan's phone, telling him that Tat was safe and back home where she belonged. It had been good to hear, of course. He'd been doing his best to keep the unpleasant possibilities out of his mind, but he couldn't deny that he'd been worried about her. He hadn't been thrown into a hysterical panic, but he'd been concerned.

He had no idea what it meant that neither Evan nor Jeff had called him with the news. Well, he guessed he knew what it meant that Evan hadn't called. They were still fighting, apparently. Which was good, because Dan was still absolutely pissed off. But why hadn't Jeff called him?

When the three of them had first started, it had always felt like Jeff was on Evan's side, but that perception had faded over the years. Now, it was back. Jeff and Evan were the real couple, and Dan was just their piece on the side. God, he was tired. And cranky, he had to admit. The whole situation would probably look a hell of a lot better once he'd had a good night's sleep. But he didn't think he'd be able to rest until some of this was settled, so he nodded to the security guard on duty at Krista's front door, then knocked. "It's Dan," he called softly.

"Come in," she answered, and he followed her voice down the hall to the kitchen. "Hi," she said, and she nodded to the pan on the stove. "I'm making hot milk. You want me to add some for you?"

"No, thanks. I'm good."

"Okay." She sank into one of the kitchen chairs. "You keep an eye on it, okay? Keep it from boiling over?"

"Yeah, okay." He picked up the spoon and stirred absentmindedly.

"What's up, Danny?"

That was a good question. "I'm sorry about Evan. I mean, sorry he treated you like that."

"Like what? Like a criminal? I hate to tell you, Danny, but—"

"But you didn't have anything to do with it. I mean, there *was* no 'it'—Tat was fine. Evan totally overreacted, and he took it out on you."

"He was worried about his sister," she said evenly.

"And I was worried about *mine.*"

"It's not really the same, Danny." She didn't explain what the difference was, and Dan couldn't keep Evan's words from returning to him. *You obviously don't care about her like I care about Tat.* Was it a contest? And if it was, had Dan already lost? Fifteen years ago, he'd run away from his abusive home and left his baby sister behind. There was no denying that, and maybe there was no way of moving past it, either.

"You don't have to stay here," he said. He could tell from her expression that he'd caught her by surprise. "I'll talk to Susan. I bet she could get the bail agreement changed, and you could stay at my place instead."

"I thought you said it was a one-bedroom?"

"I could sleep on the couch."

She frowned at him. "Danny, look around you. Why would I want to leave this place to go live in your crappy apartment? That doesn't make any sense."

He had no response. He was offering her dignity, a place

where the host's generosity wouldn't disappear at the first challenge. But apparently that didn't mean as much to her as it did to him. He distracted himself by pulling the milk off the burner and finding a mug for it. He leaned over and put the drink on the table in front of her, and said, "He may not want you here anymore. He usually calms down *fairly* quickly after one of his little fits, but he stays crazy longer when Tat's involved."

"He already apologized about it." She took a cautious sip of her milk, then smiled at him. "You don't need to worry about me. I've got him right where I want him."

"What the hell does that mean?"

Her smile shifted from sweet to patronizing. "It means that he really wants a baby. You could have been a part of it, but you were too pure for that. So I talked to Evan, and he seems really excited about becoming a father. I don't think he's going to kick the mother of his baby out of the house. Not when we've got a deal worked out."

"Wait a second." There had to be a mistake. "He just... he said he was interested, maybe. I mean... yeah, I think he wants kids." Dan could accept that much. "But he didn't make a deal with you. He said he'd have to talk it over, figure it out, get back to you... something like that." Dan tried to make this make sense.

But Krista's confidence was overwhelming. "Get back to me with the contract, sure. We've got a few details to sort out, and he needs to figure out how to make it legal. But we've got a deal." Another sip of milk and another smile. "You've been sleeping with the guy for two years, and what do you have to show for it? Me, I fucked somebody else entirely, cruised in here a month ago, and I'm going to walk away a millionaire. I guess we know who the smart Wheeler is, don't we?" She leaned forward a little and stretched her fingers out to rest on his forearm. "When he dumps you, maybe I'll let you stay with me for a bit. You can sleep on the couch at *my* place, how about?"

"Jesus Christ, Krista!" Dan didn't even know who he was

angry at. Everybody, from the feel of it. "That's your kid you're talking about. You sold your baby to a stranger, and you're *bragging* about what a sweet deal you got? Are you serious?"

"You think I should feel guilty? The kid's going to grow up in the lap of fucking luxury around here! Best toys, best schools, best start in life. You think I should have left it with you? What the fuck can *you* give a baby?"

Dan just stared at her. It wasn't like he wanted the baby for himself. Not really. Well, he'd thought about it, sure. He'd started thinking that maybe it wouldn't be that bad. Raising a kid was an incredibly important job, and maybe he didn't know exactly what to do, but he knew a hell of a lot of what *not* to do. Starting with not treating the kid like something to be bought or sold. What could he give a baby? He shook his head at his sister. "I could help it grow a conscience," he said, and he headed for the door.

Evan knew he wouldn't be able to sleep until he sorted things out with Krista. He tried not to think about Dan and dealing with his ruffled feathers. But that didn't work, and he could absolutely hear what Dan would have to say about Evan's current trip. *You're still just thinking about yourself, Evan. You think it's a big deal that you can't sleep, so you're going to go intrude on a pregnant woman whose life you've already turned upside down. You feel bad, so nobody else can rest until you feel better. Be that way if you want to, but don't pretend that you trying to soothe your conscience makes you a good guy.* Yeah, that was what Dan would say, and he wouldn't be wrong. But Evan kept walking anyway. Screw Dan and his sanctimonious bullshit.

The lights were still on in the guest house, and Evan gave a quick wave to the guard on duty before knocking on the door.

He heard Krista's voice from inside. "Dramatic exit not too satisfying?"

Evan took a moment to let that comment make any sense that it could and decided that she must not know who was at her door. "It's Evan," he called.

A pause, and then she said, "Oh." Her head appeared from the kitchen doorway. "I'd say 'come in', but it feels a bit strange inviting you into your own place."

He could remember Dan saying something similar when they'd first started out. But Evan had given Krista a hell of a lot more reasons to feel unwelcome than he'd ever given Dan, and he needed to keep working to apologize. "Is it okay if I come in?" he tried.

She shrugged. "I already said it's your place."

"Yeah, but do you mind?"

"Suit yourself," she said.

That was as close to an invitation as he was going to get, he figured, so he pulled the screen door open and stepped inside. She stepped back into the kitchen as he headed down the hall toward her, and by the time he arrived, she was sitting at the table. There was an empty mug by her elbow and a half-eaten cookie on a plate by her hand. She looked almost completely neutral. She looked like she'd never met Evan, never discussed the custody of her baby with him, never been insulted by him. He had no idea how to handle the conversation.

"I wanted to apologize again, for this afternoon. I'm sorry if I made you feel like you were under suspicion."

"You made me feel like I was under suspicion because I *was* under suspicion." She cocked her head like she was trying to figure him out. "Are you saying that you're sorry you suspected me? Are you saying that you *aren't* actually all that protective of children under your care, after all?"

Evan wished Jeff was there. Well, really he wished Dan was. When Dan was on his side, when he agreed with Evan's goals, he was a fantastic ally. There was just something pure about him, a core of strength that he couldn't be shaken from. The outside of him would thrash around and make a mess of everything if given a chance, but that core was always there, keeping him stable. And it would keep Evan stable too, when they were working together. Of course, when they were working against each other, Dan's inner strength was incredibly frustrating. So Evan didn't exactly wish Dan was there in the current situation, but he absolutely wished Dan was on his side, and there. But he wasn't, so Evan had to deal with this woman on his own. "I'm protective," he said. "But I was wrong not to trust you."

She raised an eyebrow, but didn't pursue the topic. Instead, she waved a hand to the bag of bakery cookies on the table. "Are you hungry? Dan brought them over yesterday."

"No. I'm fine, thanks." It was stupid, but Evan didn't want to eat Dan's cookies, not while Dan was still angry. It seemed wrong somehow. "I just wanted to...." Wait, he'd already said this. He couldn't apologize again, and start the whole "what are you sorry for" conversation up for another round. He might as well cut to the chase. "I wanted to talk to you about the baby. I've checked with lawyers. Specialists in this sort of thing. They say that it's illegal to give you money, straight up, for the baby. So we can't really have a contract like that. But they say that it's pretty hard to keep me from giving a friend's sister some money, if I feel like it."

"And you'd rather do that? Instead of setting up that trust, like you said? So I'd just get a big chunk of money, not the monthly allowance?"

She still seemed neutral, but he had a quick flash of something from her, something that made his business sense tingle. "The monthly allowance is still the goal," he said. Once he'd given her the money, she'd be beyond his control, and he didn't like the sound of that. "But it'll have to be a bit informal. Because of the laws. But, yeah, we can work something out."

She nodded. "We need to look at numbers. But you haven't

told Dan about this? Is that... are you planning on being a single dad? Or just you and Jeff?" She didn't seem upset about either option, just curious, and he wondered again just how this woman felt about the entire situation.

"No, I'm... I'm planning to talk to Dan. I'm just waiting for the right time. Things have been a bit hectic lately."

"He's angry about this afternoon," she said. "He thinks you were disrespectful."

"I was." Evan wondered whether they were going to loop back around to his apology. "I'm really sorry."

She frowned. "*He's* the one who's angry. And maybe part of it's because of me, but mostly, I think he's mad because you disrespected *him*." She took a bite of her cookie, chewed and swallowed, then said, "Have you apologized to *him* yet?"

"No. Not yet." Evan really wasn't sure how he wanted that conversation to go. In his fantasy world, he and Dan *both* apologized. Evan would be happy to express regret for being disrespectful if Dan would admit that he'd been insensitive to Evan during a crisis situation. Because it *had* been a crisis. Or had at least felt like one. But Tat was home. She'd shown up shortly after her call, looked somewhat chastened when she saw the full security team that had been assembled, and then breezed past Evan as if he wasn't even there. She'd been locked in her room ever since, avoiding the talk that she and Evan were going to have as soon as they both calmed down. Which maybe meant that Dan didn't have too much to apologize for, really. Evan needed to think it all through. Probably with Jeff's help. In the meantime, though, he was here, with Dan's sister, trying to make sure he was still going to be able to adopt Dan's niece or nephew, even though he hadn't managed to discuss it with Dan yet. Jesus. "I really need to talk to Dan," he said, almost to himself.

But Krista heard, of course, and she sighed. "Yeah," she said. "And it might be a little trickier than you think. He really wasn't that impressed when I told him you were going to buy the baby."

"He's not answering," Evan said. He looked at his phone. "I miss the old kind. The ones with handsets to slam down. Or at least a fucking bottom to flip closed. I mean, I want to *hang up*, not *end call*. You know?" He looked over at Jeff and Chris.

They were sitting in the same place they'd been all evening, in the big Adirondack chairs on Jeff's porch. Jeff thought maybe he'd stay there forever, sipping Wild Turkey, listening to the crickets, and letting the pain in his chest ease away. Chris had been excellent company for the entire exercise. Evan, on the other hand, was a disruption.

"I hate it when he does this. Goes all incommunicado." Evan stared at his phone some more, still trying to find a more dramatic way to express his disgust.

Jeff sighed and took a sip of his bourbon. "Maybe it's not a bad thing," he said. "Maybe you both need a little time to cool down."

"Nothing's going to change overnight," Chris agreed. "You should go inside, find a glass and maybe another bottle, and come out here to enjoy the night."

Evan didn't seem impressed with this attitude. "You don't think he and I need to talk it out?" He looked at Jeff. "You don't think we need to communicate, and share our feelings and all that?"

Jeff looked at Chris, who frowned back at him. Right. Solidarity. "We don't know. That's for you and Danny to figure out." Jeff tried to sound supportive, but firm.

Evan sat down on the porch step and peered up at Jeff, trying to get a better look at his face. "But you have an opinion, right? I mean, you want us to solve the problem? You think we're both idiots, and we need to grow up? Something like that, right?"

Jeff didn't need to look at Chris this time; he just nodded. "Yeah. I think you need to grow up." He lifted his glass for another sip.

"Are you mad at me?" Evan sounded like a confused little boy, and a significant part of Jeff wanted to comfort him. It wasn't like Jeff hadn't known what he was getting into when he started a relationship with a much younger man. And it wasn't like Jeff didn't get off on being the wise, stable one, the father figure who guided the others along. When Danny would let him, Jeff literally got off on it, playing his dom role with enthusiasm and compassion. But Danny wouldn't sub very often, and Evan had never had any interest in the game whatsoever. And out of the bedroom, they were all grown men, all equals. Chris was right; Jeff had to stop acting like the parent, mediating conflict between two squabbling children. Until he did, they had no reason to grow up and solve their own problems. His chest gave a quick pang, and he forced himself not to think about how soon they might be left without whatever guidance he'd been offering. "I'm not mad," he said honestly. "I'm just tired. You and Danny need to sort this out on your own."

"I'm not sure that's fair," Evan protested. "We're supposed to be in this, all three of us, together! You can't just back out when it gets hard."

"Bullshit, I can't," Jeff responded. There was more heat in his words than he'd expected, but he didn't feel like pulling back. "When there's something from the outside—when there's trouble with Tat, or Dan's sister, or whatever else, I'm there for you, and I will be as long as I can be. But when it's just the two of you being jackasses? When you make a deal to buy Dan's niece or nephew and don't even tell him about it? That's your mess. I warned you about it, but it's not my job to clean up after you."

"I'm not really thinking of it as 'buying' the baby," Evan corrected.

"I don't care how you're thinking of it. You're giving a woman money in exchange for her child. I'm not saying it's automatically wrong, although it sure doesn't feel right. But the words aren't what matter. The fact is, you knew Dan wouldn't like it; if you hadn't known that, you wouldn't have kept it a secret. You made your choice, and now you need to figure out a way to fix it." Jeff felt his chest tightening again, and he was pretty sure Chris was watching him more closely than usual. He took a sip of his bourbon and tried to concentrate on his breathing. Regular, not too deep, just calm and easy. He could do this.

Evan was watching him too, but he seemed to be focusing on Jeff's words, not his expression. "Do you think I'm wrong?" he asked quietly. "Do you think I should have let her give the baby to someone else? *Sell* it to someone else?"

"I have no idea, Evan." That wasn't entirely true. Jeff had *some* idea. But he and Chris had talked about this, and they'd agreed. They were going to back off, and Evan and Danny would just have to sort it out on their own. Not that Dan had shown any sign of asking for help, Jeff realized. Chris had been right there with Jeff all evening, and neither of them had gotten a call from Dan. That was a bit worrisome; it definitely made it seem like Dan was back to his "running and hiding" pattern of stress avoidance. Not Jeff's favorite thing, and obviously not Evan's, either.

But Jeff needed to have faith in both of them. Dan wouldn't run for good. And Evan wouldn't... wouldn't what? Wouldn't buy the baby without Dan's consent? Jeff really wasn't sure what the next move was for Evan. But he couldn't let himself worry about that. It was Evan's job to figure this out.

He took another sip of his bourbon and looked over to see Chris's sympathetic eyes. Chris raised his glass in a subtle toast, and Jeff actually managed a smile. There was someone looking out for him, and it felt good. It felt like something he hadn't had for far too long.

Chapter Eleven

Dan loved being the first person in the barn in the morning. He'd give the horses their hay, then go around with their feed, then check that the automatic waterers were working. And then nothing. He'd sit there and listen to them munching away, or he'd go outside and watch the farm wake up, the sun hitting the dew on the grass, the birds flitting around looking for stray oats, the fat barn cats watching the birds with interest but no activity. It was peaceful. And he definitely needed a little peace.

He hadn't slept well the night before. Leftover tension from Tat. That was part of it, sure. But mostly it was the situation with Evan. With Evan and Krista. And Chris. And maybe even Jeff. Dan hadn't spoken to him, but he assumed Jeff was on Evan's side. That was his default position, after all. Jeff and Evan had been a couple long before Dan showed up, and when things got tense, it was natural for them to fall into old patterns. The two of them against the world. The two of them against Dan.

He wandered over to Smokey's stall. The little horse pricked his ears forward and left his breakfast to see whether Dan had brought him something better. He was only fed a token handful of grain, just enough to keep him from feeling left out, and then he had to stand there and hear his barn mates still happily crunching through their feed while he was stuck with dry, boring hay. "I haven't got anything for you, buddy." Smokey turned his head, and Dan scratched along his neck, finding all the itchy spots. "I'll get you an apple later, okay? And maybe we'll go for a ride." Dan had another one of his urges; he wanted to get on his horse and go. They could ride as far as Smokey's strong legs would take them, and then rest under a tree somewhere. Dan could fish, maybe, and Smokey would do fine with just grass. They'd live off the land together, no complications, no frustrations.

Dan heard a car door slam out in the parking area. It was not yet time for the barn staff to arrive; he only had the early shift one day a week, but the others were generally more than happy to take the chance to sleep in. He looked toward the main door and wasn't all that surprised to see Evan and Jeff walk through it.

He stepped away from Smokey. The horse was pretty sensitive to Dan's emotions, and there was no need to expose him to this wave of negativity. "Hi," he said. He tried to make it sound businesslike. Evan was a partner in the barn, after all, and still owned a hell of a lot more of it than Dan did. Like the guest house, if Evan decided that he wanted to come by, he absolutely had the right.

"Hi," Evan said. He took a few steps closer. "We didn't hear from you last night. Usually you call."

"Usually somebody does," Dan agreed. They all kept their separate homes, and they didn't spend every night together, but they generally did check in. But it's not like it was Dan's job or something. He wasn't going to take responsibility for something that none of them had done.

"I tried," Evan said. "You didn't pick up."

Oh. So maybe Dan didn't really have the high ground on that argument. "I left the phone somewhere. In the truck, I guess."

"Yeah." Evan looked like he was trying to control his frustration, but Dan didn't think he was doing a very good job. "That's what you do. We have a fight, and you 'lose' your phone. I know the pattern."

"It's not lost. It's... it's probably in the truck." Dan refused to sound apologetic. He wanted to look at Jeff, wanted to see support in his eyes, but he wasn't sure it would be there, and he didn't want to take the chance. So he ignored Jeff and focused on Evan.

"It's not a great system, Dan. Makes communication kind of difficult."

And that was about it for Dan's patience. "And I know how important communication is to you. I mean, you probably wanted to tell me about buying Krista's baby, but you couldn't do it because I didn't have my phone with me all the time. You couldn't do it in person, and you couldn't call me any of the times that the phone *was* with me. No, you're right. *I'm* bad at communication, and you're a fucking broadcast network." Evan looked like he might have something to say, but Dan wasn't quite done. "But last night, *after* I found out about it, *that* was when it was suddenly essential that you talk to me. So, yeah, this whole thing is my fault. I get it."

"And why do you think I was reluctant to discuss it with you? Because you're so calm and rational about everything? Or because I knew you'd blow it out of proportion and get all crazy about it?"

"You're going to talk to me about blowing things out of proportion, after that little display yesterday? Seriously? How the fuck long do you think you can take the 'I'm calm and controlled' high road when you're having panic attacks every time Tat breathes funny? Seriously, Evan, based on yesterday—you were either totally out of control, which means you need to shut up about me being emotional, or you were *in* control, which means you're a total asshole."

"No. My sister was missing, possibly kidnapped, and I looked at the most logical suspect. I'm sorry that was your sister. I'm sorry that me treating her the way I did hurt your feelings, or upset your pride, or offended your sense of justice or whatever the fuck it is you're pissed about, but there's nothing irrational about suspecting a criminal of committing a crime." Evan wasn't trying to maintain control anymore, and his voice was just short of a yell. Jeff was standing off to the side, leaning against one of the stalls, apparently content to just watch.

Dan shook his head. "So you were totally right. Nothing to feel at all bad about."

"I've been more than generous with your sister, Dan. I paid her bail, invited her into my home, bought her gifts, let her spend time with my innocent seventeen-year-old sister ..."

"You paid her bail? What happened to the whole 'we'll use *our* money to help *our* family'? And you bought her gifts? I thought so too, until the chips were down and you decided that they weren't gifts after all, they were just loans. Shit you could take back whenever you felt like it. And seriously, dude, you're pretty inconsistent on the 'my home' line too. How many times have you tried to convince me and Jeff to move in, since we essentially live here already? Looking at the last couple days, can you understand why we weren't real enthusiastic about the idea? The next time you decide that it'd be more convenient for you if we lived here, remember this conversation. Remember why we need to have our own places, need to have something that you can't decide to take away whenever you feel like it." Dan was pretty sure he saw that hit home. Evan looked almost shaken, and Dan waited for his answer. He waited to hear Evan admit that he was wrong.

Instead, Evan said, "I really don't think you need to worry about me making that invitation again anytime soon, Dan."

Dan tried not to react. He'd be damned if he'd let Evan see how that had stung. Instead, he made his face relax, made himself smile, and said, "Okay. That conversation's not on the table. And there's not much point in going over yesterday's bullshit again. So let's cut to the chase. You think you're going to buy one of my family members, and I don't think I'm going to let that happen."

"You're not going to...." Evan had already gone way further with this fight than he'd meant to. Dan had hurt him, and he'd hurt back, and now the whole thing was out of control. But Evan didn't know how to de-escalate it, and wasn't sure he wanted to. "What do you mean? I assume you've already tried to talk Krista out of it, and I assume she's already blown you off. I don't really see what else you can do about it." They needed to fight this out, Evan was pretty sure, and then make up afterward.

But Dan wasn't fighting. His face was totally calm, totally un-Dan-like. "It's illegal to buy and sell babies, Evan. I'm sure Chris has made that clear to you. I don't know what scam he came up with to make it work, but it's not going to happen if I blow the whistle. If I tell the court the kind of deal you made, they'll shut it down. And they'll keep a close eye on Krista to make sure she doesn't make a deal with anyone else, either. Her husband's a fugitive, and she's already made it clear that his family is even less stable than hers. So you know who's going to end up with custody, Evan? Me. Anytime I want, all I have to do is find a judge who cares about kids, and your whole deal is over."

"And you'd do that?" Normally, Dan was completely transparent, and Evan could read him easily. But when he got like this, his mask was thick and solid, and Evan had no idea what was going on underneath.

Dan's shrug seemed genuinely nonchalant. "If I have to. I'd rather not, obviously. Krista's already got enough legal trouble. And you don't need the hassle, or the bad publicity. But if you think you can throw your weight around and get what you want just because you're rich, you should think again. Not everything's for sale, Evan. I'm not, and neither is my sister's kid."

It was one of the first things that had drawn Evan to Dan. Well, the very first thing had been his looks. And possibly the second, third, and fourth things had also been mainly physical. But his integrity had been what made Evan want more than a short-term fling. It was that core that Evan had been thinking about the other day, that stable, unshakeable certainty in some things. Dan wasn't for sale. Evan absolutely knew that to be true. And if Dan decided to extend the protection to his niece or nephew, he could probably manage it. Dan's integrity was admirable. But it was also absolutely infuriating. "You'd do that, just to win? I mean, what's your objection, really? Do you think I wouldn't be a good dad? That *we*, all three of us, wouldn't be good dads? Do you really think the baby would be better off somewhere else? Do you even *want* to raise it yourself? Or is this whole thing just...." Evan struggled for the words. "Is it just about being *right*, for the sake of it?"

Dan stared at him, and then let the mask fall away as he shook his head sadly. "I'm really not sure we *would* be good parents, Evan. I mean—are you planning to raise the kid with that philosophy? The ends justify the means? It's not important to do the right thing as long as you get what you want? Is that what we'd teach it?"

Evan had thought he was calming down, but apparently there was still room for his temper to rise. "So, what, you think I'm totally immoral? Ask the rest of the world, Dan. Ask them which of us would be the better father." He shook his head. "I look after my sister, I run a company that wins international awards for environmentalism and business ethics, and I contribute generously to half the charities in the damn state. You come from a family of criminals, one of whom is facing a possible life sentence, the other of whom is still a fugitive. Oh, and *you* have a criminal record too." And Evan knew he should stop himself, knew he was about to go way too far, but the words came out anyway. "You've said it yourself. You abandoned your mom when she was dying, and you abandoned your sister when she was still just a kid, leaving her to live with a man you knew was abusive. *Now* you're Mr. Family Values? You're judging *me* on my suitability to raise a child? Seriously?"

Dan and Evan had never had a physical fight. Never. But right then, Evan was pretty sure that Dan was going to punch him. He braced himself for the blow. In the split second since he'd stopped talking, he'd already begun to feel horribly guilty, and he looked forward to the pain that Dan's fist was going to cause. Evan absolutely deserved it. He'd taken things that Dan had told him in confidence, things that he knew made Dan feel vulnerable and exposed, and he'd thrown them back at him. He'd *tried* to hurt Dan, and now he very much wanted Dan to hurt him in return.

But Dan didn't. His whole body was tense and ready to go, but he didn't move, and he didn't say a word. He just stared, and then his eyes shifted to the side. Looking for support from Jeff, Evan supposed, and he was pretty damn sure Dan was going to get it. Pretty sure he *deserved* to get it. But it didn't seem that Dan liked whatever he was seeing from Jeff. His expression became confused, then concerned, and finally Evan turned his own head to see Jeff leaning against the wall, his face gray, his hands clutching at his chest.

Dan and Evan moved together, and between them, they managed to catch Jeff before he slumped all the way to the floor.

Jeff knew the fight had gone on too long, and had gotten too ugly. He'd been willing to abandon the plan he and Chris had come up with; yes, it was uncomfortable to be in the middle all the time, but better a little discomfort from that than watching the men he loved tear each other apart. He'd opened his mouth to speak, but he hadn't been able to get his breath. He realized that he'd been breathing too shallowly, remembered that the pain in his chest wasn't all emotional. He'd leaned backward, braced himself against the stall wall, and tried to get back in control. He couldn't breathe deeply, but he could speed it up a little, getting the oxygen into his body any way he could. He was dimly aware that the boys had stopped yelling, but he didn't know why. Maybe his ears had just stopped working, the blood rushing through them too loudly for anything else to penetrate. He could feel the darkness closing in around his eyes, the world beginning to fade, and he fought to control his breathing. Each breath felt like a thousand icy needles pressing into his chest, but he needed the air. He needed to live.

And then somehow he was moving. In a car, he realized, and he forced his eyes open to see Evan's almost panicked face peering down at him. They were in the back of Evan's SUV, Jeff was pretty sure, and they were in motion. Jeff tried to look forward, tried to see if Dan was driving, where Dan was, whether he was okay, but he didn't seem able to turn his head. "His eyes are open!" he heard Evan yell, and then there was a calmer female voice coming from... somewhere. From Evan's cell, maybe, set to speakerphone.

"Okay, Evan, that's good. Try to speak to him. Keep your voice calm, and tell him help's on the way."

It was Dr. Sangha, Jeff was pretty sure. Evan's family doctor. That made sense. She was physically close, and Evan trusted her. But she wouldn't know Jeff had been having pain for a while. Maybe that was just as well. Evan would be angry if he knew that Jeff had been ignoring his health. Evan's fingers were running through Jeff's hair, trembling a little but still strong. Evan took a deep breath and then started repeating the doctor's words. "Help's on the way, Jeff. We're driving to town, and they're sending an ambulance to meet us. There's a helicopter ready, if we need it. Everything's going to be okay. It's going to be okay, Jeff."

Then, Dan's voice. "Ambulance," he said, and Jeff felt a rush of air blow over him. Dan must have opened the window to flag the ambulance down. The car swerved to the right, braked hard, and then Dan turned around in his seat and peered down at Jeff. "You're okay, Jeff. The ambulance is here. It's going to be okay."

Jeff tried to believe him. He wanted to live. He needed to. He couldn't be taken away now, in the middle of everything. Dan and Evan needed him. There was movement past his head, and he realized that the door had opened, and then unfamiliar hands were on him, touching him, shifting him, taking him away from Evan and Dan. He knew he shouldn't fight, wouldn't have been able to even if he'd tried, but he felt the fear rising, felt his heart racing, and then the darkness washed over him again.

Chapter Twelve

Dan hated hospitals. Nothing good ever happened in them, and he'd been in too many. The one in Dallas, when his mom was sick. The one in Kentucky, after Justin's fall. And now, this one, shiny and almost futuristic-looking, where the ambulance had taken Jeff. They were in a private waiting room, decorated in warm colors, with rich fabrics and lots of flowers, and Dan hated it. He didn't want to be thinking about the damn décor, not while Jeff was fighting for his life down the hall.

He stood up abruptly, and Evan, who had already been pacing, shifted to the side to give Dan room. They were still being pretty careful not to look at each other, but neither had said a hostile word since Jeff had collapsed. They had a more serious fight on their hands now, and they needed to be on the same side. Dan wasn't sure how long the truce would last, or even whether it *should* last, long-term, but it was absolutely necessary for the time being.

Dan turned toward Jeff's mother, sitting next to Chris by the window. Dan had never seen Anna looking her age before, but now she did. She seemed like a frail old woman, and Dan couldn't stand it. He wanted her to be vibrant and laughing, galloping her horse up the hills, not tight and strained, sitting in a damn hospital waiting to hear whether her only child was going to survive. Dan tried not to think of Justin's parents; he really didn't want to let his mind go down that path. But it was hard to avoid it. Hard not to think about his previous loss. He could remember the last words he'd said to Justin, and the last words Justin had said to him, but he couldn't think of when he and Jeff had last spoken. They'd been at the guest house together, making sandwiches, but what had Jeff said? Anything important? Had Dan been so wrapped up in his own nonsense that he didn't even notice?

He looked over at Evan. He looked strained, but not as close to the edge as he'd seemed on the drive in. He had his own worries for the current situation, and his own terrible memories. Was this the hospital where his parents had been taken? Maybe not. Dan was pretty sure that accident had been immediately fatal. Maybe Evan had been spared this horrible waiting, that time. Of course, not waiting just meant that your last shred of hope was ripped away even faster. There was no right answer, no "good" way to deal with any of this. No way to keep yourself from going totally crazy. "I'm going to get some coffee." It wasn't like he needed the caffeine, but he did need a purpose, a distraction. "Does anybody want anything?"

"Sure," Chris agreed. He looked at Anna. "Some tea too," he suggested, and Dan nodded. Excellent. He headed out through the frosted glass door and took a moment to orient himself. That was when he saw Tat and Robyn coming down the hall. Tat's face was blotchy and red, as if she'd been crying even before she'd heard about Jeff, and Robyn's arm was tight around the younger girl's shoulders. Dan felt the weight again, the pressure that seemed to be coming from all around him, constricting his body tighter and smaller. He needed Jeff. They all did. He was the one who could deal with all this.

Tat stopped short when she saw Dan, and she looked almost afraid, as if she wasn't sure she'd be welcome. But that made no sense; Jeff had been her father's best friend even before he became Evan's lover. Tat had known him forever, and obviously loved him. "You okay, Tat?" It was a stupid question, under the circumstances, but he hoped she'd understand what he meant.

Her face crumbled. "Is *Jeff* okay?" she asked in a shaky voice.

Robyn gave Dan a warning look and made her voice louder than it needed to be when she said, "I told you, Tat, this *isn't* your fault."

Dan just stared at the girl. He had no idea what to say. His mind raced, trying to figure out what he should do, what he should say. And then he thought of Evan, his easy physical affection, and he knew what was needed. He stepped forward quickly, and Robyn smiled through tear-moist eyes as she saw him coming. She stepped away just enough for him to be able to wrap his arms around Tat. He kissed the top of her head as she resisted for half a second and then burrowed her face into his shoulder. "It's not your fault, Tat. You screwed up, and I'm not at all impressed, but that doesn't mean this is your fault. At all."

"B-but, it's *stress*, right? That's what gives people heart attacks!" Her voice was a little muffled from the fabric of his shirt, but there was enough volume behind it to make her meaning clear. It was probably just as well that she was at least somewhat muted or she'd be disturbing patients up and down the hall.

"Shhh, Tat," he said. He meant it literally, but also wanted her to be soothed. "We don't even know it's a heart attack. And *if* it is, and *if* it's from stress...." Dan gave her head another kiss, his form of an apology. "If it's from stress, that's on me and Evan, not you. He wasn't really that worried about you, brat. He knew you were fine."

"But you and Evan were fighting because of me, right?" She lifted her face to look at him, and he was reminded of Evan's complaint that she always picked up on just enough of a situation to feel bad about it, without getting the full story and context. He smiled sadly at her.

"Me and Evan were fighting because of me and Evan. You were a tiny little hiccup; the full, disgusting puke of a fight came from something else altogether."

She wrinkled her nose at his analogy, and that was a good sign. As always, Tat felt things strong and fast, and then recovered pretty well. But she did remember her feelings, and generally didn't make the same mistake twice. Although she *had* ditched her security on several separate occasions, so maybe that behavior was the exception to her learning-from-mistakes rule. Or maybe she wasn't really agreeing that it was a mistake. But that was a concern for another time.

"Evan's in the waiting room, and he'll tell you the same thing," Dan promised. It was nice to be able to say that with complete confidence. Whatever Evan's flaws, he'd been a hell of a substitute parent for his sister. And, Dan realized, it must have stung more than a little to hear Dan suggest that he couldn't do a good job looking after another little person.

"Actually, I'm right here," came Evan's voice from behind Dan. "I heard the cry of a harpooned dolphin, but that didn't make sense, so far from the sea. So I figured it must be my baby sister."

Dan grinned into Tat's hair, and he felt her body relax as she realized that Evan wasn't blaming her for Jeff's illness. Dan let his body suggest a spin, and Tat moved in the direction he'd thought of, and he effortlessly transferred her from his arms to Evan's. He reached out and ruffled her hair. "Ditching your security was totally uncool," he said, "and I know you're going to hear about it from Evan, but you're probably going to hear about it from me too. And from Jeff," he added, because he needed to remind himself as well as the others. "But this is a separate thing." He couldn't keep his eyes away from Evan's, and he caught the barely perceptible nod of acknowledgement. The truce had been in place for a while, but now it was formally acknowledged. "I'm going to the caf," Dan said to the group as a whole. "Do you guys want anything?"

"Maybe some nice mackerel for Tat," Evan suggested. "But

no tuna. She still has terrible memories of being caught in that net."

"Shut up, Evan," Tat said, but she didn't move away from his embrace. Dan grinned at her, and left a bit of the smile on his face when he looked at Evan. They both cared about the same people, and they would have to remember that before they tore more than their own relationship apart.

Evan watched Dan as he headed down the hall. It sometimes hurt to look at Dan even when they weren't fighting. He was so beautiful, so strong, and it had a strange effect on Evan. He wanted to wrap Dan up and hide him away from everyone else. Wanted to protect him. But there was also a strange urge to own him, to dominate, to make it clear that Evan loved him too much to ever let him go. In his more sane moments, Evan recognized that it wasn't a particularly healthy urge, but he really wasn't sure what to do about it. For the time being, at least, he decided to ignore it.

He turned to Robyn. "Thanks for picking her up. And for coming down yourself. Jeff's still in with the doctors—they haven't told us anything yet."

Robyn nodded. "Okay. I'm just going to go in…" And she waved her arm toward the waiting room.

"Yeah, okay." Evan waited until the door shut behind Robyn, then turned Tat's hug into a gentle shake. He wasn't sure if it was the right time or not, but he decided to go for it. "Tat, think about how you feel right now. The feeling that someone you love is in danger. That maybe you didn't do enough to protect them from it, and that there's not a damn thing you can do now to help. All you can do is stand around and go crazy with worry, and pray that the experts are going to be able to save the day." He sighed. "Think about how helpless you feel. Remember all the money you have access to, and realize that it isn't enough to buy even a little bit of control over the situation." He brought his fingers to her chin and tilted her head up so she was looking straight at him. "Think about this feeling, and remember it the next time you think it'll be fun to ditch your security and leave me to go crazy wondering where the fuck you are." He didn't usually swear around Tat, and he saw her eyes widen a little just before she nodded her understanding.

"Yeah," she said, her mouth pressed back into his shoulder. "It's frustrating, to feel trapped all the time. But I never meant to make you worry."

"Whether you mean it or not, it still happens," Evan said. "If you're so determined to be treated like an adult, that's something you need to realize. We let little kids off the hook when things go bad, because they're little kids. They can't understand what might happen. But adults are expected to know. So if you're going to use 'I'm not a baby anymore' as your tagline, you'd better understand all of what it means."

He felt her nod. "Is Jeff going to be okay?" she asked quietly.

He tightened his arms around her. "I think so. I do. We got him here fast, and he's getting the best possible care. We've done everything we can. And—" It sounded juvenile, sounded like just what he'd been warning her against, but he added, "And he has to be. We need him."

Another nod, and then she said, "And you and Dan? Are you guys going to be okay?"

That was a harder question. It was something that Evan *should* have total control over, and that *should* feel like a relief, after the powerlessness with Jeff. But somehow, things with Dan never seemed to go the way Evan planned them. He felt more out of control there than in any other aspect of his life. So he kissed Tat's head again and whispered, "I hope so." And then, because it was true, he added, "We have to be. We need him."

God bless painkillers, Jeff decided. He took a deep breath, felt only a slight twinge in his chest, and wanted to laugh. He bet *that* wouldn't hurt too much, either. Everything was just fine. Everything was excellent.

He was really stoned, he realized. Some part of his brain was trying to remind him that everything was far from excellent, and that there were serious issues still to be dealt with, his health only one among many. But that part of his brain, which was usually so dominant, was now remarkably easy to ignore. He'd much rather focus on the pattern of light coming in through the window. He was pretty sure that if he looked at it just a little longer, he'd start fading into it, and he and the light would go to sleep together and travel to wonderful places.

Then he heard something from the opposite direction, a sweeping, shushing sound, and he forced his head to roll in that direction. The sound had been his door opening, and now Dan and Evan were standing in his room, looking at him with trepidation. "They let you both in?" Jeff mumbled. It was a strange thing to focus on, but it had always been one of their concerns. The relationship had no official sanction, and if they ran into an obstreperous hospital administrator, things could be awkward.

"They wanted your mom to come," Evan said softly. "They said she was the closest relative." Even in his drugged state, Jeff could tell that Evan was seething but trying to stay calm.

"She was fierce," Dan added. "Like you'd expect. She told them we were your partners, and we'd go in first. No hesitation, no flexibility." He grinned. "I'm glad she's on our side."

"Me too," Jeff agreed. His thoughts were still jumbled, but he was beginning to come back to himself. It wasn't an altogether pleasant place to be.

"We promised we wouldn't be long, so she'd be able to pop in for a quick visit," Evan said. "And Tat wanted to come too, if that won't tire you out."

"*Tat* is not the Kaminski who tires me out," Jeff said. He wasn't quite sure what he meant by that, and wasn't quite sure how he wanted Evan to take it. What the hell, he'd just use his drugged state as an excuse to say all kinds of crazy shit and let the boys sort *him* out for a change.

Then the door swooshed open again, and a man in a white coat was standing in front of them. He glanced at Dan and Evan, then crossed the floor to speak to Jeff directly. "Mr. Stevens, I'm Dr. Kraft. I'm the cardiologist on duty, and I worked on you when you first came in."

"I don't really remember," Jeff admitted, and the doctor nodded.

"You're not expected to. But we've got a diagnosis for you, and a solid treatment plan." He glanced behind them, then back to Jeff. "Is there someone you'd like to have in here to hear about it with you? Preferably someone who will be able to take responsibility for helping you manage your care."

Put that way, maybe Jeff *should* get his mom in there. He didn't want to be a burden on the boys, didn't want them to feel they had to look after him.

But they were already moving, stepping forward to stand on either side of Jeff's bed. They turned to look at the doctor together. "That's us," Dan said.

"We'll help him with whatever he needs," Evan confirmed. He glanced toward Dan as if looking for permission, then extended his hand to the doctor. "I'm Evan Kaminski. You might recognize the last name from the Kaminski Trauma Center. Or the Kaminski Medical Research Council." He frowned thoughtfully. "I don't think we've done too much in cardiology yet." He glanced down toward Jeff before saying, "But maybe that's about to change."

The doctor shook Evan's hand, then glanced at Jeff, then

over to Dan. Jeff wished his arms would move, because he'd really like to reach out to Dan just then. But Dan didn't seem to need his support. He leaned forward enough to extend his hand to the doctor and said, "Dan Wheeler. Barn boy."

"He's part of the team," Evan said firmly, with only a slight, playful scowl in Dan's direction.

And that was just about right. Dan and Evan, working together, all part of the same team. Jeff felt the drugs reasserting their calming influence, but he barely needed them anymore. Then he remembered that the doctor was still in the room, and about to give Jeff the diagnosis he'd been avoiding for far too long.

Cardiologist, he thought. "It's my heart, then?" Jeff asked, and Dan and Evan's attention immediately returned to the doctor.

"It is. But probably not in the way you've been thinking," the doctor said, only a little distracted by the unconventional group he was speaking to. "You didn't have a heart attack. Your heart muscle appears strong and healthy, although as we have you here, we would like to do a few more tests to confirm that. What you have is called pericarditis. It's quite advanced... from what I can tell, you've been neglecting the condition for some time."

Jeff kept his eyes focused on the doctor, refusing to return either Dan's or Evan's looks. He'd deal with that later. "So what does that mean? Can it get better?"

"Yes." The doctor nodded his head firmly. "It's extremely painful, and it *can* be serious, but we think we've caught it... well, not quite *in time*, but at least before it's done permanent damage." He scowled at Jeff. "We hope." Then he returned to his more professional demeanor. "Essentially, your heart rests in a protective membrane, the pericardium. Your membrane has become inflamed. We think it's probably related to a virus, in your case, but again, we'd like to do some more tests. The treatment should be straightforward. We'll give you painkillers and anti-inflammatories, possibly antibiotics, and we'll work to determine what caused it, in case there's an underlying condition that needs to be treated." He frowned. "And because you've allowed it to become quite advanced, we'll monitor you closely to ensure that certain conditions associated with untreated pericarditis do not develop."

"But he should recover fully?" Evan was watching the doctor closely, as if alert for any hint of deception or evasiveness.

"He should," the doctor confirmed.

Jeff felt Dan's fingers wrap around his own, and tightened his grip in response. Everything was going to be okay. He was going to be okay. He looked over toward the light from the window and decided to stay awake as long as he could. He and the light could still probably travel to wonderful places together, but Jeff wasn't in any hurry to leave the place he was already in.

Chapter Thirteen

Dan smiled at Anna as she edged past him and headed into the room to visit her son. "It's good news," he told her, and he was rewarded by seeing her face relax. She looked ten years younger almost instantly. "And we'll take better care of him. I promise."

She snorted. "Good luck with that. It's not like I haven't been trying for years."

"There's two of us," Dan said, and he looked at Evan for confirmation.

"We'll gang up on him," Evan confirmed. "There will be no escape from our caring."

Anna smiled at both of them. "I like the sound of that."

"Did Tat change her mind about going in?" Dan asked. The girl was nowhere to be seen.

"She went down to the gift store to pick up some flowers. I told her Jeff wouldn't really care, but you know how she is when she gets an idea in her head."

Dan and Evan nodded in unison. They absolutely did know how Tat was. "Go see your son," Evan urged with a smile. "We'll send Tat in when she shows up, if that's okay."

"Of course," Anna agreed easily. "He'll want to see her."

"He's pretty stoned," Dan warned. "The doctor said he's on

opiates for a day or two, to let him get some rest." The guilt was heavy when he added, "I guess he hasn't been sleeping too much lately."

Anna's nod was carefully nonjudgmental, which made the whole thing worse, but Dan put on a brave smile and watched as Anna disappeared through the door. Then he turned to Evan.

They were standing close to each other, closer than they'd been in a while, and Evan was looking at Dan intently. "We need to be better," Evan said simply, and Dan nodded.

"Yeah. We still have stuff to work out. It'd be tempting to say we should leave it until Jeff gets better, but Krista's baby is coming pretty damn soon. We need to sort that out. But we need to look after Jeff too."

Evan nodded. "It's a lot. But we can do it, right?" He took a deep breath. "I'm sorry. For not talking to you about the baby. I planned to. I mean, obviously. I'm not so oblivious that I thought you wouldn't notice a baby suddenly showing up. It just never seemed like the right time."

Dan wasn't sure what to say. Did he have something to apologize for? He didn't think so. Well, the things he'd said, maybe. He'd believed them, but he knew it must have hurt to hear it. But did that mean he was sorry? He needed to think this through, but Evan was looking at him expectantly. Dan decided to keep the conversational scope limited. "Yeah, you needed to discuss that. I mean, even if it was some stranger's baby, you should have talked to me about it. But when it's my sister's kid...." And that raised an interesting point. "She said she was getting a million dollars out of it. That seems like a lot. I mean, if you decided to bypass the ethics of it all and buy a baby, couldn't you get one for a lot cheaper?"

Evan nodded slowly. "I guess. I don't know, I honestly haven't looked into it. It wasn't... it wasn't about buying a baby. I know, that's what it looks like. I get that. And maybe that's how Krista's looking at it. But for me... I just wanted your niece or nephew to be safe. And I wanted your sister to have enough money to feel secure. And I was kind of...." He looked at Dan as if trying to judge his reaction so far, and apparently wasn't alarmed by what he saw. "Jeff warned me about getting too attached to the kid. I mean, if you got custody for just while Krista was in jail, and then she got out and we had to give it back... that would be really hard. For us, and for the kid. So I thought, this way... you know. We could make it permanent. We could give the kid a safe, loving home. And we could make sure your sister was looked after, and we could make sure that it was permanent, not something that could get messed up a few years down the road."

There was a lot of good in what Evan was saying, and Dan didn't want to be cynical about it. But he still didn't really understand. "So I'm so irrational and emotionally unstable that you couldn't just explain all that to me? You had to sneak around because you honestly thought I wouldn't listen to you when you said all that?"

Evan frowned. "I don't know. I mean... no. I really don't think you're irrational, or emotionally unstable. Chris and I should probably stop saying that. I mean, it's funny when we tease you about it, but not if it's something serious. You're not unstable, you just... you make your decisions in a totally different way than I do. I don't really understand how your brain works." Evan raised his hands defensively. "I'm not saying that it doesn't work. Obviously it does. I just can't understand it. Can't predict it. So it's easier, sometimes, to kind of bypass the conversation. I know, it's a chickenshit way to do things. And I swear, I will try to stop. But, no, I don't think you're unstable." Evan's grin was quick and tentative, but when Dan let himself return it, Evan's face relaxed. "But don't go telling Chris I said that."

Dan felt a lot better about just about everything. He and Evan would figure things out. They'd fight, and they'd make up, and they'd pull their heads out of their asses and pay attention to Jeff. It would be okay. Dan let his smile deepen, and took a half step forward. Evan instantly moved to meet him.

Their kiss was quick and sweet. More than a peck, but not the full-body make-out session that Dan was suddenly craving. They were still in a public corridor, after all, and there was still a lot to work out between them. But the kiss was a good start, Dan decided, and his fingers wrapped around Evan's before he pulled away.

Evan's fingers returned the squeeze. Then his cell phone rang, and he glanced down at the screen and shook his head as he lifted the phone to his ear. "He doesn't have a favorite color, Tat. Just get whichever ones you like."

Dan's smile froze when he saw Evan's eyes widen in shock. The grip around his fingers had become viselike, and Dan braced himself for whatever was coming next.

"Your sister is with us," the male voice said. "She's safe, and will be returned unharmed, once the ransom is paid."

It was Evan's worst nightmare. No. It was the second worst. They were saying she was safe, and he'd have to believe them. But he still couldn't accept that she was gone. "She just went downstairs," he said. He knew he sounded stupid, but he was having trouble thinking at a consistent speed, or in a logical direction. "She's not missing. She's on her way back up. With flowers."

"Yeah, they were really pretty," the voice said. "She dropped them in the parking lot. Maybe you can pick them up, if they're so important to you."

There were muffled voices in the background, then the man said, "That's it for this call. I'll call back in an hour, from a different number. Make sure you pick up." Then the line disconnected, and Evan was left standing in the hospital corridor, the phone pressed against his head so hard it was crushing his ear, while

Dan stared at him in confusion.

"What's going on?" Dan demanded.

"Call Bill Albanese," Evan said. He was pretty sure Dan had the number. He hit the button to call back Tat's cell and talked as he lifted the phone to his ear. "Somebody just called from Tat's phone. Said he had Tat. Said he'd call back in an hour."

Dan was searching his own contact list, and then he hit a button and raised his own phone to his ear. "You're calling her back?"

Evan nodded. "Just voice mail, though."

Dan lifted a finger to pause Evan, then spoke into his phone. "Bill, it's Dan Wheeler. Hang on, Evan needs you."

Dan handed his phone over, and Evan tried to keep his voice under control. "Bill, They've got Tat. For real, this time."

Jeff let himself float. He'd been stupid, but now everything was better again. He'd be back on his feet, he'd take care of the boys, and yeah, maybe with Chris's help, he'd start training them to look after themselves a little. Everything else would work out fine. Everything was good.

He closed his eyes and let himself drift off into dreamland.

Chapter Fourteen

Dan had driven on the way to the hospital because Evan was bigger, and had been better able to manhandle Jeff into the backseat. He drove on the way *from* the hospital because he didn't trust Evan behind the wheel.

Dan didn't know exactly where he was going, but he could follow the GPS's directions. And Evan was a blur of activity, both of their cellphones gripped in his hands as he tried to get hold of all the people he needed, make all the reports and requests that he could, as quickly as possible. Chris had gone back to coordinate things at the house, with Robyn as his assistant, and Anna had stayed at the hospital with Jeff. Their team was spread as thin as it could be, and Dan didn't like it. He needed their solid support around him, and he suspected Evan was missing it too.

Dan questioned his reliance on the GPS when it directed him to stop in front of a nondescript three-story brick office building, but Evan hopped out of the car and strode toward the front door, so Dan followed. Apparently this *was* the headquarters for Evan's security team. Dan had always pictured something a little more futuristic-looking, and maybe something a little more sinister. He saw the row of police cars lined up in the parking lot and took it as the final confirmation that they were in the right place.

He trailed along behind Evan as he charged up the walk,

through the front door and across a small reception area. There was a security guard behind a desk who took one look at Evan's face and hit a button to unlock the door at the back of the foyer. Evan pulled it open without comment and kept moving. Dan had to jog a little to keep up.

Evan hit an elevator button on the way by, but when the doors didn't open immediately he kept walking and pushed open a door to the stairwell. Up two flights, three steps at a time, and then they were through another doorway and into a busy central room. There were twenty or thirty cubicles, and from what Dan could see each had a row of computer monitors and a human operator with a headset. Dan wasn't sure if they were watching security cameras or doing something more intricate, and there was no opportunity to ask.

"Evan." Bill Albanese stepped forward and gripped Evan's shoulder. "We're on top of it. We've got the team ready to go. We'll make it work."

Evan just nodded; his jaw was clenched so tightly he might not even be *able* to speak.

"Come on through here. We've got a command center set up. You can meet everybody, and hear what we've got so far." Bill guided Evan toward a door on the far wall, and Dan followed. But when they reached the doorway, Bill turned to face him. "Dan, I'm sorry. I need to ask you to wait out here."

Evan turned to look at both of them, but Dan just stared at Bill. "What? Why? What if Evan needs me?"

"He's with me, Bill," Evan said, his voice firm.

"I'm sorry, Evan. But...." Bill looked at Dan, then back at Evan. "Krista Wheeler. Married name Krista Russert. She's disappeared from the guest house on your property. As near as we can tell, she snuck out a window and walked away through the forest. Surveillance tapes suggest that she was picked up on the highway in a white van. Hospital surveillance shows Tatiana Kaminski being led toward a white van by a woman wearing a hat to cover her face. The woman appeared to be extremely pregnant." He turned to Dan as if wanting to see his face, then turned back to Evan. "Krista Wheeler is our only suspect in your sister's disappearance. We can't have her brother in the briefing room with us while we discuss the case."

Dan felt ill. What had Krista done? What had *Dan* done, bringing her into Tat's life? He'd wanted to be the hero, wanted to prove that he really wasn't a terrible brother. But he hadn't even proved that. He hadn't been able to do a damn thing himself, not without Evan's help, and now Evan was being repaid with betrayal and deception. It was all Dan's fault.

"It's not Dan's fault," Evan said. The words were so close to his thoughts, and yet so different, that Dan wondered if he'd misheard something somewhere. "He didn't have anything to with this."

"I'm sorry, Evan, but we can't be sure of that. There's an obvious connection, and it doesn't make sense to expose our operations to someone who has divided loyalties."

"Dan's loyalties are clear. But you're right, there *is* a connection." Evan was in his business mode, calm and authoritative. "Dan knows Krista better than any of us, so he may have insight into what the hell is going on. I want him to be part of this so we can use his knowledge." Evan paused and looked Bill straight in the eye. "There are *no* doubts about his loyalty. He loves Tat, and he'd never let her get hurt."

"More than he loves his *own* sister?" Bill shook his head doubtfully, but Evan didn't even hesitate.

"Dan does what he thinks is right. If he knew anything about this, he'd have found a way to stop it, and tried to help his sister at the same time. Dan's clean, and I want him in the room." And that was it. Evan moved forward and Bill stepped aside, letting Dan follow. The room hushed, and everyone gathered around the large central table to hear the update.

Dan found a spot standing against the wall, directly behind

Evan's chair. He was close enough, there, if Evan needed him for anything. Close enough to share whatever came.

Evan had listened to the team's update with growing impatience and growing panic. When Bill finally stopped talking, Evan took a deep breath, then said, "So you're pretty sure Krista was involved. And that's it. That's all you've got. Krista and a white van." He turned to look at the various law enforcement officers in the room. "That's what you've got too. You've got people out on this, searching and... *looking*? Is that all we're doing? Just looking around and hoping to find them?"

Sam Dekay, the FBI agent, nodded. He was older, graying around the edges, but his eyes were sharp and clear, and Evan really, really wanted to trust him. "We're going through the guest house at your residence with a fine-tooth comb. You already had arrangements in place for us to have unlimited access to your telephone and Internet records under certain circumstances, so we've been combing through that data since before you arrived. And we have an all-points bulletin out with local, state, and federal law enforcement officers. We're taking this very seriously, Mr. Kaminski, but right now, we're low on information." He checked his watch. "We've tried to use the GPS on your sister's cell phone, but it's been unreachable; we suspect the phone was either destroyed or had the battery removed. When the next call comes in, we'll try to trace it back and get a location that way."

"So until that call comes, we just wait?" Evan didn't think he could accept that. He needed to do something. Anything. He'd go out and comb the streets himself, if that was all there was.

"I know it seems like we're not doing much, but this room is basically just for communications. For telling you what the rest of our team is doing. There are a lot of officers who are very hard at work right now, I promise you."

Evan looked at the phone on the table in front of him. The officers had somehow rewired his cell signal to be received by a landline, to make their recording and tracing more effective, but it made him nervous. He checked his watch; only a few minutes left until the call was expected. What if the phone hadn't been rewired properly? What if the kidnappers called and got sent to voice mail? Jesus Christ, he shouldn't have let this happen. He should have... he didn't know what. Should have stopped them, and said not to mess with anything; he'd give the kidnappers whatever they wanted. He didn't care about catching them, he just wanted his sister back.

He stared at the phone in front of him, willing it to ring, and he was dimly aware that every other set of eyes in the room was doing something similar. There wasn't a sound as the seconds ticked away. Then there was movement behind Evan, and Dan's voice, low and careful. "My phone's on vibrate, but it's going off. I don't recognize the call-back number."

Jesus. Had Evan's phone not worked, or had they gone straight to Dan in the first place? Were they going to be pissed off? What was happening?

"Answer it on speakerphone." Sam Dekay looked around the room, the command clear. "We'll be silent. If the person on the other end objects, switch speakerphone off and repeat everything that the caller says. We've got listening equipment that will pick up their side."

Dan nodded, his face tense and pale, then hit the screen of his phone and said, "Hello?"

"Danny, it's Krista." Evan could recognize her voice, but he'd never heard her sound so tense, and she was whispering as if trying not to be overheard. "You've got people listening?"

"Yes," Dan said. Evan knew that was the right call; Krista would see through a lie, and they'd lose whatever trust she might have in them.

"Good," she said. "I don't know where we are; they kept

me in the back." Her voice was still hushed and quick, but she seemed to be trying to be thorough. "It was about an hour's drive. Maybe a bit more. We're out in the country, in some sort of cabin. Lots of trees; I think we're on a mountain. Tat's okay. But, Dan—they didn't blindfold her."

That last line seemed to have significance for Krista, and Evan could tell that the officers in the room were getting something from it too, but Evan had no idea what it meant. Dan looked confused for a moment, then his face got even paler. "Krista, you need to get her out of there. Or…." He looked around the room for help.

"This is an old phone, without GPS," Krista said hurriedly. "I've got to go, or they'll come looking for me. If I leave the phone on, can you still track it? Can you find us that way?"

Dan looked toward Sam, who had worked his way around the table and was standing next to the phone. "Leave it on," the agent said. "Try to keep the call going, if you can, so we can hear what's happening."

"Shit, I've got to go," Krista said. She sounded truly frightened. "I'll leave it on. Hurry."

There was a static-y rustling sound over the line, and Dekay reached cautiously for Dan's phone. "We'll mute the call, to be sure we can't be heard," he said, and he took the phone gently from Dan's unresisting fingers. "Stick around, in case she comes back on the line and needs to hear a familiar voice."

Dan nodded, then turned to look at Evan. Dan's eyes were wide and green, as if the reality of the situation had just hit him hard. Evan didn't want to, but he needed to press a little. He needed to know. He reached a hand out to find Dan's, and their cool fingers twined together as if they were two parts of the same body, reunited and healing together. Evan kept his grip on Dan, but turned to look at Bill. "They didn't blindfold her…." He reconsidered. Did he really want to know? No, he didn't want to, but he needed to be informed. "That means that they don't care if she sees them? Because—"

Bill's expression was pained, but he finished Evan's thought for him. "Because they don't expect her to be around to be a witness." He moved forward quickly and crouched down to bring his head to the same level as Evan's. "So this is an important break. We know not to waste too much time on putting the ransom together. We'll use that as a stalling tactic, of course, but we don't need to second-guess ourselves about whether a rescue is a good gamble. It is. We know that now, and we've got the country's best working on tracking the call right now. We're...."

Then the phone on the table rang. Evan had almost forgotten about that. He glanced at Dekay. "Don't mention Krista," the agent instructed. "If they bring her up, make it sound like you're angry at her. Make it sound the way you felt two minutes ago, before she called."

Evan wasn't sure that he wasn't still angry at Krista. At the very least, he was confused. But he needed to focus on the task at hand, so he forced himself to reach calmly for the handset and lift it to his ear. "Evan Kaminski," he said.

"Evan!" It was Tat's voice. She sounded ragged from crying, panicked and confused, but alive. "Evan, I'm sorry. Please help me."

And then there was the sound of movement over the phone, and Tat's cries became muffled and distant. "Tat! *Tat!*"

"She's fine." The man's voice was rough, but calm. "And she'll stay that way once you give us our money. You've got—"

"No, wait," Evan said. He didn't want to let this son of a bitch run the conversation. "I need to talk to my sister. That could have been...." He tried to control himself when he realized that it was true. "That could have been a recording. I need to *talk* to her, to hear her respond to what I'm saying."

"You need to get ten million dollars together by tomorrow

at 11:00 a.m.," the voice said. "You don't have time for conversations." And then the call ended.

Evan stared at the handset for a long time before gently replacing it in its cradle. He was dimly aware of some activity around Dan's cell, but the rest of the room was quiet, watching and waiting. Waiting for him. To do what? To say what?

He felt Dan's familiar hand on his shoulder, and squeezed his fingers to feel Dan's other hand still laced with his own. "We'll get her back, Evan," Dan said quietly, and Evan nodded.

Then he turned to face Bill and Sam, and he let all his fierce determination show on his face. "Get her back," he ordered. "Whatever it takes."

"Absolutely," Bill agreed. He turned and strode away, and Dekay followed him. Evan was left with Dan, and even though the room was crowded and busy, it felt like they were all alone. Evan let his head fall back to brace against Dan's stomach, and Dan gripped Evan's shoulder a little tighter. "We'll be okay," Dan said, and Evan had never wanted to believe anyone as much as he wanted to believe Dan.

Jeff knew something was wrong. His mother was still there, but she was the only one he'd seen in hours. Dan and Evan—where were they? And Tat? Hell, even Chris had disappeared. Something was going on. Something bad.

He looked at the IV dripping medicine into his body and wondered if he could detach it. He supposed he could order a nurse or doctor to do it; he was mentally competent, so they couldn't force him to stay in the hospital if he didn't want to. But he wasn't sure if he was up for the argument. He needed to save his strength for whatever it was that Dan and Evan were dealing with. He reached for the IV needle. He was pretty sure he could pull it out. Were his clothes still in the room? That would be the next challenge....

"Don't you dare." It was his mother's voice, and he looked over to see her standing in the doorway, staring at his hand on the IV. "Don't," she repeated, and he had a sudden flash of them having a similar exchange when he'd been a little boy reaching for a forbidden cookie.

"What's going on, Mom? Where is everybody? You can't expect me to just lie here while something's happening to my family."

"You can't expect me to stand here and watch the last member of *my* family killing himself," she hissed as she walked closer. "The doctors were clear. This is worse than it would have been if you'd come in when you should have, but it's not as bad as it could be if you don't take care of it." She shook her head. "And look at you. You're as weak as a kitten. Your job is to look after yourself and get better. The boys are doing all they can, and they'll let us know when they have news." She looked like she maybe regretted that last sentence, and he didn't blame her. She'd just gotten his imagination even more fired up.

"What the hell is going on, Mom?" He tried to sound calm and reasonable, and apparently she bought it.

But then it was her turn to get emotional, and he watched, stuck five feet away from her, as two fat tears rolled down her cheeks. "It's Tat," she finally said. "She's been kidnapped. For real, this time. There's been a ransom demand." She stepped forward quickly and put her hand on his chest, pushing against him as he tried to stand. "Evan's whole security department, the FBI, every police officer in the state—they're all on the job. There's nothing you can do, Jeff, and if you don't look after yourself, you're just one more thing for them to worry about."

"Mom," Jeff tried to say, but he couldn't deny that he was weak. His mother was half his size, and she was holding him in the bed without too much trouble.

"No, Jeff. There's nothing you can do. You'll stay here with me, and we'll worry ourselves sick together, out of the way." She shook her head at him. "We don't know what's happening with Tat. But we can't lose two of you at once, Jeff. You need to look after yourself first, and then take care of the boys."

"They're in the middle of a huge fight," he groaned.

"You wouldn't know it to look at them," his mother countered. "They walked out of here like they were reading each other's thoughts. Whatever the fight was, it's over, at least for now."

That was good. That was what Jeff would have hoped for. Maybe it stung his pride a little to realize they *could* take care of themselves without his interference, but mostly he was just relieved.

"Tell me what you know," he said, letting himself sink back into his pillow. "About Tat. What's going on?"

Chapter Fifteen

"We've got a tentative location," Bill said, bursting into the office where Evan and Dan had been sitting quietly. Dan was pretty sure that Evan had been praying, and he'd thought about giving it a shot himself, but decided against it. He didn't believe, and there was no point pretending he did just because it would give him some temporary comfort.

Dan and Evan stood up simultaneously. "Where?" Evan demanded.

"Come on, we're taking a command vehicle out there. I'll explain on the way."

Dan let himself and Evan be escorted outside and shown into the back of a large RV. Instead of beds and tables, the space was filled with computers, except for the weapons rack next to the large back door. There was a team of men dressed in black uniforms sitting on utilitarian benches, but otherwise it was just Dan and Evan, Bill, and the driver.

The engine had been running when they'd climbed in, and as soon as they were seated the RV started to move. Dan could see flashing lights coming through the windshield, and realized that they were part of a police convoy.

Bill Albanese was sitting next to them, and apparently he was ready for business. "We traced the signal to the cell phone tower it was coming through. They're out in the country, so there's just one tower—no way to triangulate. But we got an approximate range from the tower based on the signal strength, and we've drawn a radius out around it, and there's only three buildings in that space. Two of them are luxury homes; there's only one that anybody would call a 'cabin'. So that's where we're headed."

"And when we get there?" Evan had his calm face on again, but Dan could feel the tension running high and hot beneath the surface.

Bill grimaced. "We're trying to sort that out now, with the FBI. They're getting surveillance video—satellite and high-flying helicopters. If anybody tries to leave, we'll follow them. If they stay put, we'll surround the place, and then we'll try to negotiate them out."

"And if that doesn't work? If they won't negotiate?" The emotion was thrumming a little closer to Evan's surface now, and Dan reached out to find Jeff's traditional grip on Evan's neck. It seemed to have magic powers when Jeff used it, and Dan figured they could use all the magic they could find right then.

"If they won't negotiate, we'll have a decision to make," Bill said quietly. "Krista's phone is still live, and we're picking up bits of their conversation. They sound tense, but fairly professional." He turned to Dan almost apologetically. "We haven't found anything to suggest that it's *not* your father and brother-in-law that we're dealing with, so we're using that as a working theory. And they both have histories of being pretty calm under pressure. That works in our favor. If they know they're surrounded, hopefully they'll have sense enough to come out peacefully." He looked back toward Evan. "But we'll have snipers set up, and men in place for quick extraction, if we decide that becomes necessary. Our absolute goal is Tatiana's safe return."

He turned back to Dan, and he looked pained again. "We're not sure how to treat your sister. There was no sign that she was an unwilling participant in the initial kidnapping. But she seems to have had a change of heart. We'll treat her as gently as we can. But we have to go on the assumption that she's armed and dangerous, until we can prove otherwise."

"She's eight months pregnant," Dan said. "There's a baby to protect."

"We're keeping that in mind," Bill said.

Dan nodded. He felt strangely ambivalent about that side of things. Tat, he was worried about. Krista… he had no idea how he felt about her. She was his blood. She'd lived with him for fifteen years, longer than he'd ever known anyone else. And he saw so much of himself in her. Saw who he would have been if he hadn't been rescued, first by Justin, then by Jeff and Evan. He couldn't deny the connection to her. But he also knew that he'd never be able to forgive her if anything happened to Tat. Maybe wouldn't be able to forgive her at all, because something already *had* happened to Tat. Her naïve innocence, her assumption that the world was a safe place; that had been shattered. Dan remembered the fear in her voice over the phone, the way she'd *apologized*, for Christ's sake, as if this was somehow her fault… he wasn't sure that was something he could let go of. He wasn't sure he could ever look at his sister the same way again, knowing she'd done that to Tat. And he wasn't sure how Tat would ever be able to look at him, knowing he'd brought this into her life. Once the shock wore off, Dan wasn't sure Evan was going to forgive him, either.

But that was all something to worry about later. If this cost him Evan's trust, that was something he'd have to deal with. The important thing was getting Tat back safe and sound.

They rode in silence for far too long. It was too easy to imagine worst-case scenarios, too easy to let the panic creep in. But Dan had no idea what he could say to break the tension. He felt like he was on thin ice himself, only part of the proceedings because Evan had insisted on it. It wasn't his place to try to direct the conversation. So they drove silently, and by the time they pulled to the side of a rough dirt road, Dan was practically vibrating with unspent adrenaline, and he could tell Evan was just as bad. They needed to move, but they couldn't make any of this about them. What they *really* needed was to do as they were told and stay out of the way.

Bill had been speaking to people on the way up, and seemed to know what was going on. "A perimeter has been established, and infrared shows four live bodies in the cabin. Two of them are moving around more than the others; we're assuming those are the males. The other two are together." He glanced at Dan. "It could be that Krista's been assigned to keep Tat quiet, or it could be that she's now a hostage herself. We haven't heard enough over the cell to be sure."

"So, what now? You try to negotiate?" Evan seemed anxious for things to start moving, and Dan couldn't blame him.

"That's right. There was talk of storming the place, but we've decided against it. We don't know enough about what's going on inside. For all we know, Krista's got a gun on Tat as we speak, and she could pull the trigger before we got inside. And they've got the windows boarded up, so the easiest entrance is unavailable." He gestured for them to follow him. "I've got clearance for you to come up a little further, as long as you stay out of the way. I'm a civilian too, and this is a police operation. I've got good respect and good communication going, but I've got no real authority here."

Dan followed Evan and Bill up to the back of a black van filled with communication equipment. "They've got the batteries out of their phones," Bill said quietly. "To keep us from tracking them. I guess they didn't know Krista had one."

Just then, one of the FBI agents stepped out from behind the makeshift shelter and started toward the cabin. He was wearing heavy body armor and a helmet, but he still seemed incredibly vulnerable. Dan wondered how he was keeping his pace so steady, so relaxed. When he got about thirty feet from the cabin, he raised a megaphone to his mouth. "Attention in the cabin. This is the FBI. We have the property surrounded."

Dan's eyes were drawn to the screen showing the heat patterns of the people inside the cabin. They clustered together more tightly, and he could imagine guns being drawn and pointed. He held his breath, waiting to hear the sound of a bullet being fired, but finally exhaled into the silence.

The man lifted the megaphone again. "Come out of the cabin with your arms raised over your head. As long as you do not behave aggressively, you will not be harmed."

There was no response, but Dan could see one of the shapes moving on the infrared screen. They were too close together, too blurred at the edges for Dan to be sure who was doing what. Then one of the FBI technicians said, "The cell phone connection is dead. She's hung up on us."

Another technician said, "We've got sounds of a struggle. Voices indistinct."

There were a tense few moments as everyone waited, then a phone rang. "Mr. Kaminski's cell line," one of the technicians said.

"Patch it through to me," the man with the megaphone called, and he pulled out his own phone.

Sam Dekay, the FBI agent, appeared at Dan's side with a set of earphones. "We'd like you to listen in. See if you can identify the speaker. Give us any information that comes to you."

Dan nodded. It was a relief to have something to do. He put the earphones on his head and heard the negotiator's voice. "My name's David Bennett. My goal here is to help this situation end peacefully. I'm going to need your help to make that happen."

Dan hadn't been sure he was going to be much use at this task, but as soon as he heard the voice on the line, he knew. He listened to the man say, "Well, you're going to be a big part of that too," and he nodded toward Dekay.

"My father," he said softly. "Richard Wheeler." He saw Dekay's nod, then went back to focusing on Richard's words.

"Let me describe the situation in here. I know you've probably got those fancy cameras showing it to you, but let me make it crystal clear. My young associate is lying on the floor. And this cabin has no basement, no space underneath it, so you can't get to him from below. And he's got a lovely young lady lying on top of him, shielding his body with her own. He's got a gun to her head, and he's ready to pull the trigger." Richard paused, as if he was enjoying what he was saying. "And my lovely, pregnant daughter, the same bitch who gave away our position, is standing right by my side. You might be ready to throw her life away, but what about the little baby? What's the press going to make of that?"

The negotiator's voice was calm. "We don't want anyone to get hurt in all this. That includes you and Mr. Russert."

"I never said it was Mr. Russert," Richard protested.

"No, you didn't. But we've been listening for a while now. Not through the cell phone. Through the walls. As you said, we have some impressive equipment out here."

"And we've got some impressive advantages in here. You may not care about my daughter, but... what the fuck?" There was a pause, and the indistinct sound of voices, and then Richard came back on the line. He sounded incredulous. "Bitch's water just broke. Looks like it won't be long before we have *three* hostages to play with." Then the line went dead.

"The primary hostage is still Tatiana Kaminski," Bill said loudly enough for everyone to hear. "She is the only innocent victim here, and she needs to be our priority." He sounded like he was making a speech, trying to persuade people. But it didn't look like he was doing a great job with Sam Dekay.

"We need to get the mother to a hospital," he said. "Medical crisis trumps healthy victim."

"How long's she going to stay healthy with a psychopath holding a gun to her head?" Evan demanded.

"It's his only grandkid," Dan said softly, and Dekay turned to look at him.

"What?"

"Krista's baby. That's the only grandkid Richard's got. Maybe the only one ever; I'm sure not likely to produce any. And he's got a huge ego. He was a terrible father—couldn't handle the day-to-day shit at all. But he liked the *idea* of it. He was always going on about how he could see things about himself in each of us. The good stuff only, of course." Dan had a quick rush of uncertainty; he was in way over his head with all this, acting like he actually had a contribution to make. But Dekay was listening to him closely, and Dan forced himself to continue. "You could play it up that way. Even if he's pissed at Krista, he still wants that baby to be healthy. Because it's his grandkid, the next step in the line down from him."

Dekay nodded slowly and looked over toward the negotiator. "You got that?" he asked. "Think you can work with it?"

The negotiator nodded. "Yeah. I think I can."

Evan couldn't decide how to feel. Of course he wanted Dan's sister to get out, and of course he wanted the baby to be safe. But Bill was right: Tatiana was the primary hostage here. *She* was the one they should all be focusing on. Instead, she was apparently forgotten as everyone bustled around trying to set up for Krista's anticipated extraction. And Tat was lying in there on top of a felon with a gun held to her head.

The negotiator was working on Richard, but Evan wasn't sure how it was going. It all seemed to come down to math for him. He wasn't going to lose a hostage, no matter what. He said once there were three, they could talk about letting the baby go, but he wasn't going to sit in there with only one person to protect him. Evan heard the negotiator offer to send in an officer to replace Krista, and hope flared until he heard Richard's rough laugh. He had no intention of letting one of the enemy into his stronghold. The call ended on that note.

Evan wasn't sure he could stand any more of this. He pulled the headphones off and strode ten steps away down the road, then stopped. He wanted to howl, to fight, to attack and tear and destroy. Thousands of years of instincts told him that was what he needed to do. He wasn't sure he was civilized enough to ignore all that, to sit around and let the experts handle all of this while he just waited. He wondered what would happen if he just stormed toward the building. He'd push the agents out of the way, and they wouldn't shoot him. He could shoulder the door open... and watch as the asshole holding onto his baby sister splattered her brains all over the wall. Jesus. This had to end.

He looked over to find Dan deep in conversation with the negotiator. That was weird. Dan was being useful, sure; the negotiator probably would have come up with the whole "remind him of his grandchild" line on his own, but Dan had sped things along. And he'd had a few other insights too. But nothing that seemed to justify the intensity of the conversation he was involved in right now. Then the negotiator handed his souped-up phone to Dan, and Evan realized there was more going on than he'd been aware of. He pulled his headphones onto his ears in time to hear the phone ringing, and then Richard's gruff voice.

"You got a better offer?" he demanded.

"Yeah," Dan said. His voice was quiet and confident, practically businesslike. "It's Danny, Dick. I'm jealous of you spending all this quality time with your other kid, and I think it's time for you and me to bond a little. I think you should send Krista out and let me come in instead."

It felt like someone had thrown a bucket of icy water in Evan's face. His entire body rejected what he'd just heard. He couldn't think clearly, couldn't respond with anything but a powerful, emotional *no way*. No way he was going to allow this. He already had one of the people he loved locked in the damn cabin; there was no way he was going to let another one go in. Krista could rot in hell, and if her baby had to join her, that was a loss Evan would accept. He would *not* risk Dan. He started toward the spot Dan where was standing, intent on ripping the phone out of his hands, but he was intercepted by Bill Albanese and a few others. Bill caught him in a tight grip and spoke directly into his ear, as if hoping the path to his brain would be shorter from there. "It's not all about Krista," Bill said furiously. "Dan's fit and capable. We can't get a cop in there, we can't get one of our guys. But if the perp will accept Dan, we've got an in. We've got a better chance of getting Tat out safely."

"No," Evan growled. "Find another way."

"We're using *all* the ways," Bill said firmly. He relaxed his body just a little as Evan stopped fighting him. "We'll still negotiate. We'll still try to make this work. But having someone inside to help—that could be huge."

"Can they even do this?" Evan demanded. "The FBI? Can they trade people like this?"

"I think they're bending the rules a little," Bill acknowledged. "But the primary rule in hostage negotiations is 'do what works'. So that's the rule they're trying to follow."

Evan tried to listen to the conversation over the earphones. It sounded like Richard didn't want Dan to go in, and Evan clung to that hope. Richard wouldn't want him, Richard would say no.

Then Dan said, "Damn. I knew you were a shitty father and a general asshole, but I didn't know you were a pussy too." Evan couldn't believe that Dan was taunting the man with the gun. He couldn't believe the negotiator was letting him, was standing there watching as if he thought Dan was doing something other than being his infuriating self.

“Fuck you, boy. I'll show you who's a pussy.”

“Yeah, you're a real man, holding a fucking gun on a teenage girl and your pregnant daughter. Whatever. You're too much of a pussy to deal with your own son, even though he's just a prissy cocksucker.”

“You are a mouthy little faggot.”

“And you're a fucking pussy. I guess the apple doesn't fall far from the tree, huh?” Evan wanted to shake Dan, wanted to cover his mouth and shut him up, but everyone else was listening as if they thought this was all acceptable.

“You think I'm *scared* of you?”

“I guess.” Dan sounded annoyingly nonchalant, every bit the insolent teenager he must have been the last time his father had seen him. “I can't think of any other reason you wouldn't make the trade. You could save your daughter and your grandkid, but you won't. Why not, if you're not scared of me?”

Richard's laugh was ragged. “You really think this is going to work? You think you can fucking *dare* me to make the trade?”

“I don't give a good goddamn if you make the trade, you worthless piece of shit. I just figured there's some stuff I'd always wanted to say to you, and this seemed like as good a time as any.” Dan actually stretched his arms above his head, as if he were leaning back in a chair and taunting a parent. And his Texas drawl was sneaking back into his voice, making him sound even more infuriatingly relaxed and cocky. He brought the handset back down and said, “I figured it was a good time to make it clear to both of us that you're fucking nothing. You couldn't do right by us when we were kids, and you sure as hell ain't doing right by Krista now. I just wanted to make sure you knew that I could see that.”

“Fuck you.” Richard sounded truly enraged. “Get your ass in

here. We'll make the goddamned trade."

"Yeah, sure. Like you're not going to pussy out on the deal. You can't be trusted, can you? I mean... I don't know. I'll hand the phone over to the negotiator guy, and maybe he can figure out some way to make it work. But I doubt he can. He's not a fucking magician, right? He can't wave a wand and turn you into a stand-up guy."

"I'll send Krista out first," Richard said. "As soon as I see you walking toward me, I'll send her out. You come closer, and you strip the fuck down, because I don't need them sending in wires or weapons or whatever the fuck else they can dream up, and then you come inside. I'll have my gun on you the whole time, but the door will be open, so the cops will be able to see me. I shoot you, and the pigs will shoot me. And as much as you deserve a fucking beating, I'm not looking to get killed for shooting you."

Dan still sounded nonchalant. "Yeah, okay. I mean, if the FBI says it's okay, that works for me." He handed the phone back to the negotiator and sauntered out of the clearing. Evan followed him around behind the nearest van, and he was there to catch him when Dan slumped against the side of the vehicle and turned gray.

"Jesus Christ, Danny," Evan said. He kissed the top of Dan's head, slid down to his face and kissed his lips, wrapped his arms around him and tried to hold him there, safe, forever. "What are you doing? You can't go in there."

Dan's fingers were gripped tight around a handful of Evan's shirt. "Yeah, I can. I'm the only one he'll let in." His free hand was shaking as he brought it to the back of Evan's neck and pulled him down for a fierce kiss. "I can help. If I'm in there, I can get between... between whatever they do and Tat. I can try. Even if it's just letting her see a friendly face, that's important. But maybe I can do more. And it's good to get Krista and the baby out." He pulled away far enough so they could look into each other's eyes. "I may have been a shitty brother, but that doesn't have to keep going forever. I can change. I've changed other stuff, and I can change this too."

"You're not a bad brother," Evan said. "It was a bad situation, and you got the hell out of it. You were a kid, younger than Tat is now. You did the right thing."

"I brought this mess into your life," Dan said. "If it wasn't for me, you never would have met Krista, and none of this would have happened, and Tat would be safe."

"No," Evan started, but Dan cut him off, looking to the side where Sam Dekay was waiting impatiently.

"It's going to be okay, Evan." A quick kiss, and then Dan was stepping away. "And if it isn't—tell Jeff that I love him, okay? And get him to tell you that I love you too." Dan's smile was only a little crooked, and then he pulled his shoulders back and straightened up. His face lost its desperate expression, although it stayed gray. He turned and started back toward the cabin, and all Evan could do was watch him go.

Chapter Sixteen

Dan tried to breathe deeply. It wasn't easy. He was standing in the middle of the clearing in front of the cabin, stripping off his clothes as his father held a gun on him and his sister struggled down the stairs to the waiting paramedics. They slapped body armor on Krista as soon as she was close to them, but there was no protection for Dan. He could almost feel the bullet coming from the gun, could feel the way it would tear through his chest, destroying his heart and lungs and leaving a gaping hole in his back. Or maybe Dick would go for the headshot. Dan had no idea how good the guy's aim was.

He pulled his shirt over his head and looked at Krista. He tried to burn the image into his memory. He wasn't religious, but it was hard to believe that there was absolutely nothing after death, so he'd come up with his own little theory, one where the last moments of your life got stretched out and replayed over and over. Whatever you'd been feeling when you died was what you felt forever afterward. It was a doctrine that had tortured him ever since Justin's death, thinking of Justin being confused and afraid and in pain forever. He'd told himself that there was no justification for the belief, no support whatsoever. But he'd never been able to shake it, not entirely, and now he found himself wanting to focus on Krista, wanting to make the sense of accomplishment he had from helping her be his forever-memory. He thought back to the kiss with Evan, tried to forget about the desperation and focus on the intensity, and he hoped there was enough room for him to repeat more than one memory. He pulled his boots off, and then his jeans, and he thought about Sunday mornings at Evan's house, Evan, Jeff, and him curled around one another in that huge bed, and then shambling down to make breakfast with Tat. Yeah, if Dan had to repeat one memory forever, that would be a good one to choose.

He shoved his jeans down and stepped out of them, then looked up on the porch. "You want the full show?" he asked. "You wouldn't be the first man to want to see it all… and you wouldn't be the first man I've shown it to."

"Get in here, you little faggot," his father growled, and Dan left his clothes behind and stepped forward. He tried not to think about the wire woven through the waistband of his boxer briefs, tried to walk as if he wasn't broadcasting every sound to the crowd outside.

He stepped inside the cabin and paused to let his eyes adjust to the dim light. But Dick wasn't interested in giving him time. He kept Dan between himself and the door until he could get behind the heavy wood and slam it shut, pushing the bar down to lock it.

"That's a fucking serious log you're closing us in with," Dan said. The agents had said to describe the interior as well as he could without being obvious about it. "You guys must have been planning this for a while, to get the place all set—"

There was more that Dan had planned to say, but he somehow hadn't expected the blow. His father was using his handgun as a club, and he slammed it into the side of Dan's face. Pain exploded, and Dan staggered, bent over a little, and then felt his father's hands on the back of his neck, pushing his head down, fast and hard. Dick's knee rose to meet Dan's face, and there was another nauseating burst of pain. Dan could hear bone crunching and tried to get his hands in the way, but the angle was wrong, and he was too slow, and the whole thing was repeated, this time with Dan's head turned a little so his father's knee smashed into his cheekbone and then into his eye.

Dan wasn't supposed to be the action hero. The FBI had made that clear. He was supposed to go in and sit there, and report what he saw and get ready to duck. But he wasn't being *allowed* to fucking *sit*. He was getting beaten, maybe to the point that he'd be no use to anybody, and that needed to stop.

He stayed bent over as he charged forward, legs made strong from decades of riding, driving his hard shoulder into Dick's stomach. He heard the grunt but kept going. He drove his feet into the floorboards and pushed off, steaming ahead, and he felt the satisfying crunch as his father's ribs were compressed between Dan's body and the wall.

There was a thud that took a moment for Dan to understand, and then he was diving, scrambling, grabbing for the gun his father had dropped. Dick was bent over, gasping for breath, and Dan fell on the gun and had his hands wrapped around it just as he saw the other two bodies lying on the floor, Tat's eyes wide as they stared at him, the strange man's face an impassive mask as he straightened his arm and pointed the gun in Dan's direction. *Straightened his arm and took the gun away from Tat's head.*

"Get in here!" he screamed, loud enough that they'd hear him outside even if the underwear-mike wasn't working. He dropped onto the outstretched arm, using his full weight to keep the man from bringing the gun anywhere near Tat, ever again. He was in the process of stretching his own gun toward the man's head when the cabin just seemed to explode. A whole wall was torn away by some unseen machinery, and black-garbed commandos streamed inside, yelling and pointing guns at everyone and generally making it impossible to think.

There were a couple of loud bangs, but Dan could barely distinguish them from all the rest of the noise. The commandos were in charge, Tat grabbed and swept outside before Dan had a chance to really see that she was safe, his father pinned, the stranger grabbed, and then there was a moment when the commandos seemed to realize where the man's gun arm was. Where his gun was, and just what that meant.

Dan had realized it a few moments earlier when he'd tried to take a breath and found that it was almost impossible. The pain was part of the problem, down along his ribs and spreading fast, but there also seemed to be something wrong with his lungs, something....

He fought the panic back. He made himself focus. Jeff and Evan, smiling at him as he nuzzled into their bodies. But he wanted other people there too, so he put everyone's clothes on and set them down at the long table in the Kaminski kitchen. He felt his body being shifted, lifted, and he was dimly aware that there was way too much blood. Not that there should be any, in an ideal situation, but there sure as hell should never be this much. But that was a distraction; that was why the weak had bad afterlives. He took himself back to Evan's kitchen, and Jeff was there, and Tat and Anna and Robyn. Maybe it was Thanksgiving. Sure, why not. And Krista was there, because he wanted her to be. And since he was playing that game, he introduced everyone to Justin. He and Chris were standing off to the side, but then Tat scampered over to them, a few years younger than she was now, back when she'd been happy to be treated like a kid, and she dragged them forward, and they came willingly. And Justin smiled, and he looked happy and relaxed, not like he had after the accident. There was no pain, no fear, just love. Dan made himself focus on everyone's smiling faces until he couldn't focus on anything anymore.

They were trying to take Tat straight to the ambulance, but she was having none of it. She wrenched herself free of the paramedic trying to treat her gently and launched herself toward Evan. He stepped forward and caught her, wrapped her greedily in his arms, and rocked her like a little girl. “Tat. You’re okay? You’re okay?”

She nodded, but she was crying too hard to speak. They both knew she was anything *but* okay, in a very real sense. But she wasn’t injured. She wasn’t dying. Evan kissed her head, held her a little closer, and then looked toward the cabin. “Where’s Dan?” he asked.

Tat just cried harder, and Evan felt his body go cold. “Where is he, Tat?” But she couldn’t speak, and he whirled his body around, dragging her with him because he refused to let go, and searched the crowd for a familiar face. “Bill!” he bellowed. “Bill!”

Bill stepped off the front porch. The back wall of the cabin had been torn off and most of the activity was happening back there. If Bill was in front, he was probably just observing. “Evan,” he said seriously. He took a few steps closer, and Evan moved to meet him, Tat nestled in by his side. Bill stopped walking and said, “Dan’s been shot. We’ve got paramedics in there, and they’re giving him a quick patch and then taking him to the hospital. We don’t know how bad it is, yet....”

But Evan wasn’t listening. He was charging toward the front door, still hanging on tightly to Tat, and it was only when she actually cried out that he turned to look at her and noticed that she was pulling away from his grip, fighting, panicking... determined to not return to the room where she’d so recently been held captive. “Shit,” he said, and he stepped back toward her, let her drag him further away, then wrapped her in his arms. “I’m sorry,” he said. “I’m so sorry.”

She just sobbed and burrowed in deeper. He saw the agents and paramedics hovering nearby, wanting to get her into the ambulance, and for the first time, he decided that was a good idea. If she was somewhere safe, maybe he could go find Dan. He turned to Bill. “What the fuck happened? He was just supposed to be a hostage, not a fucking....” He trailed off. “This wasn’t supposed to happen.”

"Tat's safe," Bill said. "And we'll take good care of Dan."

Evan saw the stretcher then, being hoisted out from the ruined cabin and carried over the rough ground toward the ambulance. He saw Dan lying on it, too pale, and hooked up to too many different tubes and bags. Evan wrapped his arms around Tat a little tighter and hurried her toward the waiting ambulance.

The paramedics met her with gentle smiles and wrapped her in a warm blanket, and Evan was tempted to leave her for a moment, to go and see Dan. But the back doors of Dan's ambulance were slammed shut, and Bill was there by Evan's side. "He's unconscious, and the paramedics need room to work," Bill said. "You ride down with Tat. We're all going to the same place."

Evan nodded and climbed into the back of the ambulance. The doors were shut behind them and they began to move, but there was no siren. The only siren was the one from Dan's ambulance, and Evan listened to it as it sped further and further away and finally faded out completely.

Jeff had asked the nurse to stop giving him painkillers. He missed them, but he needed to be alert. He had no idea what was happening with the boys, but he knew he needed to be ready to help them any way he could. And Tat. Beautiful, confident, happy Tatiana. He couldn't even think about her being in danger, not without his chest tightening up and sending shooting pain down his side. Tat would be fine, and Evan and Dan would be fine, and damn it, Jeff would be fine too. That was the only acceptable solution.

His mother's phone rang, and she stood abruptly and fished it out of her purse. She saw the call display and moved closer to Jeff's bed as she answered. "Evan? Are you okay? Is Tat okay?"

She listened for a moment, her eyes locked on Jeff's, and he thought he saw her flinch, but couldn't be sure. She was stoic, his mother. "I see," she said. "Yes, all right. I'll see what I can do." She looked at Jeff as if considering something, then said, "Evan, I think Jeff needs to hear this. Would you like me to tell him, or can you tell him yourself?"

Evan obviously took the second option, because she handed Jeff the phone and then gripped his hand tightly. Jeff didn't think he wanted to hear whatever Evan was about to say. "Kid?"

"Hey, Jeff. You're okay? Your chest is okay?"

"I'm fine. What's going on? Is Tat okay?"

"Tat's okay. She's shook up, but she's okay."

That was perfect news. Had his mother been overcome by happiness, not concern? But he looked at her and saw that her face was tight, and there were tears coming to her eyes as she looked resolutely back at him. "What's wrong, then?" Jeff braced himself.

"It's Dan. He was involved in the rescue, and he got shot. I don't know how bad, but it didn't look good. He was unconscious. There was so much... so much blood." Evan sounded totally lost, and Jeff couldn't think of how to help him. He couldn't even think of how to help himself. Dan. Beautiful, strong, stubborn Dan. It was unthinkable. Unimaginable.

"They're taking him to the hospital?" Jeff tried to marshal his thoughts. There were things to be done, surely.

"Yeah. Same one you're in. Your mom's going to go down and try to meet him in the emergency room. You know, in case he's... in case he's conscious. In case he's scared."

"I'll go too," Jeff decided, and he held a hand up to still his mother's protest. "I've been walking around with this thing for a couple weeks now. I can already feel the anti-inflammatories doing their job. I'm going to go crazy sitting around up here. I'm going."

There was no answer on the other end for a long moment, then Evan said, "Yeah. If you can, that'd be good." He sounded like he was at the end of his emotional endurance, and Jeff's body ached with the need to be close to Evan, to comfort him and give him strength.

"I can," Jeff said firmly. "And when you get here, we'll wait together."

"Oh, fuck," Evan said. "I almost forgot. Krista's down there too. In the maternity ward, I guess. She went into labor."

"Jesus Christ," Jeff said. If it wasn't for Dan, it would almost be funny, this confluence of medical emergencies. But it was impossible to find any of it humorous when Dan might be fighting for his life. "Okay. I'll try to check on her too."

"Can you call Chris too? I need to be with Tat, but Chris needs to know."

"Fuck. Yeah. And Robyn."

"And Taylor, and Ryan."

"And everyone at the barn...." Jeff stopped. He couldn't think like this, couldn't let himself start listing all the people touched by Dan's life. He needed to be in control. "I'll start with Chris, though."

"Okay." Evan took a deep, shaky breath, then said, "He told me to tell you he loves you."

"He can tell me that himself," Jeff said fiercely. "Just get yourselves here, and we'll take care of it together."

"Yeah, okay," Evan said, and he ended the call.

Jeff turned his head to his mother. "Don't even argue. You know I'll go more crazy up here than I would if I were with everybody else."

"I wasn't going to argue," she said. "I was just going to get a nurse, and see if there's an extra orderly around to push you in a wheelchair." She stood up decisively. "I think it's time we spent a bit of Evan's money."

Chapter Seventeen

Everything was foggy, and when he tried to move, everything was pain. It washed over him and he let it push him back into the fog, where nothing hurt, but nothing made sense, either. He rested for a while, then tried again, forced his way back into his body, and this time he managed to get his eyes open. The light was too bright, and he closed them again, but he felt fingers tighten around his hand.

"Danny?" The familiar voice was rough and strained.

"Jeff," he tried, but he was pretty sure it came out as more of a mumble. Or a moan.

"Yeah, Tex, I'm here. So's Evan."

"Hey, man," Evan said, and then there were fingers on Dan's other hand, gentle but strong. "How you doing?"

Dan had no idea. He was pretty sure he was in a hospital. That didn't suggest that he was doing too well. Couldn't Evan ask the doctors how he was doing? They'd probably have a better idea. They might even know what the hell had happened to him. "Horse?" he tried.

Even Jeff's laugh sounded tired. "You didn't fall off a horse, Danny."

Oh. Okay. That was strange, then, because his life was really pretty safe, except for the damn horses. The fog was sneaking up on him again, and he decided to let it carry him away. Things would make more sense eventually.

Evan wasn't really sure if it was respectful for him to have done it. Dan always hated it when Evan threw his money around to get what he wanted, so doing it when Dan was unconscious, and doing it at least partly in Dan's honor... yeah, it was probably disrespectful. But that was just too damned bad. Dan could get better and yell at Evan all he wanted, and Evan would just smile and nod, because it would mean that Dan was back to himself.

So he cranked the back of his hospital bed so he was almost sitting up, and for the first time in too damn long, he let himself relax. He could look right across the aisle of the ward he'd paid to privatize, and he could see the men he loved being taken care of. Recovering. There were still too many tubes in Dan, too many machines, but the doctors were being optimistic. Two bullets at point-blank range, one going right through Dan's lung, the other passing through without hitting anything major but causing serious blood loss. But Danny was tough. He'd be okay. He had to be.

Evan looked to the bed next to him. Tat was there, curled up with Robyn snuggled in next to her, and they were both reading trashy gossip magazines. Tat was still quieter than she should be, and she was clingy, not going anywhere alone, but it was less than two days since she'd been freed. She'd get better.

Anna had the bed next to Tat's. She'd said she didn't need it, she could sleep in a chair next to Jeff's bed, but Evan had looked straight at her when he told Jeff that everyone needed to take good care of themselves in order to be strong enough to help whoever needed it next, and Anna seemed to have heard the message. Evan hoped she had, at least. The last thing their little family team needed was another illness.

Evan looked across and saw Chris sitting next to Dan. They'd all been taking turns in that seat, all waiting for another flash of lucidness. The doctors weren't worried. They said Dan's body was taking advantage of the drugs, giving him time to rest. They said that when he started fighting the narcotics, that would be time to dial them back. Evan had smiled and said that when Dan started fighting, that would be time to clear the damn room, because he wouldn't quit until he'd won. That had earned him a smile from Tat.

A nurse came into the room, and Evan caught her eye. He'd arranged for several of them to bring him regular reports from the maternity ward, but there'd been no change yet. Evan hadn't realized that labor didn't automatically start when a woman's water broke, but apparently Krista's body knew it perfectly well, and it was holding on for a while. She was in shackles, on the judge's orders, but was otherwise comfortable. Evan had paid for a private room for her. She was Dan's sister, and she had saved Tat's life. But she'd also been involved in the kidnapping in the first place, and he hadn't even considered inviting her into their family ward. There were no shackles in the world strong enough to make him feel safe with her that close to Tat.

There was a sound from Dan's bed, and Chris's head snapped up. Tat and Robyn straightened as well, and Evan hadn't even realized he was moving until his bare feet hit the cold hospital tile.

"Danny?" Chris said. "You in there, buddy?"

Evan skidded to a halt and leaned over the other side of the hospital bed. Dan's eyes were moving under his lids, frantic, almost violent shifts from side to side and up and down. If the rest of his body had been moving too, Evan would have said it was a seizure. As it was, though.... "Nightmare?"

Chris frowned. "I don't know. Maybe." He reached a gentle hand up to Dan's face. "Hey, Danielle, you little girl, you're okay. Nothing to be afraid of. Everything's good."

Evan gripped Dan's hand on his side and added his own voice to Chris's. "You're okay. You're safe. We're all here, and we're all looking after you."

"Everything's good, Tex," Jeff rumbled, his hand a familiar weight on the back of Evan's neck. Evan hadn't realized Jeff was there; when he turned to acknowledge him, he saw that Jeff wasn't the only one to join their circle.

"You're okay, Dan," Tat said from the foot of the bed, and she gripped one of Dan's feet.

Robyn was beside her and had the other foot, massaging it gently. "Everything's good, Danny."

"You're going to be fine," Anna said, and she found a spot on Chris's side of the bed.

Dan's eyes finally opened, and he looked from face to face as if he recognized them, but wasn't quite sure what they were all doing there. He muttered something Evan couldn't understand, and then said it again, more clearly. "Did I burn the turkey?" he asked.

Well, that was a bit anticlimactic. After all that buildup, all that support, the guy was still delirious. A step in the right direction, sure, but... but why was Jeff smiling so warmly?

"The turkey's good, Danny," Jeff said. "And we're all here. It's a good Thanksgiving."

Dan looked like he would have liked to have nodded, if his head wasn't so sore. Instead, he moved just his eyes and looked over at Chris. "Justin?" he asked.

Chris looked startled for a moment, but it quickly faded to sadness. "No, buddy. We'll catch up with him sometime, but not yet."

It seemed to take a while for that to sink in, and Evan waited patiently. He wasn't jealous of Justin, and he knew Jeff wasn't either. Dan loved Justin. Just because Justin was dead didn't mean the emotion was gone. But Dan could love more than one person at a time. And now Dan looked over at Evan, then Jeff, then back to Evan. "Did you tell him?" Dan asked. His voice was still slurred, but Evan liked to think that was just his Texas sleep-drawl coming through.

And he was pretty sure he understood the question anyway. "I told him. But I didn't have to. He already knew."

This time, Dan did manage a nod, a tiny shift in his head. "Yeah," he said quietly, and they all stood and watched as he drifted back to a peaceful sleep.

Jeff wasn't sure how he felt about the team-heal approach Evan had come up with. It was really the only way Evan could function, the only way he could give his support to both of his lovers *and* his traumatized sister, so Jeff would never have thought of objecting. And it *was* nice to have everyone close by, where Jeff could keep an eye on them; he just wasn't so enthusiastic about all of them being able to keep their eyes on him.

Evan was, predictably, the worst. Jeff was pretty sure that if he allowed it, Evan would be hand-feeding Jeff every meal like he was a toddler. Every trip to the bathroom was made under Evan's watchful eye, and if Jeff spent more than a couple minutes in the blessed privacy of the tiled room, Evan would be rapping on the door, making sure everything was okay. But that was Evan. Jeff had been braced for that.

It was Chris that surprised him. There wasn't the same level of careful monitoring, but there were a lot of... opportunities, Jeff supposed. Times when it just seemed natural for Jeff and Chris to have private conversations, conversations that were almost invariably guided toward Jeff's frailties, and the ways in which Jeff's compulsive need to take care of others could be addressed. At first, Jeff really hadn't realized how he was being steered and manipulated, and once he became aware, he still wasn't quite sure what to do about it.

But when he found himself awake in the middle of the night and turned on his small light so he'd be able to read, he was only a little surprised to see Chris shuffle over a few moments later. Chris was wearing sweatpants and a T-shirt, so technically he could claim that he was dressed for sleep, but his eyes were alert, without a trace of weariness, and his smile was as relaxed as if they were just having a couple beers together after work. Jeff was beginning to wonder whether Chris was partly mechanical. Some sort of therapy robot, maybe.

"Hey, man," Chris said. "You can't sleep either? It's like day and night gets turned around in here, huh?"

"Something like that," Jeff agreed warily. He set his book by his side on the bed. "You thinking of going back in to the office tomorrow?"

"Tomorrow's Sunday, champ." Chris glanced over toward Dan's bed. "If everything's smooth here, I'll go in for a bit on Monday. I think Evan's taking an indefinite leave, so, you know... here's my chance to slide into his office and start my inevitable drive for mastery of the company."

"You might want to try just *asking* for the job. I don't think company mastery has quite the same appeal for him that it used to."

Chris nodded as if thinking that over, but then said, "I don't really see the fun in being *given* control. I'm more about the seizing."

"A man needs a challenge," Jeff said.

"How 'bout you?" Chris sounded carefully casual, and that was all it took for Jeff to know that he was in for another round of whatever the hell Chris was up to. "You seeing any challenges in the near future?"

"Look around you, Chris. We've had to set up base camp in a damned hospital. I think I've got all the challenges I need, for now."

"Yeah," Chris said. "And the boys will probably be on their best behavior for a while, right? No real worries there."

There was something in Chris's tone that made Jeff careful with his answer. "There's work to be done. The two of them, but also the three of us together. But we'll make it."

"'Course you will," Chris agreed. "And you've got a plan for doing it without tearing yourself apart anymore. It'll all be good. But...." Chris leaned forward conspiratorially. "I'm in need of a plan for myself. For making sure I don't get turned into the rope of their tug-of-war anymore. So if you could fill me in on what you're going to do, that might be kinda useful."

"Does this generally work for you? Do people usually respond to this level of manipulation?" Jeff wasn't sure whether to laugh it off or be insulted. "I'm not seven years old, you know."

Chris leaned back in mock surprise. He raised his hands in a pacifying gesture and said, "Okay, slow down, don't get all worked up. I never said you were seven. I just thought we could exchange ideas, be mutually supportive, all that good stuff. But, hey, if you're not into it...."

"And now you're trying to guilt-trip me? Come on, Chris."

"Yeah. Okay. You're right. You're a savvy old fox. I can't fool you." Chris grinned suddenly. "So what do you think it means that both of them can? What do you make of the way they've got you wrapped around their little fingers?"

Jeff smiled contentedly. He'd been thinking about this, and he knew he had the answer. He looked at Chris and said, "They've got me wrapped around their little fingers because I'm in love with them. Crazy, stupid, head-over-fucking-heels in love. I know it's tough, sometimes, but the reason I get in the middle of their fights is because that's right where I want to be. No matter what they're doing, no matter how fucking immature and infuriating they are, I want to be with them. In the middle of it all. Always."

Chris had looked a little surprised at the start of Jeff's speech, but by the end, he was smiling peacefully. "So I'm on my own in trying to get loose from them?"

"You're on your own. But I'll tell you what... I bet when you give it a try, you'll end up changing *your* mind too. They're Evan and Danny, man. Where else would you rather be?"

Jeff lay back against his pillows and watched as Chris thought it all over. He saw the slow, regretful smile growing on Chris's face, and he was ready with a smile of his own when Chris looked at him. "So that's it? We just... we just keep going the same way?"

Jeff shrugged. "There's fine-tuning to be done, I think. But for me, yeah. I'm going to keep going the same way. And I'm probably going to come bitch to you about it on a fairly regular basis, so keep your bar stocked."

Chris nodded slowly. "Yeah. Okay. And it does make it better, knowing that there's someone else dealing with their stupidity." Chris frowned. "Although, you're getting sex out of the deal. What the hell is in it for me?"

"I'd guess it might be a useful tool in your quest for corporate control."

Chris leaned back in his chair. "You know, you're right. It absolutely is."

Jeff relaxed into his pillows and smiled. He'd been telling the truth when he said there was nowhere he'd rather be than stuck between Evan and Dan, but he couldn't deny that the position could be exhausting. He looked at Chris and fought the urge to lean over and ruffle his hair. It was good to have an ally. Even if the ally was a possible therapy robot.

Chapter Eighteen

"They're surprised she hasn't gone into labor," Evan said. "Apparently it usually starts within a couple days of the water breaking, but they said it doesn't always. They're monitoring for infection, but otherwise, they want to keep the baby in there for a little longer, to give it time to finish baking."

"Baking?" Dan said, and Evan nodded.

"Yeah. Cooking its lungs, or whatever. Raw lungs are gross. But they're keeping her in the hospital, just in case. But first sign that some bacteria or whatever has snuck in there—*bam*—they induce."

"*Bam*?" Dan said, and Evan nodded again.

"That's the sound of labor being induced. Not a lot of people know that, but I've been paying close attention. Did a little reading, and asked around. You know. My typical research techniques." Evan stopped pushing Dan's chair and scooted around to crouch down next to him. Dan wished he wouldn't. He'd seen his face in the mirror that morning, and he really didn't see how Evan could stand to be close to it. Dan's nose was broken, the rest of his face was purple and swollen; he looked like a monster. But Evan didn't seem to care.

"You're sure you want to do this, Danny? I mean, you're still recovering. You don't have to push yourself."

"Once she has the baby, she's going to be gone. And you said it yourself, labor could start up any time. Bam, remember?"

"Bam is for induction. Regular labor is more... splooosh!"

"Her water's already broken, dude. What's left to splooosh?"

"I haven't learned that yet. Give me time."

"Yeah, okay," Dan agreed. It was fun to talk to Evan like this. Just their general level of idiocy, nothing special, but Dan never wanted to let himself take it for granted. He never wanted to forget how grateful he was to still be around to enjoy it all.

"What are you going to say to her?" Evan asked, and Dan pulled himself back to the conversation.

"I don't really know. I mean... at all. I definitely feel like I should be going in there, but when I think it through... once I'm in, it's all a blank."

Evan nodded, then carefully said, "She *did* save Tat's life. If she hadn't called us, we never would have found them." Dan didn't like to think about that possibility, and he could tell Evan was having trouble with it too.

"If Krista hadn't helped them get her, Tat never would have been at risk in the first place." Dan needed to remember that.

"Maybe not," Evan objected. Dan let himself hope, just for a moment, that Evan had some excellent argument to make Krista's actions seem better. This was the first chance they'd had to talk, away from Tat's ears, and Dan realized that he was missing some serious details about the situation. He nodded his head in a "go on" gesture, and Evan said, "The cops found logs of their conversations—they were sending messages over the fucking Xbox. They said Krista only agreed after the men had decided to go ahead with it. They said she was at least partly motivated by trying to make it tidy. Safe for Tat."

"Bullshit." Dan wanted to see his sister in the best possible light, but he wasn't going to let himself believe things that didn't make sense. "If she'd cared about Tat's safety, she could have made one phone call and had the cops there to pick the guys up. She went along with it because she wanted the money. Ten million—even split three ways—would have been enough to get a nice start somewhere new. *Without* having to go through the damn jail time."

But apparently Evan wasn't done with his rationalizations. "She didn't agree until *after* I'd already accused her of being a kidnapper. Maybe she just felt like if she was going to be treated that way, she might as well do something to deserve it."

"Boo hoo," Dan said. "I don't care how much of an asshole *you* were; Tat was nothing but good to her. If she'd kidnapped *your* ass, you'd have an argument. But she went after Tat. There's no way to make that anything but...." But what? Dan didn't know how to classify Krista's behavior. Bad, obviously. Terrible, even. But was it evil? Unforgivable? He knew how he felt right then, but he couldn't be sure how he'd feel forever.

"Yeah," Evan said softly, and he straightened up and started to push Dan's chair again. "Okay." They rolled to the elevator, and Evan pressed the button then turned to Dan and said, "But I've been thinking about it. Maybe I was part of the problem. I mean, buying a baby. That means that people are exchangeable for money, right? That sets up this whole kidnapping business. They have a person, I have money, so let's trade. How is it different?" The expression on his face was strained, as if he was almost afraid of Dan's reaction.

The elevator door opened and Evan started to push Dan forward, but Dan got a hand down onto the rim of his wheel and stopped the motion. He raised his other hand to the people in the elevator. "Sorry," he said. "We'll catch the next one." As the elevator doors closed, Evan moved around to Dan's side and crouched down again.

"You okay?" he asked, his concern evident.

"*I'm* fine. But *you're* fucked in the head, Evan. You...." Dan tried to collect his thoughts. "You can't honestly think that what you wanted to do with the baby is the same as what they did with

Tat. I mean, you paying for the baby… you were trying to take a baby from a crazy, unsafe environment and give it a good, loving home. That's the exact *opposite* of what those fuckers did to Tat. The money… paying for the baby was like paying the damn ransom. You were willing to do what you had to do to make everyone safe." Dan lifted his hand, ignoring the way the movement pulled at the stitches along his side, and nestled his fingers in the hair at the back of Evan's neck. "I don't agree with the baby-buying. But do *not* equate it with what they did. Not at all."

Evan's eyes stayed on Dan's for a long time, and Dan forced himself to stare right back, bruised face be damned. Finally, Evan nodded. "Yeah," he said. "Okay." He stood up and hit the elevator button again.

Dan wasn't quite sure this was good enough. "I'm not playing with you, Evan. You know I'm happy to jump on you when you've done something I think is wrong. I'm not jumping."

Evan slipped his hand onto Dan's shoulder and squeezed. "Yeah. Thanks."

The elevator came then, and they rolled on board and Evan pressed the button for Krista's floor. Dan was already exhausted by the trip so far, but he needed to keep going. He'd been telling the truth when he'd said he had no idea what he wanted to say to his sister, but he knew he wanted to see her. She was… she was family. He wasn't really sure what that meant, but he felt like he had to keep trying to find out.

Evan wasn't sure he was going to be able to stay calm in front of Krista. He'd tried, for Dan's sake, to find the arguments that would let him forgive her. But the truth was, she'd betrayed him. Maybe his trust hadn't run deep, but it had been there.

The police had told him how Krista had told her partners-in-crime about Jeff's illness, and how they'd decided to capitalize on the panic to grab Tat. Tat had, through tears and sobs, told him that Krista had approached her in the hospital. Krista had said she was there for a checkup and had somehow gotten separated from her security guards. She'd asked for Tat's help, said she was afraid they'd accuse her of trying to escape. Could Tat walk her out to the van, prove that she'd been escorted the whole time and wasn't trying anything dodgy? Of course Tat had said yes. Because Tat was warm, and generous, and honest. Because she was too innocent to ever suspect someone else of doing things she could never imagine herself. At least, she *had* been too innocent.

Evan stopped pushing the chair just outside the hospital room. There was a guard there, but Evan had already gotten the okay for a brief visit. "I think I'll ask the guard if he can take you in," he said. "Or I can get an orderly, or something."

Dan craned his neck around, and Evan moved quickly to crouch beside him. The doctors had been reluctant to let Dan out of bed at all, and they had been very strict in their orders to keep him from exerting himself. His lung was patched up, but still vulnerable. His whole body seemed far too vulnerable, really, and Evan immediately changed his mind. He wasn't letting Dan out of his sight. "No, that's stupid. Sorry. I'll come in."

"Evan, chill." Evan's hand was resting on the arm of Dan's wheelchair, and Dan lifted his hand up to twine their fingers together. "Is this too much? You don't have to go in. If you don't want, *I* don't have to go in." He squirmed a little, trying to get a better view of Evan's face, and as little as he wanted to, Evan moved so he was more visible. Dan's smile was his reward. "Evan, she's family... technically. You guys... you're family for real. I want to have some sort of contact with her. At least, I *maybe* do. I want to consider it. But you guys aren't about what I want. You're what I need. If this is a problem for you, I can work around it."

Evan wasn't much of a crier. He really wasn't. But something about this sweetness, after the fear and anger of the past week... he blinked hard, took a deep breath, and he was okay. He hoped. "Thanks. For saying that. But, no, I'm with you. However you need me, I'm there. And right now, you need a wheelchair-pusher and health-monitor. I can do that. I'm okay with it."

A familiar voice from behind him said, "And are you okay with me going in too?"

Evan turned to see Tat, looking pale but determined, standing a few feet away. He straightened quickly. "Why the hell would you want to? And, no, I'm not okay with it. At all."

"But I don't need a wheelchair-pusher, or a health-monitor. If I want to go see her, you're going to have a hell of a time stopping me." Tat's chin was jutted out in her familiar stubborn expression, and Evan was so relieved to see it that he almost forgot the content of her argument. Almost.

"He didn't say you couldn't," Dan said quietly. "He said he wasn't okay with it. There's a difference."

Tat's posture relaxed as she looked at Dan, and she moved around so she was directly in front of him before sliding her back down the wall and crouching at his head level. "I don't want to steal your visiting time. I just thought it would be easier to go in as a group."

"Why do you want to go in?" Dan asked. Evan was happy to let Dan take the lead on this one. He was still trying to get himself under control, trying to fight back the instinctive urge to tackle his sister and shield her from all possible harm. Although the body-shielding could put her at risk for suffocation, considering their relative sizes.

Tat frowned thoughtfully at Dan and then looked at Evan, as if she wanted to make him understand too. "She was... after it happened. After they had us. She changed. She was afraid too. She sat beside me and held my hand, and we talked. She told me...." She looked apologetically at Dan. "She told me stories about you guys growing up. About how rough it was. And after too. Some really bad stuff. But it wasn't like she was trying for my sympathy." Tat paused as if she was mentally verifying that impression, then nodded. "Not sympathy. Understanding, maybe. Like she wanted me to know why she was... why she *is* the way she is. She said something about horses...." She frowned as she looked at Dan, as if trying to remember. "She said that some horses don't trust people to hold apples for them. She said she'd grabbed the whole apple, but it was hard to chew." She turned sharply to frown at Evan. "I'm not stupid. I know that she helped them take me. But she changed her mind. She decided to be good. I just wanted to thank her for that."

Krista had "decided to be good," Evan remembered, when she'd realized that the men were planning to kill Tat. Krista really was Dan's sister. She might flail around on the surface, and maybe her core was buried under more crap than Dan's was, but deep, deep down, she had her own moral code, and she'd lived by it. She'd decided how far she was willing to go, and she'd risked her life to make sure she didn't go any further. Krista was still unpredictable and dangerous, and Evan wasn't even a little bit sorry that she was facing a long, long stretch of prison time. But if it was important to Tat, and important to Dan, then maybe he could handle it all. He looked at Dan. "Do you want some private time with her? Or are you okay with Tat coming in too?"

"I'd be glad of the company," Dan said. He looked at Tat. "I think it's... I don't know. Maybe admirable, maybe just crazy. But it's really *something* that you want to make peace with her. But if *any* part of that is related to me... if you're doing it because she's my sister, and you think I'd want it... anything like that—you don't need to." And Evan felt better about his own almost-tears when he saw Dan's eyes shining. "*You're* my sister. You know?"

Tat didn't even try not to cry. She nodded and reached her hand out to grip Dan's slipper-clad foot. "I absolutely know. I do." She smiled through her tears. "I want to go in for *me*. But if you don't want me to, I'll stay out here. For you."

Evan decided that it was time to get this conversation on a slightly less emotional plane, or they'd never make it into the room. The security guard was already giving them weird looks. So he lightened his voice and said, "Oh, for *Dan*, you'll stay out here. For me? Nothing. No respect. Nada."

Tat slid back up the wall and raised an eyebrow at him as she brushed away her tears. "Have *you* been shot lately, Evan? Have you been shot *ever*? I mean, you call yourself my brother, but I can't think of a single time that you've been even a little bit injured trying to save me from kidnappers. Not even a scratch." She grinned and laid her hand on Dan's shoulder. "Dan has demonstrated his commitment to the cause. You... I'm still waiting."

"*The cause*? The only cause you need to know about is 'cause I say so." Evan put his imperious, authoritarian face on, and Tat reacted about the way she always did when he tried that approach.

"Whatever," she said dismissively. "Are we going in there or not?"

"We are," Dan said. He was already starting to sound a bit worn out, so Evan wanted to get him in the room and back out as soon as possible. And with as little drama as they could manage.

"Get the door, brat," Evan said, and they trundled forward. Evan wasn't sure if the guard was incompetent or just relaxed, but he didn't seem to care that there were three people going in when the permission had been for only two. And Evan didn't bother to point the discrepancy out to him.

The door opened to a medium-size room. There were no flowers, no colorful blankets brought from home, nothing to make it seem like anything but a hospital room. And in the middle of it, Krista sat, reclining against the tilted mattress.

Evan tried not to notice the shackle connecting her ankle to the bar of the hospital bed.

Krista stared at them as if they were Martians, and for longer than was comfortable, they only stared back. Finally, she looked at her brother and said, "You okay?"

He nodded slowly. "I will be. A little sore."

She looked away, but there wasn't really anything in the room to even pretend to be interested in, and it wasn't long before Krista's eyes slid back to Tat. "And you? You're okay?"

"I will be." Tat's voice was quiet but firm, and Evan really wanted to hug her.

Krista looked at Evan then. "And how pissed are you? They said that you're paying for my room here. Is that going to change when I tell you the deal's off?"

Evan honestly had no idea what she was talking about, initially, and when it came to him, it just seemed like a distant memory. "The baby, you mean?" His hand fell to Dan's shoulder and squeezed. "Yeah. It's off on my end too."

Krista looked uncertain, and then she said, "Because you don't want to give me money, or because you don't want the baby?"

"Because the way we went about it was wrong. I don't care about giving you money. Or at least, I didn't then. And I still want us to have a baby, someday—Dan and Jeff and me. But I shouldn't have snuck around behind Dan's back, and I shouldn't have set up a deal that made it seem like I was buying a human being. I screwed up, and I'm doing what I can to fix it."

"But you still want to be a dad? In theory?"

"Krista, what are you doing?" Dan said, his voice a mix of confused and exasperated. "What are you up to now?"

She looked down at her belly, and then back at Dan, and for the first time since Evan had met her, she looked almost fragile.

Almost soft. “You risked your life for me, Danny.” She shook her head. “You almost died. For... to help get Tat out, I get that, but... for me too. For my baby.”

“It seemed like a good idea at the time,” Dan said, and Evan knew he was trying to lighten the mood a little, but a bit of levity was no match for the intensity of Krista’s gaze.

“My baby still needs you, Dan. I need you to keep helping it. I’m....” She took a deep breath, and there was a jagged edge to it. She yanked her leg against the shackle, hard, and Evan could see how the metal dug into her skin with the pressure. Krista seemed oblivious to the pain. “I’m going to jail. For a long time. I want my baby raised by family. Scott’s going to be in prison for even longer than I am, and he doesn’t really have any family. You’re it, Danny. I mean, I hope Evan helps you. And Jeff—I don’t know him as well, but I hope he helps too. But I want you to be the guardian. You can get lawyers in here, and I’ll sign whatever you want me to sign, and I’m not asking for money, or anything else. I just want... if I can’t raise my baby myself, then I want my brother to do it. I want my baby to be with family.” She paused, and there were tears in her eyes. Evan was pretty sure they were genuine. “Will you do it, Danny? We had shitty parents, but I really think you can do better.” She shook her head vigorously. “No. I *know* you can.”

Evan bit his tongue, and for once, Tat showed a little restraint as well. They all stood quietly as Dan collected his thoughts. Finally, he said, “Yeah. I’ll help. And Evan and Jeff will too. And Aunt Tat, and Uncle Chris, and Grandma Anna, and Aunt Robyn. The kid’ll have more family than it can handle.”

“You can teach it to ride horses,” Krista said, and she was crying freely now. “Smokey can help.”

“I can bring it to visit its mom,” Dan said softly. He seemed like he was thinking it all through as he spoke. “We’re going to... we’re going to fall in love with this kid, Krista. We’re going to make it part of us. But that doesn’t mean it can’t be part of you too. I have no idea how long you're going to be gone for, but when you get out, you'll have family waiting." And then his voice hardened. "But if you do anything to hurt the kid, or anything to cause trouble with the rest of the family…." He shook his head. "Evan's rich, Jeff's crafty, and I am stupidly stubborn. Do not fuck with us."

She smiled through her tears. "Yeah. Okay. And that's the attitude you'll take with anyone else who might hurt the baby too. Right?"

"Absolutely," Evan said. It was a relief to finally be able to speak.

"They'll do a really good job," Tat said sincerely. "Evan made a lot of mistakes with me, but hopefully he's learned from the experience. And Jeff and Dan will help him out."

Krista nodded her understanding. Then she looked at Tat and said, "I'm sorry. For… for being part of that. For hurting you. I don't… that's all I've got. Just… I'm sorry."

Tat stood straight and tall, and Evan could see the woman she almost was when she said, "I accept your apology. And I'll try to forgive you. For the baby's sake."

"Thank you," Krista said, and again, as far as Evan could tell, she seemed sincere.

"I'll talk to a lawyer about getting papers drawn up," he volunteered. "I think it should be pretty straightforward, since Dan's family and since you obviously won't be able to take care of the kid, and since the father's looking at multiple life sentences. His behavior at the cabin made it pretty clear that he doesn't care about the baby's well-being, and I think my lawyers can take care of him no problem." He leaned forward a little and made sure Krista was looking him in the eye. "But when they write up the deal for you, I'm going to ask them to put whatever the hell there is in it to make it irreversible. To make the baby absolutely, irrevocably, in every way Dan's kid. And I'll pay for a lawyer for you too, so you can't come back and say you didn't know what you were signing."

Krista nodded. "Yeah. Okay. That's fair."

Evan pulled back a little. She was damn right it was fair. More than fair, it was necessary. He wasn't going to let the people he loved get hurt, and if he had to throw his weight around a little to make sure that happened, then he was going to do it. He knew it drove Dan crazy, but it would drive Evan crazy not to do it. So he'd restrain himself when he could, and the rest of the time, he and Dan would just be a little bit crazy together.

He looked down at Dan and noticed that he was sitting lower in the chair than he had been just moments before. The visit had obviously gone on for long enough. "We should go," he said, and Krista didn't argue.

"Get me the legal stuff as soon as you can," she said. "I think there's a waiting period, after the baby is born, but in this case...." She ran her hands over her belly. "Someone's going to need to take care of it right away. I want that to be Danny."

"I'll get on it," Evan promised, and he leaned over to put his face next to Dan's. "You ready to go?"

Dan nodded, then spoke to his sister. "You take care of yourself, okay?"

"I will. You take care of my baby."

"I will," Dan promised, and Evan wheeled him out the door, Tat following close behind.

They made it to the elevators before Tat could no longer contain herself. She whirled around in front of Dan and Evan and did a strange, shimmying dance of what Evan could only imagine was joyful celebration. "We get to keep it!" she sang. "We're going to have a baby!"

"*Dan's* going to have a baby," Evan corrected.

But Dan reached out one hand and let Tat grab hold of it.

Evan was glad to see she had sense enough to be gentle, even after Dan made his own correction and said, "*We're* going to have a baby." Then he looked up at Evan. "And we have no fucking idea what we're doing."

Jeff sat in the passenger seat of Evan's SUV. Evan was driving, and Dan was in the back, stretched out and pretending to rest. He'd only been out of the hospital for a couple days, and he'd only been allowed to go home that soon because Evan had arranged for home nursing. Jeff wasn't glad that Dan had been shot; it had been terrible, and terrifying. But he had to admit that he was glad there was someone else in worse shape than he was. He'd only been the principal invalid for a few hours, and he never, ever wanted to be in the position again.

Dan, though, seemed surprisingly okay with it all. Jeff had noticed this before. When Dan first had an injury, he was scared and defensive and cranky, but once he eased into things, he actually seemed to enjoy being treated like an invalid. Jeff's theory was that Dan needed an excuse to accept the affection that he craved, and an injury gave him that excuse. Whatever the reason, Dan had allowed Evan to wheel him out to the SUV and practically lift him into the backseat without a single word of complaint. Then he'd suggested that he might be a bit more comfortable if he had a pillow to brace against the door, and he'd winked at Jeff when Evan went sprinting back into the house to get one. Yeah, Dan was definitely enjoying himself.

Evan, on the other hand.... Jeff reached across the front of the car and lightly gripped the back of Evan's neck. "It's going to be fine, Evan. Everything's going smoothly."

"We're not ready. We need more—"

"No!" Dan and Jeff said together. Jeff glanced back at Dan and laughed before saying, "No more stuff. The first couple weeks, all the kid's going to do is eat and sleep and shit. And we've got milk, a crib, and diapers. We're set."

"The frozen breast milk was a great idea," Dan said from the backseat. "I didn't even know you could do that—I didn't know there was a bank all set up for sharing it."

"And they're going to let Krista nurse for as long as she's in the hospital," Evan said. "The first stuff is the best." He half-turned in his seat and gave Dan a quick look before returning his eyes to the road. "You're sure you're up for this? I mean, I got another room at the hospital, with a couple beds, so you can rest up. But...." Jeff could tell that Evan didn't want to say it. "But we don't have to be there. The baby's going to be around for a long time. Missing the first few hours isn't a big deal."

"Dude, we're already halfway there." Dan reached a hand through the space between the passenger seat and the side of the car and found Jeff's free hand. "We should be there for the birth." A pause, and then Dan said, "Also, I want more tapioca."

"Tia would make tapioca for you," Evan said. Jeff smiled at the understatement; after Dan's heroics, the Kaminski housekeeper would do anything Dan wanted. Hell, she'd been crazy about him *before* the rescue. Now her affection was completely out of control.

But Dan was not persuaded. "I like the hospital kind," he said firmly. "I like the way it gets a skin on top."

"Tia's would probably get a skin on top too, if she left it in the fridge uncovered for a couple days."

"So, you think I should have to wait a couple days for a snack? I think I'd rather just go in to the hospital and have some now." Dan sounded like he'd thought this through. "Also, since I'm there anyway, I think I might like to say hi to my niece or nephew."

"Yeah, okay," Evan agreed. "Since you're there anyway."

Jeff smiled and gave Evan's neck a shake while gripping Dan's fingers with his other hand. Just the night before, he'd brought up the idea of getting some counseling. Tat was seeing someone to help her through her trauma, and Dan had said that maybe they should consult a child psychologist to figure out the healthiest way to present Krista's incarceration to her child. Jeff had suggested that if they could find the right counselor, it might be good to do some work on their relationship too. Evan had been enthusiastic, Dan reluctant, but they'd both agreed. But now, driving along together, their silly, relaxed conversation lilting like cool water over smooth pebbles, it was hard to imagine that work was necessary.

Then Evan said, "But Tia *will* be really useful with the baby. She helped my mom with me and Tat; she's a pro." And Jeff felt Dan's fingers tense.

"I appreciate her help, Evan. Especially until I get better. But I still need to cut back at the barn. The kid shouldn't be raised by a 'pro'; it should be raised by family."

"Why would you need to do less of what you love, less of what you're great at, to spend time with a baby that would be just as happy with Tia? And, seriously, just because she gets paid to be there doesn't mean she's not part of the family. When you first came out here, you got paid to look after Tat around the horses; that doesn't mean you don't love Tat. And Tat and I love Tia, and she loves us; it's not about the money."

Jeff was pretty sure he was with Evan on this one, but he didn't think he needed to say so. Instead, he said, "We can talk to the therapist about that, how about? We could use it as a test case, maybe. See if we can use this discussion as a model for future disagreements."

"No," Dan said, and both Jeff and Evan turned to look at him. Evan had to look back at the road, but Jeff kept his eyes on Dan's face as he said, "I think the test case should be something else. Something where Evan isn't mostly right. Let's wait for one where Evan's mostly wrong, and use that as our model."

Another quick look back, and Evan said, "So does that mean

you'll consider moving in? After you feel better? Tat'll be gone to school in the fall, and it's not like she cares anyway. The house is big enough for all three of us, *and* a baby, and it'd be great to have Tia around to help."

Jeff was pretty sure that was pushing too hard, and sure enough, he felt Dan's fingers tighten a little more around his. "I don't think it's a good idea, Evan."

"Because you don't trust me," Evan said flatly. He looked back again, and Jeff saw how hard he was trying to not look hurt.

"I trust you with my life, Evan." Dan frowned. "That said, I'd be a lot more comfortable if you'd keep your eyes on the damn road." Evan turned obediently, and Jeff wondered whether Dan was concerned about vehicular safety or just didn't want to have to look Evan in the eye. "I just don't think it's a good situation. It's *your* place. You've lived there all your life. It's hard for me to not feel like a guest there."

"This morning you said I needed to redesign my shower stall, and then you told me which trees to cut down so you could have a better view of the barn when you ate your breakfast on the deck." Evan sounded like he wasn't hurt anymore, just exasperated.

"Well, those things would make my guest experience more satisfying. I was trying to be helpful."

"You're a prince," Evan said dryly.

Jeff decided he'd been on the sidelines long enough. "If anyone's interested... I don't want to move in either."

Evan cut a quick look in his direction. "Really? I mean, I know you didn't used to want to. But with the baby...."

"Babies are mobile," Jeff said. "And so are housekeepers. We can use *this* as our test case, if you want, but I think maybe we should look at buying a whole new place. Somewhere fresh for all of us."

"But Dan doesn't have any money for a down payment," Evan said, and he raised a hand to hold off Dan's reply. "Don't deny it, dude. I know what you make, and I know how much you pour back into buying your shares in the business. And I love it that you're doing that; I really like thinking of you owning those horses. But it doesn't leave any money behind for buying a house. And it doesn't make sense that all four of us would have to live in a tiny little place just because you're too proud to let me give you things."

"I was thinking about percentages," Dan said, and then he added, "eyes on the road!" when both Jeff and Evan turned to look at him. Evan turned around to face the front, and Dan said, "I thought maybe we could put... I don't know, I thought maybe a third, or half of our monthly income into a common pot. Just salary, Evan, not all your investments and shit. So, you know... we'd put in different amounts, but it would be sort of fair. Right? And then we could pull all our joint living expenses out of that fund. Evan makes a lot, so there'd be enough to pay a good-sized mortgage. I'd still have a fair bit of money left over to buy into the business. Jeff, it'd give you some security, with the painting—if you had a bad month or two, it wouldn't be a big deal." Dan relaxed back into his pillow. "I don't know. It was just an idea."

"You'd be okay with that?" Evan asked carefully.

Dan snorted a soft laugh. "It makes my fucking skin crawl. But I can't think of a way around it. And if we're going to be partners for raising this kid, it makes sense to have something a bit more stable with the money."

"Am I allowed to give myself a raise?" Evan asked.

Jeff braced himself, but apparently Dan's injuries were still slowing him down, because he just laughed again. "The idea's been on the table for thirty seconds, and you're already looking for a way to play it."

And then they were at the hospital. Evan pulled up to a

side door, where an orderly was waiting with a wheelchair. "You need to save your energy," Evan said when Dan started to protest.

Evan handed his keys to a man wearing a red uniform, and Jeff said, "There's valet parking at the hospital now?"

Evan looked impatient. "There's valet parking at Paulo's, and I asked if I could borrow one of their guys." Apparently Jeff should have been able to figure that out on his own. "I didn't want to have to go park while you guys went in alone." He shrugged. "I wanted us to stay together."

Jeff nodded. He wanted that too. He stepped back as Evan helped Dan out of the car and into the wheelchair, and then the three of them headed through the double doors and into the hospital. They were about to start a whole new phase of their lives, and it was scary, but Jeff knew it would be okay. It wouldn't be simple, or easy, but it would be okay. It had to be, because there was no way Jeff could imagine a world where he wasn't with Dan and Evan.

Sneak Peek at Shying Away

Chapter One

THE beat of the music was pounding into Quinn's body, pulsing against him and around him and into him, making it hard to think, or even to feel anything other than the primitive rhythm. It was exactly what he wanted. It would be nice if it was a little bit louder, enough to make conversation totally impossible instead of just difficult, but other than that, it was perfect.

He wasn't dancing, just leaning against the rail of the balcony, watching the bodies writhe on the floor beneath him. There were more women than usual, he decided, which was a bit of a nuisance. They kept him from getting a clear view of the male bodies on display, and if he couldn't see properly, how could he make his selection?

His inspection was interrupted when someone pressed in too close behind him, grinding into his ass. It would be easy enough to go along with that invitation, but he wanted to choose, not be chosen. There wasn't much in his life that he had control over, but this—this was his. He shifted forward, making his rejection as clear as possible without actually having to turn around and interact with whomever it was. Not that easy, though.

"Quinn. Hey, baby." The guy eased away from Quinn's ass

at least, but instead of leaving entirely, he shifted over to stand next to Quinn at the railing. "It's been a while. Where've you been?"

Quinn turned his head enough to see the guy's face, then turned back. He recognized him, but couldn't think of a name. He also couldn't think of a reason to care. "I've been around." Surely that was dismissive enough.

There was a bit of a pause, as if the guy had to regroup. "Well, you're here now, right? Can I buy you a drink?" Something about the way the guy said it jogged Quinn's memory. He remembered the lavish apartment, right downtown, with the incredible view over the city and the ocean. They'd been drinking something, champagne maybe, something the guy seemed to think Quinn should find impressive. And maybe there'd been coke—not Quinn's favorite drug, but not something he'd turn down, either. But he couldn't remember much else, and that wasn't a good sign. Quinn might not be able to recall every fuck he'd ever had, but he liked to think he remembered the good ones.

He took another quick look at the guy's face, and then down his chest. He was handsome enough, with a sort of aristocratic look and a long, lean body that would probably feel just right pinned under Quinn's shorter, more muscular frame. But there was no flash of attraction, none of the instinctive pull that he liked to put his trust in when selecting partners.

"I'm good, thanks." He angled his body slightly away. He wasn't trying to be rude, but he wasn't worried about it, either. There are those who pull the bandage of rejection off fast, and those who pull it off slow; Quinn liked to pull it fast. It gave both him and the other guy lots of time to find somebody more interesting. Or interested.

But this clown really wasn't getting the message. He eased in closer, the front of his body rubbing against Quinn's side, and when he spoke, instead of raising his voice to be heard over the music, as he'd been doing, he leaned in and spoke quietly into

Quinn's ear. "I've missed you. I've been looking for you. Waiting for you."

That was too much, and Quinn jerked away. Apparently he'd have to spell it out. "I'm not interested, buddy. Find somebody else to stalk."

The man looked stunned, and Quinn noticed the reaction. The guy was hot, but not scorching, so he must have a hell of a lot of money, or something else going for him, to be so confident. Quinn wracked his brain, trying to remember the sex. He really didn't think it had been too outstanding. So the guy was either rich, or maybe deluded. Either way, Quinn wasn't interested. Hell, "deluded" could be a good time, maybe—it was "rich" that was making Quinn's blood run cold. "Seriously, man. I appreciate the thought, but it's not going to happen."

"You appreciate... you appreciate the *thought*? Are you kidding me?" The man's expression was changing, anger starting to replace the surprise.

Quinn felt his body want to flinch away, but he forced himself to stand still. The guy's expression was too familiar, too soon, but Quinn had never been a victim and he'd be damned if he'd start acting like one now. This shithead had just better have the sense to back down, because Quinn sure as hell wasn't going to. "I'm not kidding. I'm just not interested." He turned to face the man. Quinn was a little shorter, maybe, but the other guy was a twig; Quinn was a stone, and he let all the cold hardness show in his eyes as he stared the man down.

It worked.

Instead of letting the anger grow, the man's expression shifted back to surprised, and then to hurt. Quinn was glad he'd seen the anger first, so he didn't have to feel bad. When the guy spoke, his voice was uncertain. "But—we had a good time, didn't we?"

"I have lots of good times, man. It doesn't guarantee a repeat." It was too bad, because Quinn liked his location, liked the view he had over the club, but discretion was the better part of valor, so he decided that he'd better find somewhere else to stand. "Cherish the memory."

That last part was a bit smart-ass, he thought as he turned and let himself melt into the crowd, but life was too short to be careful all the time. That philosophy had gotten him into trouble on more than one occasion, but he didn't think this was going to be one of them. He was in a crowded, open place, and the guy had just been arrogant, not evil. Everything would be fine. Well, maybe not "everything," in a cosmic sense, but this guy shouldn't be a problem.

He forced himself not to turn around to check if he was being followed. He wasn't a rabbit, trying to evade the fox. He was a fox himself. Or maybe a wolf. Hell, he was a tiger. The fox had better not mess with him. Quinn smiled to himself as he worked his way into the crowd around the bar. Yeah, his imaginary animal spirit could beat up anyone else's imaginary animal spirit. That was a mature outlook.

He caught the bartender's eye and raised his empty beer bottle, showing the label so he'd get the right kind as a refill. He wasn't really too picky about beer, but bartenders always seemed to want him to care, so he tried.

He paid for his drink and then turned to survey the crowd at the bar. It was quieter here, away from the dance floor, and people were having actual conversations rather than just yelling lines at each other. There were some half-familiar faces mixed into the crowd, and he nodded at Wade, down at the far end. They weren't friends, exactly, but they were—something. If neither of them had found anything better by the end of the night, they'd probably go back to Wade's place together. The sex wasn't usually outstanding, but it was reliably good, and they both knew exactly what to expect from the other. There was no need to worry about Wade getting too attached, or thinking he had a claim on Quinn's attention, or any of that crap. He and Quinn were two of a kind, and they both had sense enough to recognize it.

Quinn ran his rough hands over the smooth wood of the bar, and moved his gaze farther along through the crowd. He was trying to pick up on that hint of attraction, trying to find someone who could excite him, pull him out of himself at least for a while. He'd almost given up, almost decided that he should just go buy Wade a drink and call it a night, but then there was movement in the shadows at the end of the bar. The want and need were twisting through Quinn's stomach before he even fully understood what he was looking at.

The kid was beautiful. Tall and rangy, his shoulders taking up so much space that he was twisted around sideways, leaning into the wall in order to not crowd the man next to him. He was fair, with light skin and a disorganized thatch of blond hair, and Quinn had always liked the way that his own tanned body looked against someone paler. He liked the way it felt, even, his skin seeming warmer, as if it retained some of the heat from the sun that had darkened it. But that wasn't what was drawing Quinn in; there were plenty of well-built, fair men in the bar. This guy, though. There was something else about him, and Quinn pushed himself away from the bar and started working through the crowd, trying to get closer.

Nobody was talking to the kid, or even seeming to notice him. And that didn't make sense, because maybe he wasn't flashy, but he was definitely good-looking, by any standard. He seemed to be hiding in the shadows, as if he didn't want to be seen, and against all the bolder displays in the room, he was just fading away. Quinn himself wouldn't have noticed him if he hadn't moved at just the right time, and Quinn had been looking pretty hard.

Just as Quinn arrived, the kid moved again, setting his beer bottle down and pushing himself to his feet. Damn, he was tall. Quinn was almost six feet, and this guy was towering over him. And broad too, with those shoulders. He was wearing a simple, black button-down and loose jeans, so Quinn couldn't get a good view of his body, but he bet it was good; there didn't seem to be any fat on any of the parts that were visible. But the guy was moving again, shifting around as if trying to get past, and that spurred Quinn into action.

"Hey. You leaving?" The words weren't smooth, but they were the best he could come up with on short notice. He tried to make his tone do the work for him, hoping that he sounded seductive rather than startled.

The kid shifted his eyes toward Quinn and then dropped them. When he looked back up, it was as if he was forcing himself to do it. "I was going to. Yes."

Jesus, maybe he was just shy. Quinn normally didn't like that crap, didn't want to have to jump through extra hoops to get where he wanted to be, but somehow, on this guy, it was kind of adorable. "What's wrong? You not having fun?" The kid didn't look like he knew how to respond, so Quinn stuck his hand out. "I'm Quinn. Why don't you let me buy you a drink? I can introduce you to some people, if you want." He sincerely hoped the kid took him up on offer number one, but not offer number two.

The kid grasped the extended hand automatically, and Quinn could feel the warm strength in his grip. Damn. The guy had big hands. He still didn't seem too sure, though, and again it seemed like he was forcing himself to interact. "Hi. I'm Aaron."

"Aaron, huh? Like the aardvark?" Quinn didn't know quite what he was doing—he'd wanted to put the kid at ease, but who would be at ease when talking to someone spouting random crap like that?

The kid surprised him, though. "Yeah, like the aardvark. I don't fly an airplane, though."

"Damn—I wasn't even sure what I was talking about. But you're right—Aaron the Aardvark, flying an Airplane. What the hell is that from?"

"It's a kids' book. Like an illustrated alphabet, I think. Aaron, aardvarks, airplanes—they're all about the letter A." Aaron eased himself back down onto the barstool. He still didn't look entirely comfortable, but at least he wasn't getting ready to bolt. And this aardvark thing was actually kind of interesting.

"Yeah, that's right! There were, like, I don't know, bunnies, maybe?" Quinn was trying to trace the memories down inside his tangled brain. "Well, and aardvarks, obviously."

"Just the one aardvark, I think. Just Aaron."

And that seemed like an opportunity to get this back on the track it was supposed to be on. As soon as Quinn had thought of the bunnies, he'd realized that he probably didn't want to spend too much time chasing down that memory. "Yeah, maybe. Just the one. Just Aaron. Sitting all alone, at a bar...."

The lighting wasn't great, but it was enough that Quinn could see the blush creeping up Aaron's face. Yeah, the kid was shy. And, yeah, it was pretty damn adorable. "What are you drinking, Aaron?"

Aaron looked down at his hands as if hoping they held some clue, and then back up to Quinn. "A rum and Coke?"

It felt like a kid pretending to be all grown up, and not sure he was carrying it off. "You *are* of age, right? I'm not going to be corrupting a minor, or something?" Quinn smiled to show that he was mostly kidding, but he kept an eye out for a response even as he caught the bartender's attention.

A shy half-smile as Aaron said, "I'm twenty-two."

"All right, then." Quinn looked at the bartender. "A rum and Coke, and another one of these." He held up his half-empty bottle. He was pretty sure the kid wasn't going to be a fast drinker, so he might as well have something to keep himself occupied. Something to distract him from staring at Aaron's succulent bottom lip, or the strong tendons that led from his wrists up under his sleeves, up to hidden skin, skin that Quinn wanted to uncover. Damn, this kid was getting to him. He needed to get things back under control. "You live around here, Aaron?"

"Yeah. I just moved in, a few blocks away."

"Don't tell me you just came down for a drink, and didn't know what kind of bar you were going to...."

Another blush, but Aaron didn't look down this time. When he spoke, his voice was firm. "No. I knew where I was going."

Quinn nodded slowly, and decided that it was time to press his luck. He didn't know quite what he'd do if he got shot down, but he might as well find out; his strength was his looks, not his small talk, so if the kid wasn't hooked by now, Quinn was probably not going to get anywhere. "And did you have something specific you were looking for, here? Or just a drink?"

This time, the look was bolder, as if the kid was warming up and getting into his act. "No. Not just a drink. I was looking for something specific."

The bartender was back, then, and Quinn paid for the drinks, torn between being pissed off at the interruption and glad of the chance to regain his cool. This wasn't like him, getting so worked up over a simple hookup. He was Quinn Donahue, and this was what he was good at. He was a tiger, damn it! He wasn't going to get flustered by a cute little rabbit. Or even by a cute *big* rabbit. He watched Aaron's fingers curl around the glass of dark liquid, and brought his own bottle to his lips. He took a deep swallow as he watched Aaron's cautious sip. By the time he'd brought the bottle down to rest on the bar, he was back in control. "And this specific thing you're looking for—any chance you've found it?" Quinn had to force himself to stop talking, to not babble about damn aardvarks or something, and he was rewarded, after an agonizing few seconds, with Aaron's slow nod.

"Yeah. I guess maybe I have." Aaron's quick grin showed straight white teeth. "Or I guess maybe it found me."

That was an excellent answer, but Quinn forced himself not to jump up in the air and start waving his arms over his head in a victory celebration. Instead, he returned Aaron's smile, slow and easy. "Well, all right. You want to get out of here?"

Somehow, though, things had changed between them, shifted somewhere that Quinn wasn't used to. He wasn't supposed to be the one sitting there, waiting and hoping. And damn it if the kid didn't feel the shift in power too. Aaron had set his drink down on the bar, and he reached for it slowly, lifting it to his lips and taking another thoughtful sip, his eyes never leaving Quinn's face. He set the drink back down on the bar and waited for another several seconds before his head moved almost imperceptibly up and then down. "Yeah. Okay. Let's go."

Quinn fought to keep his cool. If nothing else, he had a reputation to protect. He took another long swallow of his drink before placing the half-empty bottle on the bar next to his earlier unfinished drink. Then he stepped back far enough to give Aaron room to move. "Your place? I'm not too far, but I'm more than three blocks." And he didn't bring hookups back to his apartment, not ever. He didn't want people to know where he lived, and he didn't want strangers in his space.

Aaron stood up as he said, "Yeah, okay." Then he waited, and Quinn started for the door. He only hoped that Aaron was behind him, and for the second time that night, he forced himself not to look backward. He wasn't sure what the hell had happened to his animal symbolism—when would a tiger hope that somebody was following him? He would certainly never care about a damn rabbit—but maybe he'd want to be followed by another tiger. In mating season, at least.

Quinn made it to the door before letting himself slow down and look back over his shoulder. Aaron was still there, thank God. He froze when Quinn looked at him, but then smiled nervously and edged forward. Quinn would have loved to be able to laugh at the guy for being nervous, but he was pretty damned edgy himself. "All right?" he managed to ask. When

Aaron nodded, Quinn pushed the door open and stepped outside.

It was a warm night, and clear, and both of those were rare for Vancouver in late September, so Quinn took a moment to breathe in and appreciate the mild weather. Neither he nor Aaron had jackets, and there wouldn't be too many more nights that they'd be able to get away with that. He glanced over and saw Aaron watching him. "Sorry. You're ready to go?"

"Don't be sorry. It's a beautiful night." Aaron stepped a little closer. "If there weren't all these lights, I bet the stars would be really clear."

Quinn glanced up at the sky, but it was just a dark backdrop to the neon of the bar's signs and the bright streetlights. "I guess." He looked back at the street, and then at Aaron. "Which way?"

Aaron wordlessly led him along the crowded sidewalk. They were on Davie Street, the heart of Vancouver's gay village, and the area was alive with other men, all out enjoying the unexpectedly warm weather. Normally, Quinn would have been distracted by the skin on display, the beautiful faces smiling and laughing and flirting all around him. He was having no trouble keeping his focus on Aaron, though.

They stopped in front of one of the tall, concrete buildings that punctuated the more common low-rise structures of the area, and Aaron punched a code into the keypad. "This is it," he explained belatedly. Quinn was pretty sure he'd been in the building before, with some other resident, but he couldn't remember details. He followed Aaron inside, and then into the elevator.

They still didn't talk as Aaron pushed a button for the sixteenth floor. The walls of the elevator were mirrored, and Quinn had to fight the urge to pull the emergency stop button. It would be delicious to undress Aaron in there, with the mirrors displaying every angle, every inch of skin, but Quinn didn't think the kid would be into that kind of public display. He didn't think he'd be into it himself, if it came down to it, but it was fun to think about. He let himself smile a little, and he knew Aaron noticed. He hoped he looked sexy and enigmatic rather than psychotic.

Another punch code got them inside the apartment. It was a bachelor, but a good-sized one, at least by downtown Vancouver standards. There were all the expected furnishings: a kitchenette in one corner, a two-person table, a brown leather couch facing a TV hung on the wall, and over toward the big window, a dresser, a bedside table, and a bed. Everything looked immaculate; the covers on the bed were even folded down, like they were in a hotel.

"Did you just move in? Or are you actually this tidy?" Quinn took a few steps into the room and looked around for any sign that the apartment was lived in. The only things that even hinted at actual habitation were the two pairs of boots lined up by the front door. They reminded him of his younger sister; she'd been deep into horses, the last he'd seen her, and she'd had boots like those. Much smaller, of course.

Aaron was watching him uncertainly, and when he spoke he sounded like he was justifying himself. "I've been here a few weeks. But, you know—I tidied up before I went out tonight."

Ah. "Because you knew you were going to bring somebody home with you."

"Well—I didn't *know*. But, yeah, I thought I might."

"So how come you were leaving, when I saw you? You'd given up?" It still didn't make sense that this kid would have any trouble at all picking up, not if he put any sort of effort into it.

Aaron dropped his eyes, and the newly familiar blush made another appearance, creeping up from the neck of his button-down. Quinn took a step forward; he really wanted to see if the kid's chest had the same beautiful pinkness. He stopped moving when Aaron looked back up. “I just felt sort of stupid, you know? I mean, I didn’t know anyone, and I was just sitting there.”

“You don’t dance?”

Aaron’s laugh was more like a snort, but he controlled himself. “No. Not—not in a way that would make anyone want to talk to me. Possibly they’d want to sedate me, and get me back to the asylum.”

“Yeah, okay.” Quinn took another step forward, so close now that he could reach out and touch the kid, if he wanted to. And he absolutely wanted to. Aaron stood frozen as Quinn lifted his hand toward his face. Quinn slowed down, although he hadn’t been going all that fast in the first place. “You okay? This is what you wanted, right?”

Aaron nodded jerkily. “Yeah. It was. It is.” He lifted his own hand and brought it tentatively toward Quinn’s chest.

Quinn shuffled forward enough that Aaron didn’t have to stretch very far, and they felt the first brush of contact, the tips of Aaron’s fingers against the cotton of Quinn’s shirt. Quinn wanted more, and he wanted it as soon as possible, but he was pretty sure Aaron needed things a bit slower. He curled his fingers around so that he could brush the side of the kid’s face with his knuckles instead of the work-hardened skin of his palms. Aaron’s eyes slid shut as if he’d been hypnotized. Hopefully that was a good thing. Quinn stretched his fingers out, rested them along Aaron’s jaw, and then curled them gently in, suggesting but not insisting.

Aaron responded, leaning down, letting himself be guided, and Quinn felt his already hardening dick throb a little more. He reached forward and gave a gentle kiss and felt Aaron’s lips move as he kissed back. Quinn deepened the kiss, and Aaron responded willingly, enthusiastically even. All of a sudden Quinn found himself being pushed backward, spun around so that he was the one with his back to the wall, and Aaron was the one on the outside. Aaron took advantage of his new freedom and moved until Quinn was shoved up against the wall by Aaron's whole body, long and hard and strong. There was no break in the kiss, not as Aaron moaned, not as he arched his body into Quinn's, and not as his hands raced all over Quinn's torso, feeling his chest, his sides, then out to his arms. It felt frantic, as if Aaron wasn't sure Quinn was real, or as if he thought he might disappear at any moment. Apparently the kid didn't need things slow after all.

And that was just fine with Quinn. He pushed off the wall, and damn it, the kid was strong, but he wasn't fighting Quinn, exactly, he was just a solid mass that needed to be moved. Quinn put a little more muscle into it and then Aaron was going along, letting himself be guided. This time it was Quinn's turn to spin them and slam into the wall. But Quinn wanted to do more than just feel Aaron's body through his clothes, and he pulled his face away while keeping their lower bodies lined up. They were both hard, pushing against their jeans. Quinn let his hips grind in. Aaron's eyes were still shut tight, but he made a little whimpering sound that was far better than any soulful gaze could ever be. Quinn's fingers attacked the buttons of Aaron's shirt, twisting them loose. He had to pull the bottom out from where it had been tucked into Aaron's jeans, he could see the effect that even that little bit of extra friction had on the kid's cock.

Once the buttons were taken care of, he shoved the fabric aside, and he got his first look at the chest in front of him. The kid was ripped, and the flush from his face was spread down over his chest, but it was arousal, now, not embarrassment. Quinn wanted to taste every inch, but he also wanted to keep staring, keep enjoying the view.

Aaron squirmed as if begging for attention, and Quinn brought his lips down to the warm skin in front of him. The kid tasted good, but the best part was the way he reacted to every kiss, every lick, every gentle nip that Quinn gave him.

One of Aaron's hands found its way to the back of Quinn's head, not guiding, just encouraging, and when Quinn found a nipple and gave it a hard suck, the fingers tightened in his hair as Aaron gasped. Quinn had never gotten all that much pleasure from his own nipples, but he loved finding guys who were sensitive there—it made things so easy. And it was hot, seeing the reactions he could get from Aaron. Quinn gave each nipple some attention while his hands were busy unbuttoning his own shirt. He shrugged the fabric off onto the floor and then straightened, bringing his bare chest into contact with Aaron's. It was skin on skin, more contact than they'd had so far. It felt perfect, especially when Aaron bent down and found Quinn's mouth, pulling their tongues together into a writhing tangle.

Then they were spinning again, and Quinn was back up against the wall as Aaron pushed in, just on the limits of too hard. Quinn shoved Aaron's shirt the rest of the way off his shoulders and then went to work on the kid's belt buckle, and then his fly. Quinn pushed the loosened fabric out of the way and eagerly felt for Aaron's cock, as big and hard as the rest of his body, straining through the thin cotton of his underwear. The initial contact was enough to make Aaron gasp away from Quinn's mouth, his breathing jagged and rough. Quinn didn't release his loose grip, but he needed a little information. "You're right on the edge, aren't you?" Aaron buried his face in the hollow of Quinn's neck, still gasping, but Quinn pulled him back so they were facing each other, and for the first time since they'd gotten started, Aaron opened his eyes. His pupils were huge, staring at Quinn like he was seeing a miracle, and okay, it was a pretty good ego-boost.

"What's your recovery time like?" But Aaron seemed to be beyond words, and Quinn figured he could take a chance. The guy was young, he was obviously horny, he could probably get hard again pretty fast. And if he couldn't, what were they going to do, sit down and have tea until he calmed down a little? "Okay, man, I'll take care of you." He eased Aaron around so that the kid was leaning against the wall again, and then dropped to his knees and used one hand to reach in and support Aaron's cock while the other pulled his underwear down.

Quinn had the same conflict as before, torn between admiring from a distance and tasting from up close, and he made the same decision, leaning in and letting his lips gently close around the head of Aaron's cock. The kid's moan was more like a shout, and Quinn tried not to worry about neighbors. Instead, he pulled off, a wet, sloppy kiss, and then opened his mouth and went for it, bobbing down as far as he could go at that angle, then back up, fast and tight and almost rough. A few more times and Aaron was keening, his fingers back in Quinn's hair, tightening, twisting, and Quinn pulled off far enough that he wouldn't choke as Aaron arched his back off the wall, his whole body spasming as he came.

Quinn swallowed while he kept his tongue and his mouth working. The kid's climax seemed to go on forever. It was exciting, feeling this sort of power over somebody else; and it was good to do something that somebody appreciated. Finally, Quinn figured he was done, and he gently moved away and then stood up. Aaron's fingers stayed in his hair as he straightened, and as soon as he was upright he was pulled in for a kiss, Aaron's lips loose and relaxed now, sloppy and easy instead of hard and demanding.

And that was all right as far as it went, but Quinn had his own interests to pursue, and he maneuvered around to bring his groin into contact with Aaron's hip. Hopefully the kid just needed a reminder.

But Aaron seemed totally oblivious, kissing gently like he wanted to just make out for a while. Quinn figured it was lucky they were standing up or the bastard would probably be falling asleep on him. He rubbed his hard cock a bit more firmly against Aaron's hip. "You still with me, here?"

Aaron's eyes flew open, and there was that blush coming up

again, and that made it pretty difficult to hold a grudge. "Shit! I'm sorry. I—uh—what should I do? I mean... I'm not very good, you know, but...."

Okay, this was more like it. Quinn was a pretty firm believer in the idea that even a bad blow job was still pretty good, but if the kid was open to other options, maybe they should be explored. "What do *you* want to do?" Aaron gave him a blank look, so Quinn decided he needed to elaborate. "Do you want to fuck?"

Aaron's blush got deeper; Quinn wouldn't have thought it was possible. The kid wasn't looking at him anymore, his eyes back down, staring toward the floor. Staring toward his own softening cock, actually, and Quinn wasn't surprised when Aaron shifted enough to get his hands free, then reached down to start doing up his pants. It was a bad sign, damn it. Quinn was going to get shut down entirely, just because he'd said what he'd been thinking? "Dude, before you get too offended about something coming out of my mouth, why don't you take a second to remember what just came *in* my mouth."

Aaron's eyes lifted. "I'm not offended! I just—I don't know. I guess...." He took a deep breath, and then blurted, "We can if you want. You know—we can 'fuck'."

This was getting annoying, and Quinn pulled his body away a little. He was getting the distinct feeling that he wasn't going to be getting off, so there was no point in continuing the tease. "Yeah, you sound really into it—that'd be a great time. Jesus, Aaron. So you suck at sucking, and you don't want to fuck. What are we looking at, then? Hand jobs? I can reach my own dick, man, I don't need you for that."

Aaron looked... damn it, he looked hurt. He was the one who'd just come his brains out, he was the one trying to weasel out of reciprocating, and Quinn was the bad guy?

Aaron stared up toward the ceiling, as if he was trying to draw strength from above. "It's just—it's my first time."

The words were so quiet Quinn wasn't sure he'd heard them, and when they eventually registered, they took a while to sink in.

When they finally did, he jerked away, leaning back against the door that led outside. "Your first time—your first time at what? Like, you've never fucked before?"

Still no eye contact. "I've never... anything. With a guy. I've—you know—done stuff with a girl. But with guys, this is... you're it."

Quinn felt cold. "Jesus Christ, Aaron. You should have told me that!"

"Oh, yeah, in all our long conversations, as we were really getting to know each other. That's when I should have told you?"

"But that's—that's the whole point! If you're a fucking *virgin*, for Christ's sake, you should be taking it slow! Getting to know somebody, trusting him—all that shit."

Now Aaron's eyes were on him, and they were fierce and angry. "Fuck you. You just admitted that you don't know me, so don't try to tell me what I *should* be doing!"

Okay, that was a pretty good point. And why was Quinn the one acting outraged here? He wasn't the violated virgin. He tried to calm down. "Yeah, okay. You're right. Sorry." The pressure of his dick against his fly was almost gone, now—if he ever needed an anti-aphrodisiac in the future, he should remember this moment. "Okay, well... not a bad night for you, then. Right? I mean, you got off, you got a bit of experience—everything's okay. Right?" Quinn didn't know quite what he was looking for; he didn't know why he was so worried that he might have brought some sort of trauma into Aaron's pure, virginal life.

"I'm not—I didn't say I wanted you to go. I didn't say we couldn't do... whatever."

"No, you didn't say it. But, you know, I was just looking for—for something simple. This is—this is over my head. You need somebody else for all this stuff."

"All *what* stuff? I'm not... *you're* the one who says I need some sort of deep emotional bond, or something. That's not me. I—I'm not looking for something complicated. I'm not."

Quinn might have believed him if it hadn't been for that final "I'm not." The rest of it had sounded all right, but just at the end there, it had seemed like the kid was trying to convince himself, not convince Quinn. And then Aaron looked at him again, blue eyes trying to be sincere, and Quinn felt the same twist of lust in his stomach that he'd felt in the bar, felt his cock twitch hopefully. He needed to get the hell out of that apartment before he did something that would destroy what little self-respect he had left.

"I gotta go, Aaron. You take care of yourself, okay?" Quinn had the door open and was easing through it, and Aaron didn't say anything more, didn't try to get him to stay. Once he was outside and the door was safely shut, Quinn took a moment to collect himself and then started down the hall. He wondered if Wade was still at the bar. He needed something to distract himself from blue, trusting eyes, pupils wide, staring at him with wonder. Somehow he doubted that Wade would be enough to erase the image entirely, but maybe he could at least help.

About the Author

Kate Sherwood, Cate Cameron, Catherine Dale... and probably a few new names, eventually. They're all one person.

One person who's lucky enough to get to live a bunch of extra lives through all the characters in her books, and who's trying desperately to keep all the lives organized into some sort of categories... so each name writes a different type of story.

But really, beneath the genre categories? All the stories will have some kind of humour, even in the darkest times. They'll all show characters who are far from perfect, but who are trying to be better.

Basic bio stuff? Kate/Cate/Catherine lives in Cottage Country, the water-filled world north of Toronto, Canada, the land where summers are sunny and crowded with visitors and winters are snowy and isolated. She loves it there. Not that she doesn't sometimes miss the city, especially when her internet is acting up or she wants something delivered!

She works full-time at a non-writing job but would love to shift into a more writing-centred life. There's a five-year plan. It might work....

Other Books by Kate Sherwood

For details, see www.booklives.com

Writing as Kate Sherwood (m/m)

All That Glitters – contemporary romance

Long Shadows, Embers, Darkness, Home Fires – four book contemporary action

Feral, Lap Dog, Twice Shy, Pure Bred – four book NA contemporary romance

Sacrati – fantasy/alt history

In Too Deep – NA contemporary romance

Chasing the Dragon – angst and adventure!

Mark of Cain – contemporary romance

The Fall, Riding Tall – two book contemporary romance

The Shift – contemporary fantasy novella – monster hunters!

Room to Grow – contemporary romance novella

The Pawn, The Knight – two book futuristic romance with plenty of angst

Poor Little Rich Boy – contemporary romance

More than Chemistry – light contemporary novella

Dark Horse, Out of the Darkness, Of Dark and Bright – three book contemporary romance with extras

Shying Away – NA romance

Lost Treasure – contemporary romance

Writing as Cate Cameron (m/f, YA)

The Billionaire's Forever Family – contemporary romance

Center Ice, Playing Defense, Winging It, Breakaway – contemporary YA hockey romance

Just a Summer Fling, Hometown Hero – contemporary small town romance

Shining Armor – contemporary romance (originally published under "Kate Sherwood")

Writing as Catherine Dale (YA, contemporary fantasy, general fiction—everything but romance!)

Dark Houses – Speculative YA

www.ingramcontent.com/pod-product-compliance
Lightning Source LLC
Chambersburg PA
CBHW051436170626
46809CB00006B/2493

* 9 7 8 1 9 8 8 7 5 2 3 5 8 *